THE LAST STAND

OF

THE CHIEF O FARRELL

BY

JAMES D FARRELL

THIS BOOK IS DEDICATED TO ALL PERSONS, PAST, PRESENT, AND FUTURE, WHO BEAR THE ANCIENT AND HONOURABLE NAME OF, (O) FARRELL – MAN OF VALOUR.

O FEARGHAIL ABU

O FARRELL FOREVER

TIME PASSES

THINGS CHANGE

THE TRUTH FORGOTTEN

Prologue

The reign of Queen Elizabeth 1 (1558 -1603) is regarded as *The Golden Age* of English history. A period of unprecedented prosperity, change, and discovery, and saw the flowering of poetry, theater, music, and literature, with the Church of England becoming independent of Rome granting the Queen absolute power over church and state. This was the age of Shakespeare, Bacon, Marlowe, and the poet's Sir Philip Sidney and Edmund Spenser to name but a few. A time when England became the greatest naval power in the world and the era of the dashing English knights and adventurers such as the swashbuckling Sir Walter Raleigh and Sir Francis Drake with tales of heroic exploits on the Spanish Main and daring raids on Hispanic ports bringing much glory and gold to the English Crown. But this was also a time when England was at war in Ireland and the final stage of the sixty-year Tudor conquest of the country ending with the defeat of the Irish at Kinsale in 1601 and the subsequent Flight of the Earls. The departure of the Irish chiefs represented the end of Irish polity, as rudimentary and underdeveloped as it was, followed by wholesale confiscation of land and displacement of the Irish nobility and clan system sowing the seeds of discontent and discord for centuries. While these Teutonic English knights and noble gentlemen, many highly educated, undoubtedly brave and chivalrous with great energies, for reasons of greed, ignorance, and religious bigotry, when coming to Ireland acted in the most brutal and despicable manner regarding the Irish as savages and a race to be exterminated. The poet laureate Edmund Spenser considered one of England's finest poets and composer of one of the longest poem in the English language the famous allegorical work *The Faerie Queene* wrote for Queen Elizabeth a treatise called *A View of the Present State of Ireland* advocating the genocide of the Irish people by famine and starvation. *Let Them Devour Each Other* stating the evils of the Irish was their laws, language, and Catholic religion. Each Lord Deputy, the Queens' head of state, came to Ireland to make their fortune or increase it, and to rule for his benefit first and the Crown second. Each of them, and every knight of high rank serving in Ireland, more brutal and murderous than the last, each vying to outdo each other with the level of barbaric cruelty they could levy against the native Irish leaving the country in a state of total devastation.

W.E.H. Lecky, the Anglo Irish historian stated: *The picture of the condition at this time (Elizabethan) is as terrible as anything in human history. The slaughter of Irishmen was looked upon as the slaughter of wild beasts. Not only men but even women and children were systematically butchered as bands of (English) soldiers' transverse tracts of the country slaying every living thing they met!*

England had no colonies and her sailors and soldiers were eager for adventure and conquest and Ireland, the small island situated on the western seaboard of Europe facing the Americas, became the first colony of England and the oldest. The English saw Ireland, their nearest neighbor as simply a colonial land there for the taking rather than seeking power and position on the more crowded and developed land of England. There were opportunities in Ireland where the land was fertile and if controlled by English settlers the land would be rich. But the Irish people, an ancient Celtic herding society, had inhabited the island for over 2,500 years with a well-developed culture and clear identity. To the Irish chiefs, the English colonists were conquerors who when they could not conquer stooped to treachery and murder with unimaginable brutality and indescribable savagery. To the Elizabethan conquistadors, the Irish were simply rebels and outlaws who never took kindly to colonisation. What resulted was a clash of a medieval and an early modern culture, between the old order of the Celtic people and the new order of colonialism and anglicisation. However, despite their endeavors, the policies and strategies of the Elizabethans were flawed and the colonisation of Ireland did not work nor did the enslavement of the Irish people. With the advent of the Protestant ascendency, the Church of Ireland members became the new ruling class with the social, economic, and political domination of Ireland by a small minority of landowners, clergy, and members of the professions. The power and wealth of this elite Protestant class reflected in the abject poverty of the majority Catholic population. The conquest of the Irish was different to most as in conjunction with the wholesale destruction of the country by war and artificial famine the Irish were subject to a repressive legal and penal system, one of the worst ever experienced by a conquered people. Of the long eventful history of Ireland, this twenty-year seminal period *The Tudor Age of Gloriana* was the most remarkable in shaping the destiny and hindering the development of the Irish people for many centuries.

This is a work of historical fiction inspired by real events and real people. It is the story of one sept of an Irish family the O Farrells during the Elizabethan conquest of Ireland and their bitter, hopeless struggle for survival culminating in their ultimate defeat. An alternative title could be *The Last Stand of the Chief O Brien, O Byrne, O Carroll, O Connor, O Daly, O Doherty, O Driscoll, O Donohue, O Dowd, O Driscoll, O Hanlon, O Kelly, O Kane, O Malley, O Murphy, O Ryan, O Shea, O Sullivan,* etc. as most Irish families suffered a similar fate during this turbulent period in one way or another.

Chapter One

Christmas Eve 1591

Thundering footsteps on bare stone slabs shattered the early morning silence as Fergal O Farrell, flinging open the ironclad doors of Longford Castle, rushed into the courtyard cursing under his breath, stopping momentarily to rub sleepiness from his eyes. His mother Megan, who was standing by the door, embraced him fondly and in a calm voice said. "My son, listen to me now and stop playing the spoiled child, you have to go with your father he's made his decision and nothing will change his mind." "Mother," he replied angrily. "Why do we have to go today can't he leave whatever business he has until the New Year, I've never been to the city before?" "No, Fergal, your father wants you with him and you must go." "But mother, why can't O Hanly accompany him as he always does. I want to stay here and help prepare for the festivities." Grabbing him firmly by the shoulders she replied in a low voice. "No, my son, you cannot question your father's decision you must obey him and listen to me now you have a long and perilous journey ahead, and you must be careful in the land of the foreigners."

In the walled courtyard, Lord O Farrell sat silent, grey hair to shoulders, slender body wrapped tightly in a three-cornered woolen mantle. Beneath him his dapple grey mare Aoifa, tail flagging, ears forward, pawing impatiently at the cobbled yard and standing impassively at his side the manservant O Hanly holding the reins of a piebald pony. A rotund, bald man came scurrying across the courtyard, two giant wolfhounds Erin and Finn yapping at his feet, and handing the rider a small silver flask said. "Lord O Farrell, sure wouldn't you be doing me a great service this day if you would fill this with the sacred waters of the ancient well of Saint Patrick sure you'll be passing the very place on your way to the city. While we have plenty of holy wells here in Longford they say this particular one is the best in the whole country. The queen of wells so to speak and its sacred qualities can cure all kinds of ailments." "Yes, Father O Duffy, I will gladly do that for you," he replied, carefully placing the flask under his mantle. "And sure Father, maybe it might cure me of my ailments and by God many the ailments I have too. Sure if I awoke in the morning without all the pains and aches wouldn't I think I was dead?" "You're a terrible man so yeh are Lord O Farrell," the priest replied laughing. "But I firmly believe if a person has faith everything's possible well it's what it says in the bible does it not." Nodding to his mother without speaking Fergal hauled himself awkwardly on to his pony, biting his lip in vexation. From the scullery, a young woman raced over and handing Lord O Farrell a leather bag said. "Sir, this contains all the items you requested everything you asked for is here." Taking the bag he swung it over Aoifa securing it to the pommel of his saddle and leaning over replied. "Thank you, Emir, you're a good girl so you are and will you ever tell your mother I am most grateful." With outstretched arm she gave Fergal a small neatly wrapped linen parcel. "Take this master," she said a coy smile on her face. "Vittles for you and your father for your long journey and listen to me now you be sure and come home safely I have something special in mind for tomorrow night." Smiling mischievously she brushed her hand affectionately across his thigh sending a charge of energy racing through his body as he sat beguiled by her vivacity and charm. The crack of a heavy walking stick on the flank of the dapple grey mare broke the spell as Aoifa lurched forward, and as they rode through the gateway of the courtyard O Hanly called after them. "May the road rise to meet you my Lord and my master, and I wish you both a safe journey." Breathing a sigh of relief he wiped his brow as he watched the figures disappear. *Much as I am devoted to the O Farrells, I'm glad to be spared the long arduous journey to the city and avoid the dreadful business Lord O Farrell has in mind for himself and his son this day.* Locking the heavy wooden gates he strolled briskly back to the castle and entered the warmth of the kitchen where his wife, Una, prepared a breakfast of oatcakes and bonnyclabber for, Lady O Farrell.

Crossing the wooden bridge over the River Camlin they reached the *Slige Assail,* one of the five legendary roads from

Tara, the common highway between the east and west of Ireland, and pushed on towards their destination. Turning in his saddle Lord O Farrell spoke to his son for the first time that morning. "Fergal, over there," he pointed his blackthorn stick into the distance. "That hill was once a most venerated and sacred place for the O Farrells in times past and sure look at it now hasn't it gone to rack and ruin." Fergal glanced with disinterest at a grass-covered mound, scattered trees, and the stark ruins of an ancient stone-walled church, and moving through the featureless landscape the stillness of the winter's day occasionally broken by the cawing and rattle call of crows perched on bare branches of tall trees who peered suspiciously at the two riders. Passing the odd bothy, or mud-built thatched cottage, no sign of life was evident except for grayish-blue wisps of smoke billowing from crude chimneys' tainting the air with a faint smell of turf, and by late afternoon they approached an earthen embankment which in the dull light gave the appearance of a giant black snake slithering across the landscape. "That my son marks the boundary of the Pale, the border between our two worlds, the world of the native Irish and the world of the English settlers, and the purpose of the ditch Fergal not to keep us out but to prevent herds of stolen cattle driven across the open ground by raiding clans." Entering the Pale, through a wide gap in the embankment at Syddan, the landscape changed from largely rugged untilled ground to well-cultivated fields with neat hedgerows and the odd farmhouse built in the English style with tall sturdy red brick chimneys' standing neat and tidy enclosed by rolling pastures of orderly tilled ground. Surrounded by darkness they reached the outskirts of a small village three miles from the city. "What is this place called father?" "This village is named Finglas by the settlers once it was called *Fionn Glas- The Clear Stream-* look," he replied, gesturing to a rivulet running along the side of the highway it's twinkling, murmuring waters, fast-flowing towards the city. Lord O Farrell, drawing the reins of his horse beckoned to Fergal. "There's the well Father O Duffy spoke about over there." Handing the flask to his son he asked. "Like a good man will you go and fill this with holy water I can't walk too far me ould leg is hurting me like mad." Barely visible, a short distance from the road, stood a low-level circular stone wall and surrounding the well, trees, and bushes, festooned with limp faded rags' waving softly as if signalling its presence to passersby's. "This Fergal is one of the most famous wells in Ireland, an ancient Celtic site and sure didn't the great Saint Patrick himself come here over a thousand years ago to convert the local Druids to Christianity, drank and blessed the water prophesying a great city would grow near this place and people have been coming here for many centuries seeking a cure. They say if you drink the water and hang strips of cloth on the trees or a bush your illness is driven into the cloth and as it rots your illness is cured, and also a person can see visions in the holy water." Approaching the well Fergal noticed, in the basin of the distant valley below, the faint glow of city lights reflected in the clear night sky and kneeling hesitated for a moment before carefully filling the flask. Scooping water in his cupped hands he supped the cold, metallic tasting liquid which numbed his mouth as a trickle, dribbling between his hands, cascaded down sending gentle ripples across the water. Something shimmering on the surface startled him and looking closely he sighted the ghostly apparition of two contorted faces illuminated in the pale moonlight, his jaw dropping at the images before him. The faces of his father and himself, grey pallor, eyes closed, two death masks floating on the translucent, gelid water. Recoiling in terror he ran back to his father and white-faced with trembling hand handed him the flask. "What's the matter son, you look as if you've seen a ghost, are you alright?" "Yes, father," he replied in a shaky voice. "I'm fine, it's nothing, nothing at all, come let us depart from this place." In Finglas village, Fergal gazed with keen interest at the neat row of whitewashed shops built in the Tudor style. A butcher, a bakery, an apothecary, and others he couldn't identify. In the village square, he reined in his horse dazzled at the sight of an ornate brightly decorated wooden pole rising high into the night sky above the shops and houses and turning to his father inquired. "Father, tell me now what is the strange device over there?" "It is Fergal what the settlers' call a maypole." "But father tell me now for I am curious to know, what would be the purpose now of such a strange and wondrous object?" "The purpose is to hang coloured ribbons from the top and at May time the settlers' dance around the pole holding the ribbons to celebrate the coming of summer, but to be honest like this practice I find all the foreigner's customs strange." Raucous laughter and cheering voices rang out across the square from a large two-story building with a sign above the door swinging gently in the faint breeze stating *The Royal Oak Inn* and through the red latticed windows they caught the odd glimpse of flickering shadows as drunken revellers' staggered across the bar room. Leaving the village they passed Finglas Abbey with its ancient carved granite Nethercross. "Fergal, I see the foreigners now use our church of Saint Canice for their Lutheran practices will these interlopers never stop, bad cess to them and their blasphemous ways." Out of the darkness appeared a wooded area with scattered clumps of gaunt trees, the air pervaded with the fusty odour of decay, and Fergal's horse shied in fear on entering the dark forbidding forest of endless shadows. "This son is Finglas Wood, once one of the greatest forests in the land but the foreigners' felled most of the ancient oak trees to construct the magnificent roof of Westminster Abbey in London, one of the finest in England, and later to build the great ships of Henry V111's navy. I can tell you now the mighty Tudor warship's *The Mary Rose* and *The Peter*

Pomegranate were built with oak trees from this forest and when the inexplicable sinking of *The Mary Rose* occurred with the loss of many lives didn't our people say it was a curse on the foreigners for felling the sacred trees. To the Celtic people oak trees were living sentient beings and a serious crime under Irish law to damage or fell an oak tree as they believed the trees were sent from heaven, a symbol of Zeus the ruler of the sky and clouds, and always held their religious ceremonies under an oak. Fergal, of all the crimes the foreigners have committed against the Irish people to destroy these ancient forests is unforgivable." "Father, tell me something now for I am very curious to know." Fergal asked a sarcastic tone in his voice. "How in God's name do you come to know all these strange and wonderful things you have a story to tell about everyone and everything don't you now?" "The bards my son," his father replied. "The poets who travel around the country from clan to clan bringing their songs and poems, but also carrying the news and gossip from far and wide, sure don't we know what Queen Bess has for breakfast before she's finished eating." Fergal uttered a low sigh of relief on leaving the dark sylvan shadows of Finglas Wood on to open ground soon reaching the outskirts of the walled city and passing over the River Liffey through Ostman's Gate the empty streets' echoing to the clip-clop of the horse's hooves clattering on cobblestones. On Merchants Quay, two ships, rigging bare with sails furled moored on the wooden quayside having sailed from England with supplies for the army and Fergal stared at the vessels' swaying gently to and fro on the flowing tide curious to observe the ship's guns. He'd heard stirring tales of the mighty English navy and the great exploits of their *Men of War* on the high seas but these ships were unarmed merchantmen in the service of the Crown, *The Ramrod* and *Nemeses,* with no sign of life aboard the vessels the sailors' enjoying the Christmas festivities in the numerous quayside taverns. Carried gently on the night air the dulcet tone of a choir singing softly in the distance caught Fergal's attention and cocking his head listened intently to the words. "My son," his father said softly. "It's the choir of Saint Patrick's church, the great cathedral of the heretics but how sweetly they do sing." Perking their ears they caught snatches of the sweet melodic sound wafting on the gentle night breeze. "But tell me now what do they sing and what are the English words of the hymn, I wish to know?" Fergal shook his head laughingly and replied. "No, father, they do not sing English words what they sing is an old Latin song called *Dulcet Jubilee.*" Lord O Farrell was intrigued. "Fergal, what do the words of the hymn mean?" "*Sweet Rejoicing* father is the meaning of the words they sing it's an old Italian Christmas hymn." Along Wine Tavern Street they passed row after row of low brick-built squat terrace houses, windows' illuminated by the flickering of tapers or candlelight, and entering Castle Street before them a grey stone behemoth, the mighty bastion of English rule in Ireland - Dublin Castle. A colossal stone structure standing foursquare, a strong tower at each corner, with the entrance gate flanked on both sides by smaller towers, and defending the gate a portcullis opening on to a drawbridge of well-trodden oak planks, and below a deep moat filled with the still murky waters of the River Poddle surrounding the castle. "Son, we have finally reached our destination and the reason for our business here this night." Fergal's heart thumped as he looked fixedly at the forbidden building before him his trepidation compounded by the gruesome spectacle of two heads' fixed on spikes above the gates who appeared to be grinning down at him, strands of waspish hair blowing lightly in the breeze. Eyes blazing with anger he turned to his father. "Are you insane, why did you bring me here to this dreadful place, I will never forgive you for this?" Nudging his horse to turn his father grabbed the reins tightly. "No, Fergal, you must follow me, you do not understand, I have my reasons, we have come this far and must finish our business here this night, let us proceed." Trudging across the drawbridge Fergal flinched at the appalling stench of raw sewerage rising from the deep ditch below with its dark stagnant water. In the flickering torchlight, from above the castle gate, a group of heavily armed soldiers' stood sentinel, clad in chainmail, steel morions on head, all carrying swords a few with pikes and muskets, laughing and joking with two young barefooted girls' wrapped tightly in black woolen shawls. At the approach of the riders the soldiers' fell silent and the Sergeant at Arms, a rough man with a cruel visage, stepped forward musket in one hand, lantern held high in the other, eyeing the pair with a steady look a mixture of curiosity and suspicion who called out with a north of England twang. "Halt strangers and state thy business here this night." Fergal, turning in his saddle asked in a low urgent voice. "Father, he wants to know what our business here is, what shall I tell him?" "Son, tell him we are here to visit a prisoner and bring him comfort." Dark clouds of rage flew across Fergal's face and he yelled angrily at his father. "I cannot believe you brought me here on Christmas Eve to this dreadful place of the foreigners. I cannot believe you would subject me to such an ordeal and for what reason. I will never forgive you for this father and tell me now, who is this prisoner we are to see?" Lord O Farrell told him and his face reddened in anger. "I've heard about him he's the son of a powerful chief, but why father?" "Listen son," he replied sharply. "I have good reason for coming here which you will learn soon enough." Shaking his head in disbelief Fergal repeated his father's words to the sergeant who, raising his musket menacingly, responded in a gruff voice. "Nay, Sirrah, ye shalt be visiting nay prisoner at this unholy hour, be off with thee now, begone, and cometh in the morrow that thee might speaketh to the constable for it is he who decides who enters the prison and who doth not."

Reaching over Lord O Farrell handed his son a small leather purse. "Fergal, tell him we will give him two coins if he allows us entrance even for a short time." "Sir," Fergal spoke in a low condescending manner. "We hast travelled since daybreak to bringeth comfort to a poor prisoner and wouldst appeal to thee as a truly Christian man to alloweth us but a short visit." Plucking two coins from the purse Fergal held out his open palm invitingly the sergeant's eyes lighting up at the sight of the shiny gold coins snatching them eagerly. "Well, I dost supposeth as a Christian man I couldst speaketh to the constable, Mister John Merryman on thy behalf he is presently at his cups in the barrack-room where the men dost celebrate the Yuletide festival." Five minutes later the sergeant returned accompanied by a tall, slender, grey-bearded man, slightly inebriated, lamp in one hand and a large bunch of jangling keys in the other. The constable stood mutely gawking at the two men then spoke slurring his words. "The sergeant informs me ye doth wisheth to see a prisoner and which prisoner wouldst it be now may I inquire?" On hearing the name, Constable Merryman stepped back and thundered in a drunken voice. "Nay, I cannot grant ye entrance at this late hour for the prisoner is in gyves and hast already been madeth secureth for the night. He tried to escape last year and we art under strict instruction from the Lord Deputy to be vigilant at all times for he be the most important prisoner in the castle, ay, if not in all the land but if ye return on the morrow I, for a modest consideration, may decideth to alloweth ye to enter and that's the end of the matter, so begone." Fergal repeated Constable Merryman's words to his father. "Son," he responded, disappointment in his voice. "I do not wish to return to this place ever again we must conclude our business tonight and get home here offer him the purse if he allows us entrance now." Greedily fingering and counting the coins the constable pocketed the jingling purse replying in a cheery relaxed manner. "Well I supposeth it canst dost nay harm but I only grant ye a short time for I am most anxious to rejoin my men, cometh follow me and tether thine horses yonder. First, I must escort thee to the barrack- room where I shalt search thy person and goods in case thee try to assist the prisoner to escapeth." Silence fell as they stepped into the large room, the soldiers' ceasing their loud bawdy conversation and ribald laughter with all eyes fixed keenly on the two strangers in their midst. The torch-lit, blank walled barrack-room reeked of burning peat, sweat, and beer, and on the large square planked table in the centre of the room, around which a group of men sat, a wooden keg of beer stood from which filling their pewter mugs to overflowing they drank freely. A large bucket of oysters and a half dozen cob loaf's sat on the table which the men gorged voraciously between greedy guzzles of strong, frothy, English ale, wiping beery whiskers from mouths. A stand of muskets' lined the wall and on the table a variety of weapons including swords, pistols, and a pair of arbalest crossbows with a stack of metal pikes in one corner and the distant corner a dusty pile of long-abandoned unstrung longbows and countless sheaves of arrow shafts. Sergeant Tiptoff, head swimming in strong beer, sat close to the smoky peat fire desperately trying to warm his frozen body having spent six hours on guard duty chilled to the bone parading the castle battlements battered by the vicious icy winds' blowing in from the Wicklow Mountains. Slouching back he fixed his drunken stare at the two men dressed in the Irish fashion who had rudely interrupted the merriment of the soldiers, one a tall gangly youth with a mop of curly black hair, glib over forehead and effeminate features, but it was the old man who intrigued him. The Sergeant at Arms had mentioned something about him being a lord or sheriff but what he saw across the room was a man bent with age, bony hands' joined as if in prayer, lowing grey hair, white haggard face, and a silver thread of green snot dangling from his bluish-red nose. *Lord above,* he thought, laughing silently to himself, *Lord Muck, Lord Benzonian of the savages, Jesu Christi these Irish have a bloody cheek and why must we English honour them trying to forge foolish chiefs into wise earls, from savagery to civility with these meaningless empty titles, more akin to a Tom O Bedlam or blind beggar in his home town of Skipton than a lord,* he laughed again. *But as he gazed at the pitiful figure before him a wave of sadness rose in his heart and tears welled in his eyes and he hadn't cried since he was a child. He wanted to give the old man his seat beside the fire to warm his cold-bent body, to give him something to eat or drink but glancing at the hardened callous faces of his fellow soldiers he knew he could not do that for the old man across the room despised him and his comrades for the dreadful misery and suffering they inflicted on his people and would kill them all given the chance. He remembered his many comrades who had died in the Irish wars snuffed out in a miserable stinking bog in the middle of nowhere all forgotten and he could still see their faces but he couldn't recall their names, and they didn't deserve to die in this God-forsaken country never to set foot in merry old England again or see their families. You couldn't trust these filthy, savage, rebel filibusters, exterminate the whole lot of them, men, women, and children, it was the only way and good riddance to them all, and he despised them for what they had done to him and what they made him become. He stared keenly at the old man who stood beside the door and he reminded him of someone-someone he hadn't seen in many years his long-forgotten father Elijah Tiptoff the way he looked after a hard day ploughing the fields of the Yorkshire Dales in wind and rain to feed his family. Old, worn out and tired, back bent crooked from long years of toil but that was home in England in Skipton and he hadn't been home for twenty years or more, he couldn't remember how long. The silence of the room was rudely shattered by the constable who barked in a strong Welsh* accent. "Here," he pointed to the table. "Open thy bag and place thine goods there that I might inspect them closely." Two manchets of wheaten bread, cuts of mutton, a capon, a small block of cheese, and a leather flagon of sweet Spanish wine including two books were spread over the table to the greedy, gluttonous, gaze of the drunken soldiers. It was the books that caught the constable's eye and snatching one he glanced briefly at the cover proclaiming scornfully. "Upon mine cock and pie what hast we here, mine own good men of England, I didst not knoweth the motley minded Irishry hadst books written in their savage tongue." The room erupted to a furious explosion of laughter and frenzied beating of fists and mugs on the table, and turning to Fergal he asked. "And tell me now churl, canst any of ye uncivilized creatures even read?" They all laughed loudly except Sergeant Tiptoff whose mind had wandered to the summertime of his youth walking hand in hand with his father Elijah under a blazing summer sun through fields of gently waving wheat in the faraway green and pleasant Yorkshire Dales. "But sir," Fergal replied naively with dry mouth, face reddened by the smarting insult. "Sir," he explained excitedly. "These art not Irish words this is a book of Latin verse." A moment's silence and the room spluttered to peals of manic laughter and hammering of fists. "Latin, dost thou tell me the prisoner thou art visiting canst read Latin." Constable Merryman yelled, holding the book disdainfully between the index finger and thumb of his outstretched hand. "Ay, sir," Fergal replied, energised by the constable's interest in the Latin primer. "Tis the custom of the Irish chiefs for their children to be tutored in the classics and many send their sons to the universities of Oxford and Cambridge in thine own country to be educated in fact mine own first cousin, Cormac O Rourke from Breffni, is presently at Oxford and," he stopped, took a deep breath continuing in an animated voice. "I sir, canst read and converse fluently in Latin and hast a good knowledge of Spanish, French, and a smidgen of Greek." Constable Merryman gritted teeth; face twisted with rage, contemptuously flung the book back on the table and shouted. "Enough of thine insolence, thou art a dullard Irishman and once a savage always a savage now prithee gather thy goods and followeth me before I dost change mine own mind." Fergal, hastily refilling the bag walked rapidly towards the door conscious of the covetous looks of the soldiers' hungrily eying the food. Constable Merryman unlocked the metal door to the Bermingham Tower, the castle's prison, a menacing circular four-story stone building, and as the door creaked open they were assailed by a gush of foul-smelling air and Fergal placed his hand over his mouth to stop himself gagging. "In God's name father," he rasped. "What is that awful smell? "That my son is the malodorous stench of death and despair and I dread to imagine the horrors we shall encounter in this dreadful place tonight." Following the dull wavering light of the constable's lamp they entered the gloomy interior of the mausoleum, the echoes of their footsteps on bare stone breaking the eerie silence. Then, out of the shadows a large cell with metal bars running from floor to ceiling dissecting the ground floor in half. At the back of the cell, barely visible, a bundle of rags stirred awoken by the clanking door and hurtling forward uttered the most diabolical screams and wails causing Fergal and his father to step back awestruck at the hideous spectacle. "What is it father, who are these people?" Fergal asked nervously. "I'm not sure son," he replied as a mass of bedraggled children, unwashed and unkempt, matted hair covering faces scrambled towards them scraggy arms poking feverously through the metal bars begging and blaring for food. Silence took hold of Fergal who winched at the sight of the desperate children. *Who could be so cruel and heartless to these innocents are these foreigners devoid of humanity, the Devil's curse on their black evil souls?* Constable Merryman, rattling his weighty bunch of keys across the metal bars, bellowed angrily. "Ye savage dogs a pox be upon thee, be quiet or I shalt order mine own men to cast thee into the River Liffey." As the awful ruckus ceased silence descended over the cell punctuated by the odd whimper and muted cry of a child weeping for its mother as they huddled together in a ragged bunch for warmth. At the top of the winding stone staircase they came to the metal-studded wooden door of the cell housing the most important prisoner in the castle, and as the door creaked open were met with the stench of urine, in the background the faint ricochet of water dripping on stone. Yellowish moonlight, penetrating the unglazed window opening, illuminated the room which was bare except for a rough wooden table and stools and on the floor the outline of a figure on straw bedding. On stepping into the room a rat scurried across the cell floor its claw's scritching on the wooden boards, Fergal flinching as it brushed lightly against his foot. Constable Merryman moving forward kicked the prisoner who awoke startled to find the constable and two strangers standing over him. Uttering a plaintive sigh he struggled to raise himself, bare feet fettered in heavy irons, his lean body wrapped tightly in a filthy, torn, woollen mantle, long frowsy red hair. "Come now, Irish churl," the constable snarled. "Thou hast visitors who didst persist in visiting this night, so I grant thee but a short time to discourse." Before them the struggling figure of a young man, shuffling frame, eyes strained in semi-darkness, who squinted keenly at his two unexpected visitors. Lord O Farrell, on seeing fear and suspicion written on his face, stepped forward placing his hands gently on the young man's shoulders and spoke softly. "My Lord, be not afeared we have come as friends to bring you comfort this night, come let us sit and talk." Fergal stared closely at the young man before him. Tall, slender, fine-featured of noble countenance, a youth with striking good looks who, on seeing the food and drink on the table his eyes brightened, and snatching the flagon took a long greedy draught of wine, wiped his mouth and exclaimed. "I thank you for these kind gifts and tell me who are you and where are you from?" "I am Lord O Farrell from Longford and this is my son, Fergal. I wished him to meet you this night; we come as fellow Irishmen and Catholics, to bring you consolation and relief from your dreadful ordeal." The young man embraced his elderly visitor, tears running down his cheeks, his slender frame shaking with a wave of emotion. "Lord O Farrell, I am most grateful to you and your son for coming this night, I can never thank you enough." "Do not cry my Lord, our people are aggrieved at your unlawful imprisonment and the whole country seeks your release from this cruel bondage. You have many friends who work ceaselessly to obtain your freedom and I can tell you now my Lord," he stopped in mid-sentence placing his hands firmly on the young man's shoulders. "Soon you will be home with your family and hunting in the forests and mountains with your friends." "Lord O Farrell, I do not cry for myself but for the pain and anguish I have caused my parents and kinsfolk by my foolishness. My poor mother was badly affected by the murder of her people on Rathlin Island and never fully recovered from the horror of the awful day and I have made it worse. My father, never disloyal to the Crown and always paid his taxes, becoming old and infirm before his time and sick with despair all because of my rashness and stupidity in trusting the foreigners; what a fool I have been. They sail a warship disguised as a Spanish merchantman into Lough Swilly with fifty soldiers' concealed in the hold. I was hunting in Fanad with my friends the Mc Sweenys my foster parents, and good kind people they are too, and the ship's captain invited us on board to taste their wine and when we did partake in many cups they overcame us and put us in chains. The ship sailed and they threw my friends overboard and bring me to this filthy dungeon. All the cunning work of Lord Deputy, John Perrot and him a friend of my father, how could he be so callous and cruel?" Constable Merryman roaring loudly abruptly ended the conversation. "Thy time is spent and ye must depart now." Fergal stood before the young man and asked. "My Lord, before we take our leave I cannot but inquire as to those poor caged creatures we did encounter on entering this place, can you tell me who they are?" A dark shadow crossed the young man's face. "We call them," he replied solemnly. "*The Unfortunates,* and there are about thirty boys in the cage aged between ten and fifteen years, the sons of Irish chiefs held here as hostages to the foreigners, and if their fathers enter into rebellion they kill them. But most of them are abandoned by their families afraid to come to this place lest they be imprisoned. They roam freely around the courtyard during the day begging and scavenging for food unless their families pay for their keep which they seldom do, so most will die of malnutrition and their bodies dumped in the river. Yes, they are indeed *The Unfortunates,* but I will keep this food you kindly brought and give them some comfort on Christmas morning."

Chapter Two

They were glad to leave behind Dublin Castle, and the dreadful misery, filthiness, and squalor of the fetid prison and crossing the wooden drawbridge Fergal glanced back at the tar-covered spiked heads on the battlement. "Father," he asked. "Who were those ill-fated men and what was their crime do you know?" "Yes, son, they are the famous O Connor brothers from Offaly, and their family has been in conflict with the Crown since Queen Mary Tudor, the daughter of Henry V111, seized their lands in 1553 under the plantation scheme of Laois and Offaly which the foreigners renamed King and Queen's counties, and bloody Mary Tudor a fervent Catholic too. The brothers were condemned by what we Irish call a *Pelham's Pardon.*" "And father, what does it mean?" "Well, son, the Queen in her infinite mercy and wisdom many years ago instructed her Lord Deputies to accept the surrender of rebels and grant them a pardon on the pledge they would disdain from future acts of rebellion thereby saving her money and the lives of her soldiers. But Sir William Pelham, the Lord Justice at the time had other ideas he was a vicious man, and such was his hatred of our people he would only accept surrender if a rebel brought him the head of a rebel more important than himself and obtain a *Pelham's Pardon.* The O Connor brothers had led a rebellion against the settler, Sir Francis Cosby who confiscated their ancestral lands in Laois, and when brutally crushed sought pardon for their deeds. Lord Deputy Fitzwilliam ordered them to the castle threatening to behead them both unless they fought a trial by battle, the winner pardoned regaining his lands and chieftaincy, and seduced by the Lord Deputy's offer the gullible young fools agreed. Fitzwilliam invited the English officials and their wives to the spectacle in the castle courtyard even supplying refreshments for the occasion and, as the ladies and gentlemen of the English stood exchanging niceties and sipping wine, the O Connor brothers engaged in a deadly duel for over an hour, their bodies barely recognizable slashed and bloodied with multiple sword wounds, until one was fatally wounded and Fitzwilliam shouted to the survivor. *Thou wilt bring the head of thy brother to me and receive thy pardon.* The exhausted O Connor decapitated his brother and brought the grizzly trophy to the Lord Deputy who immediately ordered his soldiers to behead the young man proclaiming to all present. *Once a traitor to our Queen always a traitor and to kill thine own brother in such a manner, only the savage Irish would perform such a barbaric deed.* It is a *Pelham's Pardon* a worthless English promise." "Father, I know it was your intention for us to stay in the lodging house you are acquainted with in Blackfriar's Lane, but to be honest I wish to depart with haste and find accommodation outside the city the smell of the filthy jail clings to my skin like a rag and I would not sleep well here this night." "Yes, I understand Fergal, what you witnessed this day was indeed shameful we shall ride to the village of Finglas and seek lodgings at the inn we passed earlier. If we leave at first light shall be home in time for the festivities." Leaving Dublin Castle unknown to them they were watched from an office above the barrack-room by the most powerful of the Queen's men in the land the Lord Deputy of Ireland, Sir William Fitzwilliam. "Secretary Fitton," he ordered. "Go at once to the constable and findeth the names of those gents, where they hail from and to whom didst they maketh visitation in the prison tower. Methinks mischief may be abroad and instruct the constable to keep a record of all persons coming here to see any of the prisoners."

Approaching Finglas village, a light flutter of snow carpeted the landscape in a thin veil of white and reaching the Royal Oak Inn they dismounted, tethered their horses and entered the dimly lit public house which was empty, the drunken crowd having long departed, except for four men sitting in a far corner bent over in discussion who took no notice of the new arrivals. The bar room smelt of wood smoke and stale beer, and a large log fire burned brightly on the far wall, the red glow of the dancing flames making the room warm and inviting. The Innkeeper Geogarty, a bald, red-faced, portly man, was behind the bar filling bottles of whiskey from a large wooden cask and on seeing the strangers stopped what he was doing eyeing the pair with a mixture of curiously and suspicion and placing his two hands flat on the bar leaned forward and inquired. "Good evening to ye strangers, and tell me now what service doth ye require this night?" Lord O Farrell spread a handful of coins across the counter. "Son, tell him we need food, a bed for the night, and the horses to be tended and fed." At the sight of the coins, the Inn keeper's face brightened his suspicion vanishing but not his curiosity. "And what brings ye strangers to Finglas village on the eve of Christmas?" he asked. "We wert in Dublin on business." Fergal replied nonchalantly. "Well strangers, alloweth me to inform ye thou art in the company of important persons tonight," he muttered, gesturing towards the group of men. "Over yonder is the high and mighty Lord Fingal, he who owns the land from Finglas to Dunshaughlin, where he doth abide in his fancy castle with his half Irish wife and that be the sheriff's men at his table. They didst hold an assize here the present day, serious business indeed, for they didst condemn one of Lord Fingal's tenants to hang at Newgate Prison in the town for the murder of a mere Irish ploughman." Stopping in mid-sentence he grabbed a pewter tankard from under the bar counter, and taking a long greedy swig of beer wiped foamy suds from his lips with a dirty cloth and continued. "The poor beggar, a loyal English man called, Elias Boykin, him hailing from Bristol and methinks he shouldst hast been rewarded for his valorous service to our Queen but the sheriff's men didst place poor Elias in jail. Anyway, strangers, taketh a seat yonder and I shalt fetch thee food and drink and instruct the horse boy to attend to thy mounts, the servant girl wilt maketh ready thine quarters presently." Sitting at a table by the door they slumped back wearily as the Innkeeper fetched two wooden platters and bending low over the fire scooped a dollop of pottage onto each plate which he placed unceremoniously on the table producing two wooden spoons, two pewter tankards of warm English beer, and a trencher with a loaf of coarse black bread. "Bon appetite to ye strangers and I dost hope thee enjoy mine own cooking," he chirped, a wry grin on his face. "*A Iosa Criost -Jesus Christ,*" Lord O Farrell uttered on tasting the pottage tainted with the pungent scent of damp wood and a faint tang of smoke, but they were hungry eating with gusto their burnt offering. "And I complain about Mrs. O Hanly's cooking," he continued, stopping momentarily to spit out a lump of fat and gristle. "But, never again Fergal, I can promise you, never again." On tasting the flat, vinous English ale, he coughed and spluttered. "In God's name Fergal, what taste do these people have no wonder the foreigners' always look pale and sickly, and now I know why." But hunger making a good sauce they devoured the pottage and drank the tepid, bitter-tasting English beer, and when finished Fergal rose. "Father, I must use the privy, and while outside I will check if the horses are watered and fed." Lord O Farrell, his hunger and thirst satiated, pursed his lips as he sipped the warm flat bitter contemplating the events of the day. *He knew he made the correct decision to visit Dublin Castle, and glad he had brought his son, it was important the O Farrells were known to the prisoner and especially Fergal. What if the prophecy about the young Lord came true? God only knows what the future would hold or which way the wind might blow and he had to take whatever measures necessary to protect his family and the O Farrell people.* The door bursting open sent a gush of cold snow sprinkled air into the room and glancing up he was confronted by the awesome sight of a stocky man smothered in a fine dusting of white standing squarely in the doorway, a glowering look on his face and brandishing an evil looking billhook. Stumbling into the room the man on seeing Lord Fingal staggered over grabbing the collar of his jacket. "Thou renegade Irish upstart," he roared angrily. "Thou hast condemned mine brother Elias to the hangman's noose and him loyal and true for the killing of an Irishman." Lord Fingal turning recognized the man as his tenant Wesley Bodkin who, raising his arm to strike with such swiftness, the sheriff's men froze momentarily. Fergal returning witnessed the event and glanced at his father who gestured to the shillelagh which lay across the table. Fergal, hands shaking, heart palpitating, instinctively grabbed the heavy walking stick, a loaded stick with a lead-filled knob, and rushing forward walloped the man on the back of the head with such force as he could muster. The dazed man staggered and reeled backward as the sheriff's men, propelled into sudden action, pinned him to the floor. Lord Fingal astonished at the suddenness of the attack leaped to his feet and shouted excitedly to Fergal. "Young man, thou hast this night saved mine own life. I thank thee from the bottom of my heart, mine wife wouldst be a widow and mine children orphaned hadst it not been for thy bravery and speedy course of action." He hugged Fergal and barked orders to the sheriff's men. "Soldiers, depart thee to the city and take this varlet Boykin to Newgate prison, I shalt arrange for Judge Monks to try him at the next assizes." A wide grin crossed his face and turning to Fergal he said. "How canst I ever thank thee mine own gratitude is profound, who art thou and what bringeth thee to this place on the eve of Christmas?" He glanced across the room at the old man who sat glowing with pride astounded at the deed he had witnessed. "Mine own father, sir," Fergal replied. Lord Fingal approached the table and grasping the old man's hand shook it firmly. "Sir," he announced in a joyous voice. "Thine presence hereth on this night hast been mine savior, how canst I ever thank thee, I am forever in thy debt. I am Luke Plunkett, Lord Fingal at thy service." Turning he called loudly to the Innkeeper. "Bringeth us thy finest aqua vitae Geogarty, and not the gut rot poteen thou dost serveth the yeomen." Sitting, he poured large measures of whiskey into pewter cups the Innkeeper left on the table and on raising his cup exclaimed. "Mine own good friends, alloweth us drinketh to thy health." On tasting the aqua vitae Fergal, not accustomed to strong drink, began to splutter and choke gasping for breath, his face reddening with the flush of raw alcohol. "Young cousin." Lord Fingal said laughingly. "Thou canst certainly striketh a shillelagh as good as any man but thou certainly cannot drinketh liketh one. But sirs, I drinketh to thine good health for I am forever in thy debt for what thou didst for me here this night." Looking inquisitively at the old man he inquired. "Prithee Sir, tell me now who art thou and what bringeth thee hither on this night?" The old man sat mutely staring blank-faced at Lord Fingal. "What is the matter, sir?" he queried, baffled by the man's silence. "Lord Fingal," Fergal responded. "Mine own father sir; thou must forgive him for he speaketh not the English tongue and canst only understand the odd word." Lord Fingal shaking his head replied warmly. "Ay, I see, now I understand, therefore I shalt converse with thy father in the native tongue." Lord O Farrell sat back surprised on hearing Lord Fingal address him. "Do not look so shocked," he said warmly. "Sure wasn't I fostered to an Irish family and suckled at the breast of a fine decent Irishwoman, Mrs. O Madden in Dubber Cross, not far from here and at the breast of the same woman didn't I learn the Irish, the natural language of the country before I could utter one word of the English, and sure don't most of us old English of the Pale speak Irish, and don't we use the language in the Privy Council to annoy the Lord Deputy and the English civil servants and that's a fact so it is." Raising his glass he saluted cheerfully. "Slainte, my good friends, Slainte, and good health to the both of you and I thank the Lord above you were here this night now I must ask who are you and where do you come from?" Lord O Farrell told him and nodding his head replied. "Yes, I know of Longford, I am a member of the Queen's Privy Council serving Lord Deputy Fitzwilliam, and one of my fellow councilors, Christopher Nugent lives near Longford you will know him to be sure?" Lord O Farrell shaking his head replied disparagingly. "Yes, my Lord, he is well known to the O Farrells and does do us much harm if the opportunity arises since his family came with the Norman conquest many years ago and drove us off our land but we soon learned their ways of war and managed to reconquer what was rightfully ours and this the Nugents' resent. The man is a villain and causes much disturbance to the native people." "Yes, you are right, Lord O Farrell, Nugent is indeed greedy and unscrupulous, and a fostered man like myself and strangely enough his relative Sir John Nugent, the Chief Justice was hung by Grey the Lord Deputy on a false charge and yet he is the most loyal of us old English. Do you know Christopher Nugent has composed an Irish primer for Queen Elizabeth as she wishes to speak certain words of the language to indicate a level of knowledge and gain the confidence of the Irish chiefs but more importantly, Lord O Farrell why are you here in the Royal Oak this night though glad I am? You're a long way from your home in the company of strangers but please do not look on me as a stranger for I am your friend and if ever I can do you or your family a good deed it is what I shall do." Stopping momentarily he took a long swig of whiskey and continued. "Lord O Farrell, do tell me now why you came here this night for I must know?" "Lord Fingal, it was our true intention to seek shelter in a lodging house in the city which I am familiar with and travel home in the morning, the distance here and back been too long for a day's journey. The lady of the house, Mrs. O Ryan is Irish and I can converse with her and be informed of all the news of Dublin as my wife likes me to carry home the gossip which gives her great amusement as she has much curiosity as to the ways of the English in the city. But after the unspeakable things we witnessed this day Fergal was loath to spend the night in the town hence we came here." Lord Fingal finished his drink and leaning forward inquired. "What did you witness, please tell me now for I am much intrigued?" Lord O Farrell hesitated for a moment. "My Lord, we were in Dublin Castle to visit a prisoner and bring him consolation, and the misery and suffering we encountered greatly distressed my son." Lord Fingal fixed his gaze on the old man and in a low drawn voice said. "Lord O Farrell, this night your presence here saved me from certain death at the hands of that bumpkin, Wesley

Bodkin and now you inform me you travelled from Longford to see a prisoner in the castle on Christmas Eve. You are indeed a noble and Christian man but I am curious, may I ask the name of the prisoner?" On hearing the name a dark cloud crossed his face and reaching over he placed his hand on Lord O Farrell's shoulder. "My good friend, do you not know the mortal danger of your enterprise as Christian a gesture as it may be. Are you not aware this young man is the most important prisoner in the castle and to be honest you risked your life and your sons by visiting this man? So, I beg you now do not go to the castle again it is more than your life's worth. I could not help you with this matter. The Lord Deputy is a devious man and no friend of mine sure didn't he levy a heavy tax on all the old English landowners of the Pale to pay for his army to suppress the Irish chiefs, and when we objected to the Queen he took spite against us and especially myself as the spokesperson. We old English bear little malice against the native Irish as long as they cease from raiding the Pale and causing much damage and theft as does the rogue O Byrne in south Dublin. Live and let live is what I do believe but this is not the governments' stance and their stratagem is one of deviousness and perfidy. The Lord Deputy regards this prisoner as the greatest threat to the English colonisation of this country, you are lucky indeed I am lucky, you left the castle unharmed. Fitzwilliam has learned of the prophecy and it is why they keep the young man so closely watched and heavily fettered." Refilling his cup he looked keenly at the old man and inquired. "My good friend, do you know of the prophecy concerning the prisoner?" Lord O Farrell took a deep drink without replying and after a few moments, Lord Fingal broke the silence. "The soldiers' captured a Jesuit priest named O Rogan in Wicklow who under torture revealed he came from Spain carrying news of an ancient Irish manuscript written by Saint Colmcille he discovered at the Irish college in Salamanca referring to a prophecy regarding the person you visited in the castle." Lord O Farrell dropped his cup spilling the contents over the table, startled look on face. "What is the matter Lord O Farrell, are you acquainted with the priest O Rogan?" "No, of course not, it was the strong drink it caught the back of my throat." "Father like son, not to worry now," Lord Fingal replied smiling. "My new friends, I must draw this night to a close, my good wife will be awaiting me and I beg you heed my words carefully; these are dangerous times." When he departed Fergal inquired. "Father, what did Lord Fingal mean when he spoke of a prophecy, is it something to do with the prisoner we visited. I still cannot fully understand why we came all this distance to visit this young man, why is he so important?" "Son," he replied. "It is time for slumber we have a long journey ahead in the morning, come let us go." Climbing wearily up the narrow wooden stairs to their attic bedchamber and pulling off their boots, they clambered onto the cold straw-filled mattress, and in the early hours of a cold Christmas morning huddled together for warmth still fully clothed. Their bellies full, their hearts warmed by copious amounts of the finest aqua vitae, and their minds rich with pleasing thoughts of the good deeds they had executed. "Fergal," Lord O Farrell whispered in the darkness. "Listen to me carefully now, you must never speak or inquire about the prophecy Luke Plunkett did refer to, it is too dangerous. If the foreigners or their spies found out you know of this matter you could be hung but not before the hot coals of torture." "Yes, father," Fergal replied sleepily as fleeting images of his beautiful Emir danced across his mind.

 Morning came quickly for the pair and at first light, mounted on their well-fed and well-rested steeds, began their silent journey home under leaden skies through the deep velvet silence of the snow-covered landscape.

Chapter Three

The loud barking of Erin and Finn, sensing the imminent arrival of their much-loved master, heralded their safe homecoming, and crossing the Camlin they entered the courtyard of Longford Castle, a four-story square fortified tower house protected by a high stone boundary wall. Lady O Farrell stood patiently with the priest as the tenants and their families gave a tumultuous cheer, the men throwing their hats in the air, at the sight of their Lord and his son. Lord O Farrell slid wearily off his horse and embraced his wife fondly his faithful hounds gently nudging at his heels in gladness at his presence. "My husband, how glad we are for your safe return I was worried about you both but by God's good grace you're home and tell me now," she asked inquisitively. "How did you fare, did you complete your task successfully?" Lord O Farrell nodded a satisfied grin on his face. "Yes, my Lady, we did indeed and without too much bother although we did have a little excitement at the inn where we lodged last night." Handing the priest the flask he said. "Father O Duffy, good to see you, and here take this Fergal filled it at the well as you requested and Father I have something important to tell you." Taking the priest to one side he spoke softly. "Your unfortunate friend Father O Rogan, has revealed the prophecy of Saint Colmcille to the foreigners, so I was informed last night in Finglas, but come let us make our way to the great hall for I am weary and in need of refreshments, there I shall relate to you the tale of our little adventure in the Royal Oak Inn." Lord O Farrell, his wife Megan at his side, strolled through the castle doorway into the torch-lit building and entering the great hall took their places at the top of a long U shaped wooden board table with bench seating. In a neat row on the trestle table sat countless jugs of mead and beer in readiness for the great feast. Each year, as was the custom, Lord O Farrell invited his people to the castle for a lavish meal with much drink, music, and merriment, everybody treated as equal, and this year was no exception. The great hall, as it was termed, comprised a large refectory adjacent to the kitchen and scullery where Mrs. O Hanly toiled feverously preparing the munificent Christmas feast, the hall looking splendid and welcoming with a large turf fire blazing in the centre of the rush strewn, stone flagged floor, smoke rising unvented to an opening in the roof tainting the air with a faint acrid smell. The bare stone walls beautifully decorated with garlands of holly and ivy with the odd judicially placed sprig of mistletoe, the hall illuminated by a series of rush torches set at intervals around the room, the soft yellow glow of the flickering flames' casting long dancing shadows on the whitewashed walls. At the top table, five places were set with pewter plates, goblets, and cutlery, with Lord O Farrell sitting at the center, his wife to one side, his son to the other, and the priest beside Fergal. The fifth-place alongside Lady O Farrell set for dining but the seat empty. With pride and bravado, Lord O Farrell related the happenings at the Royal Oak to his wife, the priest, and all within earshot explaining in great detail, occasionally waving his shillelagh above his head in jubilation, how his brave son by his quick action and courage saved the life of Lord Fingal. Word spread quickly around the hall of the heroic exploits of Fergal, and Father O Duffy standing, raising his hands for silence addressed the crowd. "All present, fill your cups and drink to the brave and noble son of Lord O Farrell, Fergal, who has done us all proud by his mighty and gallant deed in saving a man's life last night in Dublin, and not any man but the wealthy and powerful Lord Fingal a member of the Privy Council." To the cheers and roars of the people Fergal, red-faced, stood and lifted his tankard in acknowledgment blushing, even more, when Emir, who from a large clay jug refilled tankards of beer, kissed him brazenly on the cheek and whispered. "My brave handsome Irish hero, meet me later in the orchard for I must reward my gallant warrior of the O Farrells for his noble act of courage and valour." Her seductive words' sending waves of excitement coursing through his body as with gaping mouth and gleaming eyes he watched her neat, slim, figure skipping barefoot across the floor bringing laughter and joy to all present, occasionally whirling fleet-footed to a lively jig, jug of beer on head without spilling as much as one drop. Platters of roasted meats, pies, brawn, and freshly baked bread, were carried to the table by the cook and her army of servants, the manservant O Hanly managing the affair in a most dutiful and organised manner. Lord O Farrell spared no expense for the special occasion with many beasts of the field slaughtered, a rare occasion, and umpteen barrels of beer procured in Mullingar, with casks of whiskey flavoured with raisins and fennel including countless jars of mead. In the background, the harper strumming his eight-string instrument gave out a sweet melodic tune, the music echoing through the hall barely audible above the laughter and shouting as the rollicking people danced and sang, carousing until the early hours. Lord O Farrell ran his eyes along the sea of laughing faces before him and turning glanced admiringly at his wife who sat contented smile on face. *Megan, still beautiful after all these years and her dressed in the finest silk gown he'd brought from Dublin but behind the happy countenance he knew her heart still grieved for her youngest son, Cahir. She always held a special place in her heart for the boy who was so like her father, but he broke their hearts and almost ruined them when he disowned his family and ran off to Wicklow to join the army of O Byrne, fighting a bloody war against the foreigners over ten years ago and they hadn't seen him since, and he could be dead or alive for all they knew. At his feet, his dogs dozed in the warmth of the fire their bellies full of scraps thrown from the table, his faithful dogs, his protectors who walked steadfastly by his side keeping a careful watch on their master. One time he had a band of trained men as his bodyguards, Gallowglass, highly trained Scottish or Irish mercenaries' clad in armor with heavy long-handled battleaxes, fierce men of war who would have died to protect Lord O Farrell or more correctly the Chief O Farrell as he was known then. But sure didn't Sir Henry Sidney of the English put an end to the Gallowglass, and much more besides. Sidney changed their ancient ways forever and took away his true worth and self-respect. Bad cess to the cursed foreigners and Henry Sidney for the misfortune he'd brought on him and the O Farrells. Those were the days,* he thought, smiling to himself, *oh how he missed those days, the old days of cattle raids their favourite pastime, and on one such occasion, a raiding party from the O Reillys' stole a couple of hundred cows from the O Farrells. The chief was a young man then and he and his fellow clansmen were in hot pursuit of the fleeing O Reillys when a warrior hurled an ash spear piercing his thigh. His comrades carried him on a makeshift litter back to the castle where the skill and devotion of their physician, Doctor O Hickey saved not only his life but the loss of his leg and since the time of the injury, he could only walk with the aid of a stick.*

Refilling his goblet to overflowing he instinctively touched his thigh grimacing at the throbbing pain. "*A Iosa Criost,*" he uttered, swallowing his drink in one swift gulp, the many drams of whiskey failing to dull the edges of the pain, and placing his head on his folded arms his memory began to wander. *Once he was the powerful, Chief O Farrell of the ancient lands of Teffia and Annaly, now renamed by the foreigners the county of Longford but to him and his people it would forever be Teffia and Annaly as it had been for a thousand years -Christ these heretics, these foreign interlopers, contaminating the pure soil of their country and he remembered his father saying. One country- one people means peace; one country- two peoples mean war, and his father was right. The O Farrells were ill-fated as their lands the first in Ireland to be shired by the Lord Deputy, Sir Henry Sidney in 1570, the same year the priest came with the news the pope had excommunicated Queen Elizabeth. The location of Teffia and Annaly was their misfortune, situated in the centre of Ireland a relatively short distance from Dublin, a frontier between Gaelic Ireland and the English Pale, and a gateway to Connaught. Their land was flat with few mountain ranges or forests where they could fight in the Irish way of ambuscades to inflict damage on approaching English armies like his brother in law, O Rourke had managed to do for several years in Breffni, but look at what was happening to him, his land and people destroyed trying to resist the foreigners. They might be good at skirmishing and hit and run tactics in the bogs and forests but had not the arms or means to fight a well trained disciplined army with heavy cavalry and modern weaponry. This Sidney knew and his spies keep him well informed about the strength and capability of the O Farrells to resist his iron will, and so their ancient tribal lands were shired in the English fashion and parceled out to various septs and lesser men than him, and men without a claim under Irish law were granted portions of O Farrell's land with Sidney exercising the tried and tested English policy of divide and conquer, and the O Farrells subject to Sidney's devious stratagem of Surrender and Regrant introduced by, Henry V111 whereby the land was surrendered to the Crown and the Irish chiefs' granted a new title and the land held in tenure under English law and the protection of the Crown. So, he swapped his Irish title the Chief O Farrell for the English feudal titles of Lord O Farrell and Sheriff of Longford, but these were empty and meaningless as the power rested with the Queens' Commissioners in Mullingar where the Lord Deputy had appointed an Englishman, Richard Steynes to act as sheriff all because he couldn't speak the English tongue. The new titles were granted under strict conditions including abandoning all Irish customs and law, paying taxes, even outlawing their ancient sport of hurling, and most importantly swearing allegiance to the Queen. He soon learned the Irish lord must tow the feudal line with the sword of Damocles hanging over his head, and it was the beginning of the end for Lord O Farrell. Many of his people despised him for going over to the English, and even his younger son had deserted him.*

Under English law the eldest son inherited his father's title and wealth, however under Irish Brehon law of it was not the eldest son who automatically inherited his father's estate but the person the clan considered the ablest and most suitable to become the leader and the father's wealth divided into equal portions among his sons. The O Farrell people wanted Cahir to succeed him but now as the eldest son, Fergal would inherit his title and estate under English law. The people saw Fergal as a scholar and Cahir as a natural leader and trained warrior but he believed his eldest son Fergal with his fine education and proficiency in the English language and Latin was the right person to deal effectively with the Queen's Commissioners and manage the affairs of the family, so he instructed O Hanly and Father O Duffy never to discuss Irish matters or the wars against the English with Fergal and to shelter him from hot-headed Irish politics, and when O Rogan the Jesuit came and told them about the prophecy of Saint Colmcille he made sure Fergal knew nothing of the matter. He didn't want the flames of discontentment and insurrection with dangerous talk of rebellion to lick at his son's soul.

A cloak of drowsiness enveloped Lord O Farrell and drifting into slumber relived the warrior days of his youth fighting great battles and driving vast herds of stolen cattle across the flat open plains of the midlands at the head of his brave band of warriors. In the background, the sound of revelry reverberated noisily around the great hall with singing, dancing, and the reciting of ancient war songs and ballads' lamenting the coming of the foreigners, the destruction of the ancient oak forests, and the courage and bravery of the O Farrells at the Battle of Clontarf when, under the leadership of the High King of Ireland, Brian Boru they drove the Danes out of Ireland six hundred years before!

Lady O Farrell touched her husband affectionately on the shoulder as he lay slumped over, head cradled on folded arms, snoring softly, empty goblet grasped rigid in hand. *Him, old and grey, the story of his life etched on his face with the constant worry of keeping on the right side of the Crown and the burden of the heavy tax the government levied against the family. A kind generous man he was too, and when he travelled to the city each year to pay what taxes he could he brought her back plenty of gossip about the settlers and always a new silk dress in the English style. Once he was different, a brave, strong, proud warrior chief of the O Farrells, and not a care in the world. They were so young and innocent when they married all those years ago. She bore him many children, she couldn't recall how many, seven maybe eight or nine but only two survived, two boys, Cahir and Fergal her oldest who sat at her side. Her handsome scholar, a healthy youth with studious face, and the brave deed he had done in Dublin saving a man's life brought a smile to her face and made her chest swell with pride. But he was born a sickly child and they were unsure if he would survive and only by the skill of Doctor O Hickey did they manage to keep him alive and for the first few years of his life he was confined to bed needing constant attention and because of his poor health wasn't fostered as was the Irish way like his brother Cahir. It was by God's good grace Father O Duffy sought sanctuary with them when he did becoming Fergal's tutor, and an excellent tutor he was too. When her brother Cormac attended university at Oxford her father wanted Fergal to join him but Lord O Farrell point blank refused to let his son leave Ireland as he considered Father O Duffy a better tutor than the heretics in England. How many years was it now since Cahir left home, many, many years and not one day passed she did not think about him and worry about him, and each day she asked Father O Duffy to say a prayer for the Lord above to keep him safe in the wars against the foreigners. Cahir had been fostered by her own family the O Rourkes in Breffni and trained in the art of war and an expert horseman but he bitterly resented his father for going over to the English as he knew it meant he could never be the leader of his people and inherit what he believed was rightfully his and would rather fight and die than to be a slave to the English. Everything turned bad the day the monstrous tyrant, the petulant Lord Deputy, Henry Sidney arrived at Longford Castle with his band of thieving knights. Sir Big Harry of the Beer- Henri Na Beara the people called him because he drank beer instead of water and travelled with mules laden with barrels of English ale. They knew of his awful deeds of carnage at Rathlin Island and Mullaghamast, and how someone could be so violent especially to all those poor defenseless women and helpless children. She shuddered at the thought of the brutality and inhumanity of this man and his people, terrorising every corner of the land bringing death and destruction in his path. Fat, pompous, Saxon oppressor and him with his army of armor-clad knights mounted on powerful warhorses. The people called them The Soldiers of London and were terrified of these ruthless, brutish men and their modern weapons. He demanded her husband surrender the lands of the O Farrells his family held for almost six hundred years since the time of Brian Boruma the mighty High King of Ireland. Sure wasn't it because of the bravery of the clan at the Battle of Clontarf in 1014 when the victorious Irish army drove the Danes out of Ireland they called them the O Fearghails –O Farrells –Man of Valour and her husband was indeed a man of valour but she understood his predicament entirely; how could he resist. If he refused to surrender the land they would be driven off and face extermination at the hands of Sidney and his band of killers. The English not satisfied taking their lands and their livings would kill them under the pretense of the law and so her husband rode to Mullingar, signed away his birthright and proud and ancient heritage. Many of his people despised him for this act, for turning his back on the old ways, but what choice did he have. Her father, King Brian O Rourke refused to surrender his title and was locked in a vicious war with the English but he was in a different place, a place called Breffni in the wilderness of Connaught with the whole area covered with forests and mountains where he could fight running skirmishes, and where it was difficult for the English to operate as they could never confront the Irish in open warfare. But all her reckless and brave father succeeded in doing was prolonging his day of reckoning with the foreigners, destroying the country and causing much hardship and suffering to his people, bringing a famine on their heads, and she heard tales of the terrible slaughter of her people in Breffni by the President of Connaught, George Bingham and his cutthroat brothers. But she was proud of her father especially the day a priest called a year ago and told her he came from Breffni where he had delivered a letter directly from Philip the King of Spain personally thanking her father for sheltering eight hundred Spanish soldiers in his castle at Lough Gill saving them from certain death at the hands of the English after the sinking of the Armada ships on the Irish coast. The priest made her laugh when he told her father had made a wooden effigy of Queen Elizabeth sitting on a mock throne which his soldiers used for target practice and knew spies would report this insult to George Bingham knowing full well this would certainly reach the ears of the Queen, but it would only make the Crown more determined to destroy him and destroy him they would. The awful night her husband returned from*

Mullingar, white-faced barely able to speak, his body paralysed with fear as he told her what happened. Walking to where Sir Henry Sidney had set up his camp for the Surrender and Regrant ceremony he froze in horror at the sight confronting him. Both sides of the path were lined with the blank staring, bloody heads of vanquished local chiefs all known to him, the ones who refused to pledge allegiance to the Crown. His cousins, uncles, friends, all staring at him in muted horror, blood still dripping from their severed heads, mouths twisted and open as if trying to utter a warning of the fate awaiting him at the hands of the English. Sir Big Harry's objective to terrorise the Irish worked and all but the bravest refused to sign over their titles and lands, the foreigners, bringers of death and mayhem to her people, a cruel, callous, treacherous race of men and lesser men than the Irish and us with our own language, traditions and culture, just why do they want our people to be like them? A lump rose in her throat looking at her husband and his broken countenance as grimacing dark clouds' filled her soul thinking of the fate awaiting him and the O Farrells.

A multitude of thoughts crossed Fergal O Farrell's mind as he sat, a grin as wide as the ocean on his face, a warm glow of pride burning deep in his chest. *While he had not wished to travel to the city with his father the incident in the Royal Oak made it worthwhile and how he found the courage and presence of mind to do what he did he still could not fathom.*

He'd saved a man's life, a rich and powerful Lord, and into the bargain made his father and their people proud and tonight was the first time many of the tenants ever acknowledged him, and most importantly he had impressed Emir. His body trembled with excitement thinking about what would happen when they met later in the orchard and he had decided the time was right to reveal his plans for them both. His father objected to his relationship with Emir who he saw as a loyal servant but unfit for the future Lord O Farrell wishing him instead to marry a person of rank anyone who might improve their situation even one of the old English from the Pale would be acceptable but he had other plans for Emir and himself. He was sick and tired of the constant money problems and the troublesome tenants so he had made the decision they should elope and go to Mullingar where he could teach Latin and abandon the Irish ways and might even disown his Catholic fate and become a Lutheran if it benefited him although it was something he would have to consider carefully. He didn't share the burning passion of many of his fellow Irishmen for resisting the English. He just didn't care and would never be like his brother and the other hotheads. He would join the foreigners for a better life for himself and Emir. Sure hadn't his cousin Sean O Farrell changed his name to John Shane forsaking his Irish ways becoming a Protestant and lived in Mullingar working as a translator for the foreigners in the courts. Yes, it was the way forward, join the English and not resist them. Let the greedy Saxon interlopers have the land and be done with it, let them deal with the tenants and pay the taxes. What life would he and Emir have in Longford with the English snapping at their heels and many of the people resenting him as Lord O Farrell? He would reveal all to Emir later and they could begin planning for their future it was the most important thing and the man he saved in Finglas could help him secure a position of standing with the English, the man owed him his life did he not. But what about the prophecy Lord Fingal mentioned and his father's reaction, what did it all mean. While it was good to bring comfort to the prisoner in Dublin Castle, he knew his father was a kind decent man, but the risk he took Lord Fingal had said so, surely there must be another reason and his father always had a good reason for everything he did. It was ten years since Cahir left and he wondered what he would think about him saving a man's life he was sure he would be proud but he was angry at Cahir for going to the wars. It was not the way forward in dealing with the foreigners, his father's way was the right way and Cahir had broken his parent's hearts by leaving and jeopardising the family's credibility with the Crown. He could have ended up a hostage in that awful Dublin castle with the Unfortunates all because of his brother's rashness. His father had to bribe the Queen's Commissioners with gifts of a hundred cows and six sacks of Spanish wine and publicly disown Cahir to stop them from taking punitive action against the O Farrells.

Father O Duffy sat gazing into the blazing fire reflecting on his lengthy career and time in the service of the O Farrells. *Forty years ago his family had sent him as a youth from his home in County Meath to train as a Jesuit scholar with many other Irishmen at the Irish College of Colegio Del Arzobispo in Salamanca, Southern Spain in the province of Castile. He had received a stipend from the King of Spain to be ordained into the priesthood in order to return to his native land to maintain his cherished Catholic religion which was outlawed in Ireland and he was lucky to be alive. When the pope excommunicated Queen Elizabeth in 1570, he returned to Ireland and on his arrival journeyed to his home in County Meath to visit his elderly parents. Little did he know about the state of affairs in the country as he had been exiled for many years? The heretics had spies everywhere and to be a priest was punishable by immediate death without trial, the punishment proscribed. A close friend of his, Father Brian O Riordan, a fellow Jesuit who had studied with him in Spain and returned with him to Ireland, had been captured in Wexford and subject to an awful death, and only a year ago his old tutor, Professor O Rogan came to visit him at Longford and told him of a great prophecy of Saint Colmcille he had discovered in an old Irish manuscript at the Irish college about a Savior King who would unite the Irish clans and drive out the heretics but poor O Rogan was captured by the soldiers, tortured, and taken to a forge, arms and legs broken, and left the night to suffer*

57

agonising pains and in the morning disemboweled. No surprise he told the foreigners about the prophecy and now it would be common knowledge throughout the land. No quarter was given to Catholic clergy and they were hunted mercilessly, and if you were lucky the soldiers might use you as target practice discharging their leaden bullets and grant you a speedy end. When he returned to his village someone reported his presence to the Queen's Commissioner and a posse of soldiers came to arrest him but by good luck managed to escape. Friends told him the O Farrells of Longford Castle who at great risk were known as devout Catholics and for harbouring fugitive Catholic clergy, and so he sought refuge with the family and never left. By chance, shortly after the time of his arrival, Lady O Farrell gave birth to a son who was born with a malady and required the constant attention of Doctor O Hickey to keep him alive and at the age of one year he was destined to be sent for fostering by a surrogate family but his mother refused, the strong-willed woman she was, unwilling to let him leave the castle for fear of losing her beloved eldest son. So, in contrast to the Irish custom, and much to the consternation and disagreement of her husband, the child stayed with his parents and he became tutor to the boy, Fergal O Farrell teaching him the language of the English, Latin, and the classics to ensure he would become a well versed and educated young man. The family was kind and generous treating him like one of their own and Lord O

Farrell let it be known he was in his service as a tutor to his son but he covertly celebrated mass every Sunday in the great hall and administered the sacraments bringing comfort and solace to the O Farrell people. Long hours were spent each day tutoring Fergal who was intelligent, and soon fluent in the English and Latin tongues, and would make a good leader of the O Farrells, and his skills useful in his dealings with the foreigners, and Lord O Farrell was correct to shelter his son from the infernal machinations of the Irish rebels like his brother Cahir. The impetuousness of the hot-headed fool nearly ruining the family, and he firmly believed Lord O Farrell made the right decision in accepting the Surrender and Regrant Agreement from the heretic, Sir Henry Sidney. Tacit obedience and cunning were the best ways forward until the prophecy was fulfilled and the time right to crush the foreigners and drive the English heretics from Ireland and restore the true religion of Christ.

Chapter Four

Much taken in strong drink, Cahir O Farrell slumped back, wistful smile on face, as fleeting memories of his home and family raced through his mind. *He missed Annaly, the ancient land of the O Farrells, and he missed those long summer days swimming and fishing in the Camlin, him and Fergal running with mad gambol along the banks of the river. He missed everything about Longford, but this night he was in a different place with different people, his comrades in arms, in the great wooden hall of the fort of the Irish chief, Fiach Mc Hugh O Byrne, Lord of Ranaleagh, deep in the valley of Glenmalure in the rugged mountains of County Wicklow. Here he served in the army of O Byrne who controlled an area south from Glendalough to the woods of Shillelagh in Wexford, and west to the borders of Carlow, a vast territory of forests and mountains rich in hiding places. Lifting his goblet in both hands he drank long and deep from his cup of joy, scanning the faces of his comrades scattered around the hall in small groups laughing and joking. Wiry dark-haired mountain men, and amongst them tall young men of noble countenance, the sons of Irish chiefs like himself. The men from different worlds but bonded together in a brutal war of resistance against the foreigners. Ronan O Byrne, the chief's eldest son the centre of attention as always, the bravest man he ever met who saved his life on more than one occasion with his band of kern, the lightly armed, fleet-footed soldiers of O Byrne, and beside him the ever-smiling mischief-maker Phelim O Doherty from Buncrana in Inishowen disowned by his father Sir John O Doherty, the Queens most loyal Irish chief in Ulster, and alongside him the tall handsome Manus O Sullivan from Kerry his closest comrade, and with him the wise and proud Liam O Griofa from the woods of Galway, all brave and gallant men of the cavalry squadron in the army of Fiach Mc Hugh O Byrne. He glanced over at the two Tyrone men sitting chatting in the corner, big strong fearsome warriors of the Great Hugh O Neill, Earl of Tyrone. Once there were twelve of them but Captain Tom Lee and his soldiers' killed their comrades during the last raid when the foreigners burned down the fort at Ballinacor. Rising clumsily he staggered towards Chief O Byrne, who sat with his wife the beautiful Rose O Toole, and approaching the table raised his drink in salute. A wide grin crossed O Byrne face in acknowledgment and lifting his goblet he nodded to his much-loved Captain of Horse who stared back keenly at his chief, a man of invincible courage, a brilliant soldier, and a natural leader known to the English as the Raven. But O Byrne told him how he wasn't always the fearless warrior and, as his father had done, avoided contact with the foreigners living a remote life in the fastness of the woods and glens. But things changed when the Queen's Commissioners, Crispin Harington and Fulke Wesley, came into the lands of the Cavanaghs in Carlow, a defenseless people who did not speak English or understand the ways of the foreigners. Harington, greedy for their land hung forty innocent men and women, and this single act infuriated O Byrne as he had been fostered by the Cavanaghs and loved their people. So, he forsook his remote life determined to avenge his foster family declaring war on the foreigners becoming a formidable marauder and a constant thorn in their side. Frequently raiding and burning the settler's outlying villages almost to the gates of Dublin Castle which was twenty-five miles from his fort and no matter how hard they tried the English could not capture or destroy O Byrne, who became the paladin of the Irish people, deathly to the English, and the reason why himself and the sons of Irish chiefs joined the army of O Byrne. His new life in Wicklow was hard and disciplined, and as the son of a Lord he always had the luxury of a soft bed and a full belly, but here it was different. The soldiers slept on a bare clay floor, feet towards the fire, mantles wrapped tightly for warmth, eating what food they killed in the forest or caught in the rivers or lakes, and many a day his belly grumbled. When Captain Lee burned down the fort at Ballinacor they slept for four months on the forest floor while rebuilding their stronghold further up the valley. It was a bitterly cold winter and they huddled together for warmth, and he would lie at night on a carpet of soft damp earth counting the twinkling stars visible through the canopy of trees and wake up frozen to the bone, and often the old and infirm never waking. Times they were reduced to surviving on squirrel meat becoming experts at laying traps, and often their only source of food. But he came to love his new Spartan life in a sylvan world of dark forests and deep valleys, days spent hunting and fishing or raiding the settlers of the Pale. He'd been hardened and grown callous by the brutal adversity, and how many men he had killed he did not know, and killing became his life and death his constant companion. He had been trained in the ways of Irish warfare by his uncle and foster father, Brian O Rourke becoming a skilled horseman deadly with the Irish light spear. O Byrne made him captain of a squad of twenty horsemen called hobblers who, on their small sturdy Irish horse without stirrups, could move swiftly over rough terrain and mountainous slopes easily outrunning the heavy English cavalry. One night they would raid the suburbs of Dublin, and a few days later burn and pillage settler's villages in Carlow, forever evading the English and leading them into carefully laid traps where the light-footed and lightly armed O Byrne kern would decimate the pursuing troopers. A soldier of his cavalry squadron could hurl an ash spear with deadly accuracy and the steel tip pierce an English knight at ten yards, and while the armour afforded protection the impact would often dismount the rider, and like a swarm of locusts, the kern would descend on the man stabbing and thrusting with practiced dexterity, stripping the soldier to the bare skin in sixty seconds. After their deadly work he would often gaze at the naked corpses of the English knights' lying in the dirt, bare breasts' gashed, eyes' open heavenward with mouth agape, and always the same innocent, childlike countenance, when stripped of their armour, pomposity, and arrogance. It was ten years since he had answered O Byrnes clarion call for men to join his army. Spies in Dublin Castle had informed him of a plan by the English to invade his territory with a huge army fresh from England, to destroy him and his people and drive them from the forests. For the turn of a coin, the Queens' most loyal subject would furnish information and Fiach had many spies in the castle and informed this army was led by the new Lord Deputy, Baron Arthur Grey de Wilton, a Buckinghamshire knight with three thousand newly levied men. He smiled recalling the time O Byrne swaggered around the great hall mocking the new Lord Deputy. "Listen to me now you Irish dogs," he mimicked in a clipped accent. "I am the one and only, the mighty invincible, Baron Arthur Grey de Wilton the Fourteenth, and I am going to teach you Irish savages a lesson in English manners," pinching his nose and speaking in a mock English accent to the hysterical laughter of the men. O Byrne was informed the new Lord Deputy was a vainglorious man full of pomp and ceremony, knowing little of Ireland or its people, but with his new well-equipped army intended to crush the Desmond rebellion, to which O Byrne gave support, and destroy the clan to end their consistent raiding and burning of which the people of the Pale complained bitterly, but the resourceful O Byrne had different ideas intending to teach the Lord Deputy a lesson in Irish manners. Hugh O Neill, Earl of Tyrone had secretly sent him twelve of his best soldiers trained in the use of firearms and a cart heavily laden with Spanish muskets with an ample supply of black powder and ball and O Byrne gathered an army of eight hundred well trained and armed men to defend himself and his people against the onslaught of Baron Arthur Grey de Wilton, and his army fresh from England.*

The wily and cunning O Byrne set a trap to snare Lord Deputy Grey and the English forces. It was the night of the handing over of the sword ceremony in Dublin Castle and the army captains, Crown officials and their wives, present in the King's Hall to partake in a sumptuous feast and enjoy the glorious and extravagant spectacle of the Queen's representatives' swearing-in ceremony. On learning of the event, O Byrne dispatched Cahir O Farrell and his horse to strike at the Pale causing as much havoc as their small band could. Moving swiftly from Ballinacor they rode within three miles of the city sacking the settler's villages of Crumlin, Drimnagh, and Inchicore, setting fire to low thatched houses their progress marked with the lurid glare of burning buildings, and killing anyone who opposed them. In the King's Hall, Lord Deputy Grey made merry with his officials who lauded him on his new role when Sergeant Tiptoff came with the news the O Byrnes were burning and killing a couple of miles from the city. The indignant Lord Deputy jumped to his feet declaring. "Mine own valorous captain's of the Queen, this night the woodsman, O Byrne, hast the temerity to interrupt our state proceeding we must, therefore, teachest these wild mountain men a lesson and bridle the unruly Irish colts with a sharp English bit. In the morn, men of England, we shalt fly the Saint George's cross over the Raven's fort, and they shalt taste the punitory whip of English rule, the rough mountaineer put to silence and his head fixed over the castle gate." Against the advice of his commanders, the army mustered and three thousand men began their march to the hills of Wicklow and the fort of Ballinacor. The soldiers, mainly raw recruits from Wales and Yorkshire, dressed in scarlet or buff uniforms with puffed sleeves and heavily armed with muskets and pikes with seasoned captains' leading the column. At Lugnaquilla, O Byrnes scouts' caught sight of the approaching army over a mile away easily detected by their garish uniforms. Cahir O Farrell and his squad rode temptingly close to Greys' forward column luring the English into pursuing them, and passing through the Glen of Imaal entered the rocky valley of Glenmalure, a deep U shaped ravine surrounded by woods and bogs, each side covered with bracken, a stream snaking along the bottom. Lord Grey, looking every bit the knight as he rode at the head of the column, clad in shining armour with breast and back plates, cuirass and chain mail, wide ruffs, and polished steel plumed helmet, and believing he had trapped O Byrne and his ragged army shouted to his captain. "Captain Lee, order the men to throweth up a rough earthwork across the mouth of the valley to prevent any escapeth, methinks this day we shalt flush out the prey and ruffle the feathers of the Raven, what dost thou surmise?" The captain, shrugging his shoulders without replying glanced scornfully at his commander. *Another dangerous fool, how many men would be slaughtered this day for the popinjay jack knows nothing of the wily O Byrne, the firebrand of the mountains, a man he'd been trying to kill for many years.* Lord Grey barked orders to his general of the Queen's Kern. "Cosby, get thee up the valley with the kern and flush out the savages that we shalt maketh an easy kill." Captain Lee shook his head as he glared at the corpulent red-faced Cosby puffing and huffing as he tripped and stumbled down the side of the valley trying to find his footing. *Christ, this is all too easy and poor Cosby, though brave and experienced, is seventy years of age and what match would he be against the fleet-footed O Byrne kern- another pompous English fool.* Turning in his saddle the Lord Deputy addressed a knight newly arrived from England. "Sir Walter Raleigh," he commanded. "Thou art strictly forbidden to partake in action this day, the Queen hast ordered it so, for she is of the mind thee lack experience in Irish warfare and wishes to keepeth thee safe for future enterprises. Methinks Sir, thou hast much favour with her gracious Majesty, Master Raleigh, dost thou not?" Lord Grey, with his bodyguard of mounted troopers, stood expectantly at the head of the ravine as a double file of men and scattered horse led by General Cosby moved deeper into the valley which echoed to the grunts and groans of cursing men with no enemy in sight. Further along on the lip of the ravine, O Byrne stood surrounded by his squadron of horse. "Cahir, my captain, I cannot believe the foolishness of Grey sending his men into the valley they greatly outnumber and outgun us are you sure this is not a cunning strategy to deceive us, could they have more soldiers to the rear?" No, chief," his captain replied confidently. "Our scouts report no troop movement for ten miles except for Greys' column; the man is a pompous English fool." O Byrne lifted his sword. "Well captain, the time is right for our musketeers to begin their work; I shall give the order to fire." The men began sniping with arquebus muskets their deadly fusillade of ball taking a heavy toll on the marching column causing panic amongst the inexperienced troops who began to falter, stumbling and tripping on the slippery stones of the stream. To the sound of Irish war pipes, O Byrne's kern followed by their allies the O Tooles and the Cavanaghs who, concealed in the bracken and trees, sprang forth from the sides of the valley pouring down the craggy slopes and falling on the flanks of the long array of men strung along the basin of the ravine. The ferocity of the attack broke the English lines causing the recruits to drop their weapons and in blind panic hurtle back along the valley the kern at their backs stabbing and hacking, a handful of lingering stragglers tripping and slipping on loose stones to be brutally cut down. A cloud of thunder came over Lord Grey's face as he watched in dismay, his self assured hubris badly shaken, the retreating mass of soldiers' charging down the valley towards him. On the ledge above, Cahir watched as the red mass of teeming figures poured wildly down the ravine a black swarm of kern in hot pursuit and spurring his horse into action moved rapidly followed by his squadron of hobblers. Lord Grey sat upright in his saddle startled to see a group of horsemen thundered towards him like hobs of hell, spears above heads, pointed with deadly intent. "Lord Deputy Grey." Captain Lee snapped. "Methinks this day the valorous Lord above hast forsaken us and the hunter hast becometh the hunted." Stirring into action the captain's aid, Trooper Tom Churchyard nudged his horse forward into the path of the leading rider who galloped furiously at him, coming head to head with an Irish youth without armour, spear held high aimed directly at him. Raising and levelling his heavy metal cavalry lance under his arm to make short work of the Irish upstart he was taken aback when at close distance the youth let fly his spear which struck him hard on the chest splintering on impact with only the steel tip piercing his breastplate puncturing his skin forcing him to drop his lance. Drawing his petronel cavalry pistol from his holster he cocked the weapon discharging a shot at close range the ball grazing the rider's shoulder. Trooper Churchyard, giving his reins a sharp tug, caused his horse to turn sharply riding swiftly back to his party who had fled the scene in chaos for the safety of their citadel leaving the valley basin strewn with the bodies of eight hundred men including several captains and a general. As the noise of battle receded the O Byrne kern began the grisly task of dispatching with sword or musket butt those still breathing and stepping over bloody corpses yanked off boots, ripped off shirts and tunics, piling high discarded bits of armour, muskets, swords, and pikes, as they shouted obscenities and waved captured flags and banners wildly in the air to the crack of the odd musket shot. Skirmishing with the remnants of Grey's soldiers to the gates of the castle, Cahir O Farrell's small band returned to their stronghold triumphant in their devastating victory over the mighty army of the Lord Deputy, Baron Arthur Grey de Wilton the Fourteenth.

To a tree outside O Byrnes fort, a man was tied naked and bloody as a group of young girls flayed their captive until no skin was left on his body, his flesh exposed raw red to the elements. Such was his pity, Cahir drew his sword to bring a quick and merciful end to the man's sufferings but a hand grabbed his arm firmly and his comrade, Ronan O Byrne spoke. "No, Cahir, let it be my friend, death is too good for him and he deserves to suffer for the devil of a man is the notorious general of the Queen's Kern, Francis Cosby and those." He pointed to the group of hysteric young girls savagely beating their captive. "Those are the orphans of this English heretic who did hang their parents, a vile creature devoid of a spark of human decency. Let it be Cahir, it is their revenge they will cease soon and leave him to die under the rays of the sun and the cold of the wind for the English way of torture is the forge and hammer and this is ours, and we leave such work to the women."

Chapter Five

The office over the barrack-room was a sparse affair with creaky, bare planked wooden floor, waist-high hardwood wainscoting, and rough stone walls largely unadorned save for a portrait of the Queen, the air in the small, dusty, musty room permeated by the fusty odour of damp and decay. At his desk piled high with state papers, a well-thumbed bible, and a miniature silver-framed portrait of his wife, Agnes, the Lord Deputy stooped forward quill in ink-stained hand, occasionally dipping into ink well, writing slantingly in a neat and tidy hand. A man of nimble mind and pauca verba, crafty, cautious, and treacherous, of recent times inflicted by the maladies of old age, ill-health, and ill-temper. Hailing from Milton Hall in Northhamptonshire, William Fitzwilliam was born into a wealthy family his father, William, Sheriff of London, and treasurer to Cardinal Wolsey. He served previously in Ireland when his brother-in-law Sir Henry Sidney, the Lord Deputy, appointed him Vice Deputy Treasurer and later Lord Justice, but was accused of corruption by, Lord Justice Rokeby barely escaping charges. His previous official post was in England supervising the execution of Mary Queen of Scots at Fotheringhay Castle, a task he was proud of as Sir William was a devout puritan and loathed Catholicism. While rumours of corruption hung over him like a dark cloud and he was not a soldier, the Queen considered him a safe pair of hands with a good knowledge of Ireland returning him as Lord Deputy and here he sat, as he did every day, reading the latest dispatches from England delivered on the tide that morning from Bristol aboard *The Ramrod*. Breaking the royal seal he opened the voluminous document leafing deftly through the weighty sheaf of Crown dispatches. *Always the same, the parsimonious Queen complaining about the money spent on the army which cost twice as much as the tax gathered in Ireland, and rising steadily with every outbreak of rebellion, always fearing the wars in Ireland would bankrupt the Crown. Oh, how this abominable land of Ireland hath exhausted our promised land of England. The first dispatch stated his request for two thousand soldiers and additional monies for the upkeep of Dublin Castle, which was falling into a ruinous state, was refused although he informed the Queen, in person, that everything in the castle was either rotten or rusty, and he even paid out of his own pocket for repairs to the roof of his living quarters to stop rainwater dripping on his face as he lay sleeping. He had not received his salary for six months and the army was operating on credit from Dublin merchants who charged two pennies a loaf of bread which cost one penny in Chester or Bristol. Everything in this godforsaken place swallowed money even armies and nobody in England cared about Ireland. Was he expected to finance the army himself and he already in debt? How could he face another year of penury and God forbid if something happened to him, the ignobility of leaving his son William to inherit his debts and leaving his poor wife Agnes penniless, oh how he missed his wife and family? Why did he ever adventure his reputation in this place, he had gained nothing from the fruits of his travails during his Irish service which he prayed God almighty might soon deliver him and he'd already requested to be stood down on grounds of ill health?*

His secretary Fitton approached the desk and addressed him softly. "Lord Deputy, I apologise for the intrusion but there is a Trooper Churchyard outside who wishes to speaketh with thee and present this petition." Carefully placing his quill in the ink well he laid the parchment document neatly across his desk scrutinising the contents which read:

Petition of Thomas Churchyard Trooper her Majesties Army of Ireland

Thomas Oliver Churchyard hath served valorously in the Irish armies of her gracious Majesty for the past thirty-five years and hath in all his services received diver's wounds which canst be seen on his body and never received any recompense from the Queen. May it, therefore, please her Majesty to bestow on him a yearly pension and grant him an honorable discharge from his lengthy and honorable military service.

Signed: Captain Thomas Lee of the Queen's Horse (Army of Ireland)

The Lord Deputy was taken aback. *A soldier with thirty-five years service in the Irish wars; remarkable. He must be the longest-serving soldier in the Queen's army and him still alive to tell the tale, and I can only imagine what tales this man could tell.* "Secretary Fitton," he ordered. "Bringeth this man to me immediately and I wilt hold discourse with him and instruct the servants to bringeth refreshments, wine and toast for myself and ale for the trooper. I wager I shalt be some time while he relates his experiences in the army of which I hast much interest." The door flung open and a heavily built man entered the room, morion in hand, dressed in the attire of the Queen's cavalry. "Mine own Lord," he bowed respectfully. "I dost giveth thee thanks for meeting with me." Without replying the Lord Deputy gestured for the trooper to sit staring keenly at the man before him. Truculent countenance, bull-necked with a pronounced crescent-shaped scar on his brown-tinted, weather-beaten face a reminder of a long healed battle wound. Placing his morion and broadsword on the desk the trooper sat upright directly facing the Lord Deputy. "Trooper Churchyard, thou hast given long and valorous service to our gracious Queen hast thee not," the Lord Deputy said, casting a furtive glance at the petition as he filled a goblet with wine and a tankard with English ale.

"Trooper, partake in a little refreshment and prithee tell me about thy lengthy service in the army, dost taketh thy time. I am most curious to learneth of thine experiences in the Irish wars for I shalt tell thee now thy Lord Deputy is but a humble administrator and no soldier, and the only weapon I ever didst holdeth wast this quill." The trooper sat forward cleared his throat and in a gravelly voice replied. "Mine own Lord, where rebellion doth breaketh out in Ireland, I am present and hast suffered all the maladies of the common soldier, sleeping in every ditch in the land, hast endured every discomfort and mine own best captains' hast been hunger, cold, toil, and sickness, and I cannot recall how many horses were killed under me or how many men I hast killed." The Lord Deputy sat back heavily in his chair and inquired. "With whom didst thee first serve trooper, and prithee tell me all as I dost wish to learn of thine experiences, and the stratagems' used by thy commanders in the service of her Majesty." Trooper Churchyard placed both hands flatly on the table and leaning forward began. "Mine own Lord," he paused on seeing the Lord Deputy stare fixedly at his hands. *The hands of a common flesher in Cheapside, two fingers missing from one hand and both hands crisscrossed with fine red scars etched markedly into his skin.* "This one," the trooper affirmed gesturing indifferently to his hands. "The sword work of the O Kellys, the O Driscolls, the O

Murphys, and a Gallowglass took my fingers in Monaghan, the rest I hast long forgotten." Folding his arms he sat back and continued. "Now, Lord Deputy, I shalt begin mine own tale which I dost desire thee findeth of interest. At the age of fifteen, I wast employed as an apprenticed blacksmith in Chester and pressed into service by, Sheriff Roderick Babington to come to this country in the service of, Thomas Radclyffe the Third Earl of Sussex in the year 1556, to quell the rebellion of Shane O Neill in Ulster." The Lord Deputy had heard the tale about the haughty Shane the Proud as they called him. The Queen wanted the Irish chiefs to adopt the English language and dress and in defiance, O Neill had the temerity to arrive at court in London wearing full Irish garb accompanied by a guard of axe bearing Galloglasses' clad in shirts of mail, iron caps, and linen garments dyed with saffron. Shane with his band of Scottish redshank desperados marched defiantly into the Star Chamber to the utter amazement of the Queen and her courtiers and for his insolence, Sussex sent him poisoned draughts of wine as a gift but the poisoner poor at his task, and Shane and his comrade drinking the wine survived but swore revenge on Sussex. "Search as we didst, mine own Lord," he continued. "We couldst not findeth the rebel O Neill and his men who melted into the hills and bogs and in frustration, Sussex changed tactics and we burned the crops and farms bringing a great famine on the people of Tyrone even slaughtering four thousand of O Neill's cattle and I canst tell thee, mine own Lord, us soldiers' feasted well on meat for many a day while the Irish ate grass or watercress and the beef we couldst not eat we burned or threw in the river and thou couldst ride fifty miles across Tyrone not seeing one living thing, man or beast. We even slaughtered O Neill's broodmares to stop the supply of horse to the Irish cavalry. But, Lord Deputy, Shane the Proud didst not alloweth our deeds against his people rest, and as we retreated we camped at a place called Monaghan, not even posting guards at nightfall such wast our confidence." Stopping to refill his tankard he took a long swig and continued. "They came out of the darkness, five hundred axe yielding O Neill Gallowglass, screaming their accursed Irish war cries in tight battle formation cutting a bloody swath through our ranks and killing over four hundred of our men. The Irish called it *The Battle of the Red Sagums* because Sussex hadst us soldiers wear red coats but Lord Deputy it wast no battle more like a slaughter and I didst taste the steel of a Scottish battleaxe that night to remindeth me always of Shane the Proud, and they sayeth a handful of the Gallowglass who slaughtered us hadst been to the Queen's court earlier that year with O Neill. Anyway, mine own Lord, Sussex was a better soldier at killing cattle and starving women and children than Irish soldiers." "Trooper," the Lord Deputy asked. "What about the murder of Shane O Neill's kith and kin in Belfast, wert thou present on that occasion?" "Ay mine own Lord, a treacherous affair, if I dost sayeth The Betrayal of the Clandeboye, is what tis called and I wast at the time serving under the First Earl of Essex, Walter Devereux who wished to be more merciless than his predecessors and granted the whole of Ulster to colonise by the Queen, but he couldst not defeat the O Neills a powerful family who didst hold the lands for a thousand years. To make peace, Chief Brian O Neill of Clandeboye invited Walter Devereux to his principal castle at Castlereagh- the Grey Castle outside Belfast for days of feasting and drinking, and the Irish knoweth how to dresseth a table well, but Essex hadst other plans besides feastings and parleying with Brian O Neill. Upon entering the castle Devereux gaveth the order and us men of the Queen didst commence the slaughter of two hundred unarmed servants and attendants, men, and women, breaking the Irish custom and strict rules of hospitality while the terrified Brian and his wife, both who wast later hanged, gazed on in horror. Nasty business but the Earl of Essex frustrated at his lack of success carried out this vile murderous act to sendeth an aggressive and threatening message to the Irish chiefs. But Lord Deputy, it changed nothing and only madeth the Irish hate us more and even greater murder didst we inflict on the clan of Sorley Boy Mc Donnell, the Scottish allies of the

Irish. Sir Henry Sidney didst order the second Earl of Essex, Robert Devereux the son of Walter and his captain Sir John Norris to march on the Scots in Antrim and annihilate them but Mc Sorley was informed of our approach and to protect the women, children and infirm of his clan, shipped those folk over to Rathin Island three miles off the coast of Antrim. But Robert Devereux wanted to teachest the Scots a hard lesson to defer them from aiding the Irish and the famous buccaneer, Sir Francis Drake didst carry us on his fine ship *The Falcon* to the island whither stood a castle held by a handful of Scottish soldiers but Captain Drake didst bombard the walls with his cannonade and they soon surrendered on promise of their lives but we butchered them. When the women and children fled and hid in the caves we hunted them down and threw every last one of them over the cliffs into the sea. A fine day's work and the said Sorley Boy Mc Donnell running wild in anguish along the shore in Antrim witnessing the slaughter from a distance powerless to lift a hand to defend his helpless people. But mine own Lord, this terrible deed didst not chasten the Scots but madeth them and the Irish more determined to defeat us." "Trooper Churchyard," the Lord Deputy declared, raising his goblet. "I dost sayeth thou hast executed many valorous deeds for the Crown in the extermination of the savage Irish and the mercenary Scots. I drinketh a toast to thy brave deeds and pray continue." "Sir, after service in Ulster I didst join the cavalry squadron of Captain Tom Lee, he who hast signed the petition, and I shalt tell thee of mine own first service with the said captain. A certain English settler named Sir Francis Cosby, a knight who came into Ireland during the reign of King Harry, a Nottingham gentleman who dwelled in Queen's County in a fine mansion called Stradbally House built on lands confiscated from a clan of the name O Connor under the plantation scheme of Queen Mary Tudor. He wast the most brutal and greedy of men and much feared by the Irish and it wast told to me by Captain Tom Lee, and I dost believeth what the good captain doth sayeth, that Cosby hadst an immense tree growing outside his house from which he wouldst hangeth the local men, women, and children, and took much delight watching infants hung by the long hair of their mothers and be vexed if the tree was bare and sayeth. *You seem to me my tree shrouded with great sadness and no wonder for you have long been childless however I shall speedily relieve your mourning and shortly adorn your bough with more Irish corpses.* "However, by his brutal methods he didst sorely whip the O Connors into a rebellious frenzy and our squadron ordered south to quell the uprising before in blazed far and wide. Cosby and his ally, Robert Hartpole anxious to defeat the Irish devised a plot to rid the land of the chiefs of Laois, so they summoned four hundred of gentlemen of rank the Irish dost call *An Daoine Uaisle* for a gathering in a rath or ancient round-shaped Irish fort known as Mullaghmast, and Cosby ordered them to come unarmed as a sign of trust to make terms and the fools didst just that and we wast waiting and well prepared for our bloody deed, and a bloody deed it wast. When they entered the circular mound we barred the gates and commenced to butcher them one by one until none of the Irish wast left standing and their screams and wails' echoed around the walls of the fort like the sound of wild beasts been slaughtered and so much blood wast spilled the fields outside the rath turned red and this affair the Irish calleth *The Murder of the Seven Septs of Laois* or *The Field of Blood* and Lord Deputy it wast murder indeed in cold blood and us soldiers who didst the slaying, slipping and sliding on the bloody gory mess which flowed liketh a river beneath our feet." "And, tell me trooper," the Lord Deputy asked. "Didst this brutal act bring peace and order to the land?" "Ay, things were peaceful for many years Sir William until the arrival of a new Lord Deputy, the Baron Arthur Grey de Wilton with a large army of raw recruits all levied men from Yorkshire and Wales but he wast an arrogant and impetuous man who kneweth nothing of Ireland, and nearly cost mine own life at the Glenmalure of which thou wilt no dowbt be familiar. "Indeed trooper," the Lord Deputy replied. "A day lacking valour for our rightful cause and her Majesty, pray tell me more of the matter for I am keen to learneth." "Mine own Lord; the Queen's army didst lose many men on that black day and much equipment including our war banners. I accompanied Deputy Grey with Captain Lee and Sir Walter Raleigh when a band of hobblers, that is the Irish cavalry, well if thou wouldst calleth them cavalry for they art poorly armed and ride a small horse they dost call a hobble without stirrup but they art brave enough and the Irish horse canst cover all manner of rough ground and terrain. This band didst charge our party to dispatch Lord Grey when a reckless young churl cast his spear piercing mine breastplate nearly killing me. I managed to let loose a ball with mine petronel which but grazed the upstart on the shoulder. On the day many of our captains were killed including General Francis Cosby, the one I hast related too, although strangely we never found his body and a host of common soldiers, all levied men. But the pride of the Baron Grey de Wilton wast bitterly stung and didst but bide his time till he couldst regain his lost honour and reputation and so he didst two months later when the opportunity arose however not against the Irish but unfortunate mercenaries sent by the shaveling devil, Pope Gregory to aid the Desmond rebellion, misfits from Italy. These unfortunate men were not soldiers, but largely vagabonds and convicts from every jail in Rome, the scum of Italy and further afield and the native Irish called these men the Romans Soldiers. They landed at a craggy, rocky place opposite the town of Dingle under the command of Hercules Pisano with plenty of supplies of weapons and ammunition." The Lord Deputy sat back eyes widening with interest. "Ay, the famous occurrence at Smerwick, and tell me trooper wast thou present and didst witness what occurred?" Trooper Churchyard bent forward with grimaced face. "Ay," he confirmed, nodding his head. "Ay, mine own Lord; I wast there that day alright and didst much slaughter on the orders of Lord Arthur Grey." "Didst not mine own good friend, Sir Walter Raleigh plays a part in the affair Trooper Churchyard?" "Ay, Lord Deputy, he was indeed present as wast the poet Edmund Spenser and Sir Walter didst most eagerly lead our party who dispatched many a poor unfortunate soul to Hades that eventful day. Mine own Lord, methinks the devil himself wast at the place of death and smiled at the butchery we carried out. Firstly, we didst hang, without pity or remorse, six or seven Irish women we found in the fort and two of them heavily pregnant. Then we stripped the prisoners of their armour and set about our bloody work of hewing and paunching which, Lord Deputy, is a cut to the neck or a stab to the belly which wast the proscribed method of mass execution. The inside of the fort echoed to the screaming and howling of the defenseless Italians who clung together in corners like frightened children with some running wild around the fort to escape our blades and I canst inform thee, my Lord, for mine many years as a man of war never didst I exert so much effort in the art of butchery, and when the Queen's work ceased our arms were sore from much hacking, cutting, and thrusting of the sword, our uniforms splattered in blood and our weapons blunt and dented, our ears ringing with the screams of men being butchered mercilessly. Then we threw the bloody corpses on to the beach where we counted over six hundred bodies and many of our men didst hast an uneasy conscience for partaking in this killing which they thought wast unnecessary and Grey's revenge for his base humiliation at Glenmalure." The Lord Deputy leaned forward eyes flashing with anger. "And wherefore trooper?" he snarled. "Is it not a soldier's duty to killeth the enemy of our Queen and our true religion? Dost thee not know Aristotle's infallible rule or the golden words of Cicero regarding such matters of state?" "Nay, sir, I dost not," he replied, eyes fixed to floor. "Well trooper, I shalt inform thee. Aristotle didst sayeth *Commonwealths are wounded by leniency and cured by severity* and Cicero *Send force and then justice* and soldier art these not wise words?" Trooper Churchyard caught the vexation in the Lord Deputies' voice. "Mine own Lord, tis so, but," he hesitated momentarily. "Lord Grey didst promise those men their lives and liberty if they didst lay down their arms and surrender. They bore no threat but Lord Grey having given his pledge of sparing their lives ordered us to the task of butchery and these men, mainly boys were but poor simple ragged bisogonos, those gents wast not soldiers and we believed it wast to salve Lord Greys' smitten vanity so he hast the good and true men of the Queen play the butcher for his revenge. And mine Lord, he didst stroll along the line of naked corpses laid out on the shore wringing his hands in glee and congratulating himself at the wonderful deed he hadst completed for the Queen, but he never hadst drawn his sword or bloodied his hands on the day. Then he ordered us to behead the poor souls and throw their bodies into the sea and we didst bury their heads in a field which the natives call *The Field of Heads* and that night, Lord Deputy, us men of the Queen were ordered to assemble where we didst kneeleth as one, washed by moonlight as the waves thundering on the beach, and the chaplain conducted a service of thanksgiving for the valorous work done for our Queen. I dost confess I didst simmer with rage when I perceived Lord Grey and Edmund Spenser kneeling in solemn gratitude to their savior, eyes raised heavenward in thanksgiving, and they with clean hands, clean swords, and even cleaner consciences, and I didst feel sadder than the lapping waves of the sea for what I hast done that day for I am in the service of our gracious Queen as a soldier and not a butcher." The Lord Deputy sat back impassively hands-on chin. "Ere we conclude trooper, I wish to knoweth more about Captain Lee to which thou dost refer?" "He is a fine soldier Lord Deputy, a bawcock who hast done our gracious Queen much valorous service in the field." The Lord Deputy knew the man was circumspect in his reply. "Trooper, thou must be honest with me and trust thy Lord Deputy for tis I, is it not, who shalt recommend thy petition to the Queen is met." "Mine own Lord", the trooper replied hesitantly. "I hast given thee much discourse of the wars in Ireland and the hard service I hast suffered for our Queen but," he hesitated, casting a look of trepidation at the Lord Deputy. "I might not but be truthful about Captain Tom Lee and let me tell thee. I hast nothing except diver wounds on mine own body and a restless sleep each night, mine wages are in arrears and art forever in arrears, but Captain Lee is a wealthy man who is married to a rich Catholic, Elizabeth Peppard the widow of Lord Eustace who hast considerable wealth. Mine own Lord, whilst we the common soldier risk our lives each day and slaughter ruthlessly, what the captains' gain we lose," he hesitated momentarily. "What is it Trooper Churchyard, prithee tell me what dost thee wisheth to sayeth?" "Lord Deputy Fitzwilliam, tis rumoured amongst the men Captain Tom Lee is a papist and in league with the Irish chiefs and is known to be on good terms with O Neill, the Earl of

Tyrone. To be blunt, Sir William, there are two types of men in the Queen's Irish army, the men in pay, although always in arrears, and the gentleman adventures' liketh Captain Lee, and whilst us simple soldiers dost giveth our service and our lives for our Queen and country it is the captains' who dost reap the rich rewards."

Without replying the Lord Deputy stood, eyes fixed keenly on the trooper. "Trooper Churchyard, I dost thanketh thee for thy discourse which I hast found of great interest and methinks thee to be a man of much valour and coragio. I shalt dispatch thy petition to the Queen's secretary, Francis Walsingham for her majesties' consideration." Trooper Churchyard, shaking the Lord Deputies' hand firmly replied. "Lord Deputy, I hast grown tired of playing the butcher, and mine soul is hurting and mine conscience dost trouble me, so I prayeth thou shalt grant me peace that I may return home to England. I hast nothing, no wife, no family, and mine only reward for hard service is bad dreams and a body covered in scars. I dost thanketh thee for hearing mine tale and accepting mine own humble petition. I am much in thy debt, Lord Deputy Fitzwilliam."

Chapter Six

It was a bitterly cold January night as a heavy fall of snow blanketed the city of Dublin and its environs in a carpet of white. Constable Merryman stood close to the glowing barrack-room turf fire in the company of Sergeant Tiptoff and a recruit called Throckmorton from Chester. "Cock a hoop on that barrel yonder liketh the good man thou art Sodger Tiptoff, and alloweth us to filleth our cups with good hearty English bouse and warm our hearts on this freezing night for I hast been informed tis a special brew cameth in on the tide from Bristol this morning." Filling their tankards to the brim they chugged back the strong frothy English ale in long, greedy glugs, wiping foamy dribbles from their beards. "Hearty cheers to thee, mine own valorous men of England, and let us prayeth the heavy snow doth keepeth that flibbertigibbet they dost calleth the Raven holed up in the forest this night that he might leaveth the decent settlers of the Pale at peace. Last week it wast reported he killed half a dozen innocents and burned two villages, black Irish scoundrel that he be." "Sodger Throckmorton," Constable Merryman inquired. "Prithee tell me now, mine own good fellow, how dost thee liketh thy service in the Queen's army in Ireland." Taking a mouthful of beer the soldier, pausing for a moment, replied. "Well constable, to be honest, I dost not liketh the place too well for us pressed men dread the name of Ireland, and it never stops raining, but the whiskey is wholesome and good for the damp climate. Ay, constable, I dost liketh the odd noggin or two of whiskey which I findeth most lush but I dost not liketh the natives in this town as they be none too friendly with us soldiers. In Chester, we hast a proverb constable, and it sayeth. *Tis better to be hanged in England than to die liketh a dog in Ireland* and tis how most people at home think about this place?" Constable Merryman shaking his head replied. "Nay, Sodger Throckmorton, thou hast not been out of the Pale and hast seen nothing of the real savage Irish or their heathen ways. These people here in Dublin art not the native Irish, nay they be half English corrupted by this country and its ways. Now mine own good fellows, I shalt relate to thee both what I hast seen of the true Irish, and I shalt tell thee of their filthy habits. Five years ago, ere I wast appointed Constable of the Castle, I hadst reason to be in the far north of the island in a place they call Donegal in the service of our Queen, and I canst tell thee I beheld sights that wouldst turneth thy stomach. Now, this land they doth calleth Donegal or Tyrconnell is a wild and desolate place whither the real savages liveth liketh vipers and slovens and dost eat chaff with swine, and in that far away place I didst gazeth in disbelief at the sights I didst behold before mine own eyes. Firstly, dost thee knoweth the wild Irish feed mostly on white meats and esteem greatly for dainty sour curds they vulgarly dost calleth bonnyclabber, and tis said that the common people only eat meat once a year at Yuletide. But sodgers, the great wealth of the Irish tis their cattle and for this cause they dost watchfully keepeth their cows and fight for them as for religion and life and even when they be starving they wilt not killeth a cow except it is old and bears no milk, and in wartime drive their great herds of cows before them and when hungry they shalt open a vein and drink the blood or mix it with oats to make what we dost call in England, a pudding." As he related his observations of the native Irish in far away Donegal his two companions sat silent, wide-eyed in astonishment. "Ay, Sodger's Throckmorton and Tiptoff, they dost place much worth on their cows as only a few grow crops liketh civilized men and those that dost tillage useth rude husbandry and this ye shalt not believeth, they dost pulleth the plough by using the tail of the horse." The soldiers shook their heads in disbelief. "Tis true, tis true, for I hast seen this barbarous custom with mine own eyes, and they art lazy and dost burn the oats from the straw to make cakes without threshing as is the English custom. Now, I didst visit a local chief's castle, a filthy hovel it wast too, as they dost keep animals in the castle at night afeared they be stolen and the whole lodging stinking with the funk of animal dung disgusting it wast but this chief, a wild Irishman called Mc Sweeny, a big hairy beast of a man didst invite me and mine comrades to breaketh bread with him and God's sooth what they didst eat for supper thou wouldst never comprehend." Stopping momentarily he took a swig of beer as the two soldiers' waited with bated breath for him to continue. "Go on constable, tell us more," Throckmorton yelled. "We art keen to knoweth, tell us now constable." "Well, mine own lads, in the centre of the smoke-filled room, reechy with the smell of peat, wast an open fire and on the fire a large cauldron didst cook and thou wouldst never believeth what they didst cook for dinner. A stew madeth with the entrails of an unknown beast and floating on top of the greasy mess of pottage wast big lumps of butter, and hairy butter to boot, too loathsome to describe. I canst tell thee, mine own sodgers, we didst not filleth our bellies that night, and in God's sooth that be the way of the savage Irish a slovenly race they art and no dowbt about it for they wilt put on a saffron shirt of coarse linen and shalt weareth it without a change of shirt till it be worn out." "Constable Merryman," recruit Throckmorton inquired audaciously, tongue loosened by several quarts of strong Bristol ale. "Tell us now, sir, how thee landed the cushy number as, Constable of the Castle and it be known the post is a lucrative one with many coins to be made from the sale of food and drink to the prisoners?" Constable Merryman refilling his tankard sat back and continued. "I shalt tell thee sodgers, and I wilt tell thee now. By God's good grace I wast granted this high post by the illustrious Lord Deputy, John Perrot he who preceded Deputy

Fitzwilliam." "Constable," recruit Throckmorton interrupted. "Wast not the said John Perrot rumoured to be the miscreate son of King Henry V111?" "Ay, tis true sodger, and he didst hast the countenance and majesty of the great King Harry. Well, mine own good men, believeth it or not but I wast master of a frigate called *The Gift of God* in the service of John Perrot who wast Vice-Admiral of the Welsh seas and Council of the Marches." Sergeant Tiptoff pointed his finger at the constable. "Ay, I dost perceive now, Mister Merryman, wherefore thee hast the gait of a man who hast been a seafarer for many the year." The constable clearing his throat continued. "Ay, Ay, sodgers tis true, anyways we wast part of a naval squadron charged by her Majesty to the interception of foreign ships off the coast of Ireland, her gracious Queen fearing aid reaching the rebel Irish. One night, in hot pursuit of a Spanish ship off the coast of Kerry, we were struck by a storm so bad we though all on board wouldst perish with the wind howling liketh the banshee and the waves as high as a mountain rolling over the ship but using my mariner's skills I saved the ship and crew including John Perrot's young son, Thomas who happened to be on board that night, and so the gentleman wast much indebted to me and we didst striketh up a strong friendship, him and I, good Welshmen that we be, both of us hailing from Haverford in Pembrokeshire, so we forged a strong bond. We that be of Welsh personage dost be most inclined to trust each other more than another especially the Irish, and even as we speaketh many of the servants in the castle and indeed Secretary Fitton are Welsh-born and all placed in position by the good John Perrot as he liked to be surrounded by people of his race. In the year of the Lord 1587, he summoned me to sail to Ireland on important business for the Crown, entrusting me for a bold and daring task and if I didst succeed mine own reward to be the much prized and envied position as, Constable of the Castle here in Dublin, and having completed the task in question he appointed me as constable, and so the story dost end." Constable Merryman rose, glanced out the window at the clock on the courtyard wall, and announced. "Sodger's Tiptoff and Throckmorton, as the bawdy hand of the clock is now upon the hour of midnight I shalt take mine leave and shalt bid thee, fine men of the Queen, adieu as I must riseth early in the morn. I'm weary and mine old seafarer's legs ache, so I dost bid goodnight to thee both." Sergeant Tiptoff racing over stood squarely in the doorway blocking his exit. "Nay, Constable Merryman, nay sir, thou cannot depart at this time till thee relate the rest of the story, tis of great interest to us. We art much intrigued, come be seated now and tell us what thee didst for Lord Deputy, Perrot to be granted this prized possession of, Constable of the Castle, prithee tell us now." The constable threw several pieces of turf on the fire and sat a smug look on his face. "Well, if thee insist men I shalt finish mine own story. I suppose it canst dost no harm but I shalt tell thee now few men hast heard the tale before so, mine own sodgers, count yourselves as privileged. Lord Deputy Perrot, a clever and devious man, and well versed in the stratagem of politics, didst devised a cunning plan for Red Hugh the youngest son of Black Hugh O Donnell, Lord of Tyrconnell to be kidnapped and madeth hostage here in the castle to ensure an alliance couldst not develop between the two most powerful clans in Ulster, the O Donnells and the O Neills. He wast a wise man indeed, and that be the God's sooth and no dowbt his father's bastard son, and as I hast said much resembled King Harry and far cleverer than many of the Deputies including the present Lord Deputy Fitzwilliam, him a cruel, greedy old fox. King Brian O Rourke of Breffni, drunk one-night didst inform John Perrot of a prophecy concerning the young O Donnell and he decided to taketh action even though the boy's father was loyal to the Queen, well as loyal as the deceitful Irish canst be for they don and doff their loyalty liketh the ebb and flow of the evening tide. Anyway sodgers, without the Queen's knowledge or the approval of the Privy Council, Perrot devised a daring and cunning plan to take the fifteen-year-old O Donnell boy captive and it be a highly secret venture he didst entrust to myself, such mine own standing with his honour, responsibility for its execution and the plan wast this, and a cunning plan it wast too. We didst disguise *The Gift of God* to appear liketh a foreign merchant ship, a Spanish wine Barque to be exact, removing the gunwales and cannons and filling the ship with much wine captured from a Spanish vessel in the straits. So, we sailed around the coast by Howth Head and soon we anchored in the choppy waters of Lough Swilly in Donegal and sent out a welcome to all the local chiefs to cometh aboard and taste their fill of wine and the Irishry dost hast a particular fondness for Spanish wine which they dost call *The King of Spain's Daughter*. After a week most of the chiefs had come aboard to sample our fine offerings but not an O Donnell, so we planned to raise anchor and sail back to Dublin on the next tide when a boat appeared carrying five youths who announced they were a party of young nobles accompanying Red Hugh O Donnell. Oh, what sweet joy and what a catch, and they came on board and madeth merry and when the youths be filled with many cups of wine our soldiers concealed in the hold didst pounce on them, as a cat pounces on a mouse, and disarming them we didst place O Donnell in chains in the ship's brig and brought him forth to this place and that's where he hast been nearly five years and his companions we didst throw overboard." The soldiers sat silently, shaking their heads in wonderment at the brave exploits of sea captain or more correctly, Constable Merryman. "Although," he continued. "Lord Perrot and indeed mine own good self didst almost lose everything including our heads on one occasion." "Go on constable, relate to us thy tale," Throckmorton shouted. "Well sodgers, this is what didst occureth. We were chasing pirates off the coast of

Cornwall and spied a fast carrack a French vessel from Marseilles, and she be named *The Peter and Paul* and Perrot believed she carried contraband or worse so we brought the ship into the port of Cork to search her and found she wast loaded with bales of pepper and soap but no contraband goods or weapons for the rebels but during the search we found a bag of pearls and many jewels which the good Lord Perrot pocketed for himself. Now, mine own sailors' wast angry as they didst not receive a share of the loot and one fellow didst inform none other than Francis Walsingham the Queen's secretary and when told the goods were worth £2,500.00 on God's sooth good Queen Bess wast mighty vexed at having been shortchanged out of this large sum of money and so pursued Lord Perrot and." The door bursting open stopped the constable in mid-sentence as a prison guard charged into the barrack-room. "Constable Merryman raiseth the alarm, there hast been an escape, the prisoner O Donnell and two of his companions hast vanished from the refectory." Constable Merryman sprung to his feet spilling the contents of his tankard over the table. "What dost thou mean they hast vanished, sodger." "Constable, they wert in the refectory having supper when they asked to go the privy unaccompanied as there was no danger with the three of them in iron fetters, and after a time I checked on them and low and behold they were gone, their irons lying on the floor, they must have escaped into the privy chute and into the moat below." The constable thundered out of the barrack-room into the courtyard barking orders for the drummer boy to sound the alarm and minutes later the full castle complement of fourteen soldiers and six gunners assembled in the yard. "Constable," a soldier yelled. "We cannot open the gates they art locked from the outside." "Go to the battlements sodger," the constable responded. "Calleth to passersby's to open the gate." Minutes later a plank was removed and racing out they found the discarded coats of the fugitives on the outer bank of the moat. "Sodger Adams," the constable ordered. "Ride to Beggars Bush barracks with much haste and summon the Captain of the Troop to dispatch search parties they cannot hast gotten too far they wilt not go unnoticed, searcheth everywhere and block all roads out of the city for they must be apprehended at any cost." Heart filled with dread the constable trudged across the courtyard to the quarters of the Lord Deputy, cursing to himself and stepping into the office, Sir William Fitzwilliam, sitting at his desk reading the bible in flickering candlelight glanced inquiringly at the constable. "Constable, what is the commotion, what hast occurred?" Constable Merryman stood, eyes to the floor, cap in hand. "Lord Deputy," he replied in a timorous voice. "The prisoner O Donnell has escaped with two of his friends." Fitzwilliam pushing back his chair scurried forward hitting the constable hard on the face with his bible causing him to reel back reddened face smarting from the blow. "Jesu Christi, thou art indeed a miserable scoundrel, what dost thee mean thou hast alloweth the most dangerous prisoner in the castle to escapeth?" The constable holding his stinging face stepping forward replied meekly. "But Lord Deputy, tis no new thing prisoner's escapeth, and tis no new thing they be recaptured, they shalt not travel far. We shalt catch O Donnell and his friends this night as we didst on his last escapade, didst we not?" The Lord Deputy, pointing his finger squarely at the constable yelled. "Merryman, thou art a blinking idiot, a dullard and there is no mistaking that and what John Perrot saw in thee I dost not knoweth for thou art but a simple lubberworth." "But Lord Deputy, they cannot last long in this weather and we caught them easy enough the last time and they must hast received assistance from within the castle for they had a key for the fetters and there art but two keys, and I hast mine own here look," he said lifting his bunch of keys. "The other is in thy possession, is it not?" The Lord Deputy stood silent staring blankly at the constable with gimlet eye, replying sternly. "Mister Merryman, thou must payeth for thine incompetence. I shalt fine thee fifty marks which the paymaster shalt deduct from thy stipend whilst I consider what further punishment thou deserve. Begone now and findeth the prisoners and be thou thankful I am a most merciful and Christian man." Closing the door softly behind him the constable muttered to himself. *Ay, methinks a lucky escape for O Donnell, and an even luckier escape for me.*

Six miles away Red Hugh O Donnell, accompanied by his two friends Art and Henry O Neill, struggled through a heavy snowstorm towards the safety and sanctuary of the Wicklow hills. Using the precious key of freedom O Donnell and his companions threw off their irons leaving behind their shoes lest they would hinder them and climbing into the open chute of the privy discharged at a considerable distance into the moat below. Swimming with great difficulty in the cold, filthy, ditch water they reached the outer bank where they discarded their much soiled and wet outer garments and passing through the main gate, which by good fortune was unguarded, lifted a heavy plank used to keep the gate ajar sliding the timber through the metal keepers effectively locking the gate from the outside and gaining them precious time. The intelligence received from the trusted servant of the Great Hugh O Neill, the horse boy, Sean O Hagan was good and when he visited him in jail passed Red Hugh the key. The horse boy waited outside the castle to guide them out of the city and passing along empty streets down Tennis Court Lane on to New Row finally reaching Saint James' Street and leaving behind Saint Catherine's Church they passed through Saint James' Gate which was open and moved towards the outer perimeter of the city through a gap in the Pale pushing south to Powerscourt. In the blinding storm, they lost the youngest of the three, Henry O Neill causing them much consternation but plodded on relentlessly towards their destination distancing themselves from pursuing troops. Shoeless and poorly dressed against the bitter cold and wind, teeth clattering, they blew breath into numb fingers for warmth, eventually succumbing to exhaustion taking shelter in a recess under a cliff called the Table Mountain, the pair clinging together desperately for warmth and comfort. O Hagan, their faithful guide who was mounted trudging ahead to alert O Byrne to their presence as in scant shelter they lay entwined drifting into a numb sleep of unconsciousness. O Hagan reached Glenmalure where Fiach and his followers were overjoyed at the news of the successful escape of Red Hugh O Donnell. O Byrne, raising his sword in jubilation roared. "Men, our time has come and the prophecy will be fulfilled. Red Hugh will lead us victoriously against the foreigners and we shall drive them from our land." A great cheer erupted from the gathered men and O Hagan grabbing O Byrne pleaded. "Chief," we must make haste if they are to survive we must go now." "Cahir O Farrell, where is O Farrell?" the chief thundered over the crowd, and running forward Ronan O Byrne yelled. "Father, he is not here his squadron is on a raid to Carlow, chasing down a band of renegade foreigners under Tom Lee, who are causing havoc to the people and has not yet returned they may have taken shelter from the storm." "Ronan my son," he responded. "You must go immediately, follow the guide, and bring your best men; O Donnell must be saved at all costs." Knee-deep in a thick blanket of snow they struggled to follow the guide stumbling blindly through the blizzard until finally reaching the craggy outcrop where O Hagan had left, O Donnell and O Neill. "Captain O Byrne," the guide yelled frantically. "This is the place I am sure of it, we must dig." Seeing nothing in the flurry of swirling snow they anxiously searched using the blunt end of their spears to prod the deep mounds until by good fortune Ronan O Byrne felt something soft beneath him buried in the dark depths. Digging desperately with their bare hands they finally found the two stiff lifeless bodies clung together, arms entwined, frozen in painless oblivion. Ronan, wiping the snow and ice off their ashen faces, forced a little aqua vitae into their blue-tinged lips until at last the flickering of eyelashes and opening of dull eyes followed by the stirring and shivering of limbs. O Donnell was alive but barely, his feet badly swollen inflicted with severe frostbite, his companion, Art O Neill had fallen into a deep, peaceful slumber of no return, a frozen corpse. Astonished at the survival of O Donnell, Sean O Byrne turning to Ronan asked. "Captain, how is he still alive nobody could live through these conditions it is a miracle, he must be of strong body?" "No Sean, it was not his strength of body that saved him but his strength of mind and his burning desire for revenge against his cruel oppressors." Placing O Donnell gently on horseback, a soldier each side to keep his much-weakened body-steady, they made their way to the safety and warmth of O Byrnes wooden fortress returning the next morning to bury Art O Neill in an oak forest at a remote place called Granabeg to ensure the English soldiers would not find and desecrate his body.

Despite his ordeal, O Donnell survived slowly regaining his strength, but such was the severity of his injuries the surgeons' amputated his frostbitten toes leaving him a cripple. The news of his escape travelled throughout the land bringing much joy and hope to the people that, as the prophecy of Saint Colmcille predicted and as Moses had freed the Jews, the predestined Savior King, Red Hugh O Donnell, would free the Irish people from their bondage and drive out the foreign heretics.

Chapter Seven

With the threatening words of Richard Steynes running through his mind Lord O Farrell, shillelagh in hand, paced the courtyard contemplating his meeting with the Queen's Commissioner who had called that morning demanding taxation monies owed to the Crown. *The utter madness of having to pay tax on lands his family-owned for six hundred years. He had just over a hundred tenants' paying rent, barely enough to meet his dues, and many of them poor herdsmen with little income. Since he had sworn allegiance to the Crown he encouraged his people to grow crops and tillage in the English fashion but those few tenants who did sow crops prepared their land by tying the tails of their horses to the plough, the old Celtic way, much to the amusement of the Crown officials. He was three years in arrears and warned of the consequence of his failing by Steynes. He could lose his land and property by default as stipulated under the terms of his Surrender and Regrant Agreement. For all his passivity and obedience they kept tightening the noose, facing him with the stark reality the whole Surrender and Regrant Agreement was nothing more than an elaborate subterfuge to force confiscation of the Irish chief's land. Maybe his brother in law, O Rourke, and the other rebel chiefs were correct- better to fight than be a slave to the inevitable but what dreadful fate would they encounter. For a moment he could see the jagged line of decapitated heads at Mullingar, and the O Connors on the castle gates. What could he do without weapons or soldiers, and look at the faith that befell the rebel Desmond, James FitzMaurice, and the horrific slaughter at Smerwick, and him with plenty of money and arms and the backing of the pope, he shuddered thinking about it.*

James FitzMaurice FitzGerald, the Earl of Desmond was *Lord of the South* leader of the Geraldines, a powerful old English family, loyal to the Crown but Catholic, owning huge areas of fertile land in Munster. As the Elizabethan conquest began in earnest the Geraldines were pushed reluctantly into rebellion in the name of the Catholic cause by the greedy English knight's, Carew and Gilbert. The old and crippled Fitzmaurice was lifted on to his horse sword in hand with his Irish tenants' behind him to face the onslaught of the English army beginning a war of total destruction followed by famine, and it was reported a person could travel for weeks through Munster without seeing a living soul. FitzMaurice became hated by his people for being the cause of their misfortune and forced to flee the country. On appealing to Pope Gregory for aid in his crusade against the heretics returned to Ireland, the pope sending him six hundred soldiers and substantial military supplies to aid the Catholic cause. These largely untrained men landed at Smerwick in Kerry where they encamped in a fort called Dun an Or and were surrounded by the English forces under Lord Grey on land and Richard Bingham at sea, and after a heavy bombardment surrendered on Greys' pledge to spare their lives however on leaving the fort the unarmed men were brutally slaughtered.

The barking of the dogs startled him and looking over saw a rider approach, a man known to him, his wife's brother Cormac the oldest son of, King Brian O Rourke. Cantering over, wooden target and light ash spears in one hand, reins held tight in the other, his brother in law drawing in his horse addressed him in a sneering manner. "How are you Lord O Farrell, or should I say how are your English masters, you are a fool and a coward to bow to the foreigners because you do not dare to fight back like my father. Why can't you be like your son Cahir, I am informed he is doing good service for O Byrne in Wicklow?" Lord O Farrell, stung by the insulting words responded curtly. "Yes, Cormac, but where does all this fighting get you, hunted day and night by the Binghams, your people starving, and everything destroyed by the foreigners." "It is true," Cormac responded sharply. "We suffer at the hands of Bingham, but we fight with honour and dignity and do many injuries to the foreigners and will never submit, and if you and your cohorts had joined my father things might be different, yes, you and the other cowards are the real cause of our servitude. Future generations of Irishmen will remember my father's name and his brave deeds while you and your bedfellows will be long forgotten, and we will die but once but you renegade Irishmen, a thousand times." Lady O Farrell alerted to the arrival of the rider approached her brother, Fergal at her side. "Cormac, I see you have traded your Latin classics for a spear and shield." "Yes my sister," he replied. "Father summoned me home from England before he took up arms against the foreigners concerned they would take me as a hostage or murder me. But Megan, I have to say during my two years at university in England, I had friends and in fairness, the students and tutors treated me well. It's only here in Ireland the English turn into heartless monsters and father believes is not Queen Bess that is our misfortune but the greedy English knights like the Binghams, but sister we give Richard Bingham and his brothers' sore treatment." Turning to Lord O Farrell he continued. "And you, high and mighty Lord of the manor, and what manor is that now with your lands taken and you reduced to penury. I take you for a fool and a coward, and Fergal my cousin," he continued. "I hope you are well and your studies progressing although I still cannot understand how the priest O Duffy would be a better tutor than the scholars at Oxford." "Good to see you cousin," Fergal replied. "But not good to see you bearing arms in a fight you cannot win." "Maybe not Fergal, but at least I have the courage to die trying unlike you and your father." "Cormac," Lady O Farrell said. "I am sorry you abandoned your studies to take to the sword for I do believe you would make a better scholar than a swordsman." "Sister, it was my place to be at father's side and I am proud to fight against the murdering Richard Bingham and his brothers who are out to destroy us and kill our people, and when they are done with the O Rourkes who do you think they will turn on next?" Lady O Farrell glared at her brother defiantly. "Cormac, we have nothing to fear from Richard Bingham, and why should we, they cannot touch us this family has the protection of the Crown." Cormac, throwing back his head laughed mockingly. "My sister Megan, I never took you for a fool, your husband yes but never you, but heed me now the greedy murderous Binghams will never stop their lust for blood and land is insatiable but now I must go. I carry news of great importance to the Burkes and other clans in the west, but before I depart I bring these gifts from father he asked me to give them to you," he said handing her a beautiful Spanish cloak and a pair of gold spurs. "These spurs are for Cahir, father is proud of his foster son and so he should be, and how is my brave and courageous cousin?" Large tears welled in Lady O Farrell's eyes and in a low voice replied. "Cormac, to tell the truth, I do not know we have not seen him in ten years and I fear he will be killed in the wars, I miss him so much." "Hold your tears, Megan, you should be rejoicing your son dared to fight and the wit not to trust the foreigners like that husband of yours, coward that he is. Your son is fighting for a noble cause and Cahir is a brave and skillful warrior." Nudging his horse forward he pointed his spear menacingly at his brother-in-law. "You backed the wrong side O Farrell, and soon will be punished for your cowardice and betrayal of our people the time of reckoning is coming for you and your fellow cowards." "What do you mean by these words O Rourke, punished by whom?" Lord O Farrell responded angrily. "What are you talking about we have the protection of the Queen?" Cormac shook his head and laughed scornfully. "The protection of the Queen, soon there will be no English soldiers or settlers in our land they all will be driven into the sea, have you not been told the great and joyful news, O Farrell? The whole of Ireland is ablaze, our time has finally come when the great leaders of the Irish will unite the clans." "What great leaders are you talking about O Rourke, tell us now?" The whole country is aflame with the blood of resistance. Red Hugh O Donnell has escaped from his chains of bondage and is free and with the aid of our great captain the all-powerful Earl of Tyrone, Hugh O Neill, we will raise our war banners behind the mighty Irish army that is why I go to spread the news and raise the people, and you, traitor." He stopped in mid-sentence fixing his gaze at Lord O Farrell. "I give you warning, yes, you coward, you betrayer of your people now you will pay the price. Red Hugh O Donnell will come and take your head and burn your castle in punishment for disowning your heritage for a worthless Saxon title. You mighty lord of the English will soon pay for your cowardice." "No," Lord O Farrell returned with raised voice. "O Donnell will be no threat to me or my family you bringer of death, leave now." Cormac turned to his sister. "Megan, I bid you farewell and you, Fergal. I wish you good luck which you will need with this coward and mark my words you will all pay dearly for your allegiance to the foreigner." With a brisk kick to the ribs, he spurred his horse forward and as her brother disappeared into the distance Lady O Farrell turned to her husband. "My Lord," she inquired wryly. "Tell me now; did you assist O Donnell in escaping from the castle?" "No, my Lady, I did not have the means to execute such a mammoth task that I left to better men than I, but he did need our support and consolation and it is what we gave with good reason." "Father," Fergal asked. "I know you forbade me to speak of the matter but what did Cormac mean when he spoke of the prophecy, it now seems everyone speaks of the prophecy." "Yes son I did, but the time has now come to reveal all. Father O Duffy, explain to us the significance of the prophecy much talked about and why has it excited the people of Ireland in such a manner, my son is keen to know." "Yes, my Lord," the priest replied. "It is the custom of this land that a holy man or saint would by divine intervention foretell a future event something of great magnitude affecting the lives of the Irish people. It has been written in the Annals of the Four Masters over a thousand years ago that Saint Colmcille in his *Great Book of Prophecies* foresaw the subjected Irish people drive the foreign invaders out of the country led by a king called, Red Hugh O Donnell, and the prophecy of the great and holy Saint Colmcille states:

The man of high renown shall come

He shall bring weeping and woe in every land

He shall be the goodly prince

And he shall be king for nine years

"But Father O Duffy, tell me now. "Fergal questioned. "How can we believe in a prophecy written a thousand years ago, is it not a dangerous prediction that could lead to rebellion and destruction across the whole country?" "Yes," the priest affirmed. "But the Irish people place great faith in the prophecies of the holy men. Fergal, look at the prophecy of Saint Patrick at the holy well in Finglas, sure didn't the great man himself stand at the place a thousand years ago and state. *A great city would arise at The Ford of the Hurdles in the valley below* and has not the city of Dublin sprung up as predicted, and you've seen it yourself have you not?" Fergal nodded in agreement and the priest continued. "What about the terrible massacre at Mullaghmast in Laois, did not Saint Malachy predict this horrific event five hundred years before calling it *The Field of Blood* and on the day of the massacre at Mullaghmast only one gentleman, a man named Lalor of the Irish, escaped because he knew of the prophecy and was suspicious, so held back on entering the rath where the

English had set their deadly trap. He waited all day watching his friends go in and none come out, so he fled and saved his life and all because of the vision of Saint Malachy, so why would we doubt the prophecy of Saint Colmcille?" "Yes, Father O Duffy," Lord O Farrell responded. "But the truth is simple, prophecy or no prophecy, we can never defeat the foreigners, yes, we may drive them out but they will return, and if we did defeat them the chiefs with the usual jealousies and envy of the Irish would be at war with each other for land and power and as Fergal wisely said the only thing this prophecy will achieve is more futile bloodshed and suffering." "But, Lord O Farrell," the priest replied. "A man must have hope, sure without hope we are doomed are we not. At the Jesuit College in Salamanca, we were taught that faith, hope, and love, was the essence of man and without these virtues, all men are doomed and in this philosophy, I truly believe?" "Fine words, Father O Duffy, fine words indeed," he replied. "But my good friend, it is simple- the crux of the matter is the English are too strong for us to defeat. If we did defeat them it will only be a Pyrrhic victory and they would come back wave after wave their resources are infinite and they have the strongest navy in the world. The English on their peril can never lose Ireland that fact is simple, we are Catholics and as such they must control us to prevent an invasion by Spain their mortal enemy. They did the same thing against the Scots many years ago in *The War of the Rough Wooing* when King Henry brought in the Reformation and the French threatened to invade England through Scotland. They will do anything to protect themselves and the bastard Queen has many enemies abroad and they would use Ireland, even to the detriment of our people, as a stepping stone to destroy the bastion of the heretics. No matter what the prophecy says they cannot be defeated. Yes, we may win many battles but will never win the war. Fergal is right; this bravado will cause nothing but mayhem across the country. O Donnell allied with O Neill will be a powerful force and will indeed have victories but the old rivalries of the less powerful clans will turn against them and O Neill will turn on O Donnell to take control of the whole country. This family will take no part in rebellion we have lost too much already and we would only end up losing everything and," he continued. "O Donnell will do us no harm, Fergal and I at great risk have made sure of that, but you must excuse me now for I have an important matter to attend too."

The manservant was busy helping his wife prepare the evening meal when Lord O Farrell stepped into the kitchen. "O Hanly, I need you to do me a good service. I require you to leave first thing in the morning, take the best horse we have from the stable and go to Donegal with greetings from the O Farrells to Red Hugh O Donnell, and our acknowledgment of his new chieftaincy; he will remember us from our visit to the prison. One week later O Hanly returned with the gift of a beautiful stallion for Lord O Farrell bearing the name *O Donnell*. "My Lord," O Hanly stated. "Red Hugh O Donnell sends his warmest greeting to you and your family, and told me he will never forget your kindness and for the comfort, you and Fergal brought him in prison last Christmas, and also if he can ever repay your family he will gladly do so." A wide grin of satisfaction crossed Lord O Farrell's face as he looked admiringly at the horse running his hand gently along the forelock. "It is indeed a fine stallion and worthy of the name it bears." Turning to O Hanly he announced. "My loyal servant, this is indeed good news you bring, and as always you have performed your task well and as a reward, I wish you to keep *O Donnell* for all your years of faithful service. Come now, tell me everything about the O Donnell castle and the preparations for war, come now and tell me all."

Chapter Eight

Lord Deputy Fitzwilliam endeavored to make sense of Captain Tom Lee's report regarding the prophecy of Red Hugh O Donnell. *The captain had obtained the information from a popish priest under torture, so how reliable was the information, a man will tell many a fanciful tale with his feet in burning oil- will he not? His predecessor, John Perrot had threatened the relative peace in the north by having Red Hugh O Donnell a youth of fifteen years, the eldest son of the Lord of Tyrconnell and his vixen of a wife Finola Mc Donnell, Black Hugh and the Dark Daughter as they were called, kidnapped and interred in the castle's dungeon as a hostage incurring the wrath of the Queen for his rashness and many of the English of the Pale could not understand the reason for what they perceived as his indiscreet action which could have serious consequences for them all. The O Donnells were a wealthy and powerful family having sworn allegiance to the Crown during the reign of King Henry V111. He heard the rumors John Perrot was the illegitimate son of King Harry, having the qualities of a king and statesman and definitely with the same choleric temper as the King and strangely the Irish liked him and the chiefs' trusted him although he could be brutal when necessary and on his departure from Dublin the Irish lined the streets, and even one of the O Neill chiefs came to see him return to England. Yet this man planned and ordered the kidnap of the son of a powerful Irish family. Yes, they were contravening English law with their frequent cattle raiding and feuding between the rival clans of O Donnell and O Neill, but so what, let the savage beggars kill each other, it would suit our purposes well. But to snatch young O Donnell in such a manner, and his actions had jeopardized the delicate peace in the north, but Perrot was a shrewd and wise old fox acting no doubt for a good reason but for what reason?*

"Fitton," he called, summoning his secretary who was painstakingly copying parchments in an adjoining room. "Tell me now Fitton, didst thee not serve under Lord Deputy, Sir John Perrot?" "Ay, mine own Lord," he replied. "Sir John granted me this post as secretary as he didst liketh fellow Welshmen in his service." "Fitton, O Donnell wast taken hostage and imprisoned here by John Perrot, tell me now what dost thee knoweth of the matter?" "Well, Lord Deputy, if I might speak freely without disrespect I, and indeed many of the people working in the castle wert much surprised by his action and sorry for the boy. Lord Deputy, the boy's father, Black Hugh of the Fish, wast a regular visitor to the castle and with the aid of a translator didst hold long discourse with John Perrot in this very room and it wast a spectacle to behold at which hour he came yearly to payeth his dues to the Queen. His followers with their Irish ponies and many pack mules laden with kegs of aqua vitae, Spanish wine, and barrels of salted salmon for the Lord Deputy. One year he gave Sir Perrot a pair of the most magnificent Irish hunting dogs and his servants never failed to leave a barrel of fish and a keg of whiskey in the barrack room for the soldiers, and although a mere Irishman, Black Hugh O Donnell didst display so much generosity and nobleness that the soldiers and castle servants liked him and Lord Deputy he dressed in the finest of clothes and," stopping mid-sentence a wide grin crossed his face. "When he came to speaketh with John Perrot he wouldst always giveth me a gift and never forgot mine own name, and tis wherefore at their peril many of the older soldiers, fond of Lord O Donnell, didst taketh pity on the son and at which hour he wast starving in the grate they wouldst smuggle him morsels of food which no dowbt hath kept him alive, and all those employed in the castle didst consider it strange when the boy arrived in chains one night and they sayeth Constable Merryman might hast played a part in the kidnap and wast master of the brig that seteth the trap for the boy. The father and mother didst visit Red Hugh but only once, and it wast shocking to perceive how Lord O Donnell hadst declined and barely recognizable as he was much perturbed at the captivity of his son and couldst not comprehend wherefore he wast kept in such durance vile. I canst tell thee now, mine own Lord," he said sarcastically. "We received nay generosity or kindness from Lord O Donnell on the occasion of his last visit, and hast never seen him since." "Secretary," the Lord Deputy asked abruptly changing the subject. "What is the nameth of the papist priest turned true Christian, the scholar who hast done her Majesty service by translating the bible into the blasphemous Irish language although wherefore such a vile deed wouldst be executed I cannot pertain?" Secretary Fitton, rummaging with nimble fingers through a hefty pile of Crown documents found the paper containing the name which he handed to the Lord Deputy who, throwing a perfunctory glance at the paper, flung it disdainfully on his desk. "These accursed Irish names, I cannot understand this barbaric language. Fitton thou speaketh Welsh, dost thee understand the savage Irish tongue." "Lord Deputy," he replied. "Welsh and Irish art Celtic languages but of different branches, Welsh is Brythonic as is the Breton and Cornish languages, and Irish is Gaelic as is the native language of Scotland and the Isle of Man, although some words art similar they art two different languages entirely, therefore, I cannot sayeth I speaketh Irish well but years of writing the Irish names hast given me an understanding of the words and pronunciations and," picking up the paper he looked briefly at the name. "This man thou seeketh is named, Uilliam O Domhnaill, which is a relatively easy one and translates roughly into English as, William Daniels." "What dost thou mean by translates roughly Secretary Fitton, what thou sayeth doth not maketh sense."

"Well, mine own Lord, as there is nay direct translation of Irish names into English, we anglicise their words as best we canst for example we calleth the northern province Ulster, but this word means nothing, nothing whatsoever, the true name is Ulaidh, and what we call Munster is actually Mumu, and so they hast been called for a thousand years." "Mumu, for God's sake Fitton, what sort of a ridiculously absurd name is that?" The Lord Deputy questioned in a scornful voice. "Tis the ancient Celtic name, mine own Lord, and I dost suppose our English names sound as strange to the Irish people as their Irish names sound to us. The anglicised names we useth mean nothing and art but a very crude translation based solely on the interpretation and understanding of the common soldier or clerk who translates the names in an intuitive manner of their understanding." The Lord Deputy sat back a perplexed look on his face. "Prithee, continue secretary, is there anything more thou wisheth to disclose regarding this matter." "Ay mine own Lord," Fitton continued. "The most common error we maketh is the use of the prefix *O* we dost place ere Irish names which to us means *son of* when the proper prefix is *Ui* or *Ua,* and as I hast stated Lord Deputy, a common soldier or clerk hast translated and mispronounced the *Ui* or *Ua* in intuitive English into an *O* and also the prefix *O* doesn't mean *son of* it means *grandson*. Also, I hast cometh across townlands and villages with a dozen anglicised names and this causes our administration much confusion, and thy predecessor, John Perrot wanted to replace every single Irish name in the country with a new English alternative, and this thou shalt find difficult to comprehend Lord Deputy. The illustrious John Perrot didst inform me that the Irish language is a thousand years older than the English language and one of the oldest languages in the world first spoken at the time of King Solomon and," he continued. "Also the oldest literature in Europe is written in the Irish language." With raised eyebrows, the Lord Deputy leaned forward and in a mordant voice replied. "Secretary Fitton, this I dost find hard to believeth, even if it cameth from the mouth of the illustrious John Perrot, and he be a wise and knowledgeable man. Fitton, art thou telling me now the common names we use for every person and every place in Ireland art incorrect." "Ay, mine own Lord, to varying degrees depending on the person who translated the names in the first place and Lord Deputy, our soldier's art the worst as most of them cannot even read or write English and art base ignorant, but the simple fact is as we cannot understand the native language of the Irish people we must translate as best we canst, and that is the way we manage?" The Lord Deputy banged his fist on the desk. "Enough Fitton, enough of this madness, howbeit everything in this backward country is always difficult and nothing ever straightforward or as messemes, but one last question before we conclude and prithee tell me I am in this instance correct." "Ay, Lord Deputy, what is the question, prithee tell me?" The Lord Deputy sat upright an eager look on his face. "Secretary Fitton, this land we seek to conquer and colonise, tell me now the proper name is Ireland isn't it?" Secretary Fitton shaking his head replied. "Well, mine own Lord, nay, strictly speaking, the correct name of this country is Eire, and that is what the Irish call it and hast named the country so for over 2,000 years." "Ah, Fitton, now I dost understand, we English use Ireland as the anglicized name for Eire do we not," he stated a smug grin on his face. "Nay, Secretary Fitton replied diffidently. "Nay, Lord Deputy, the anglicised name for Eire is in fact, Erin." The Lord Deputy slumped back in his chair shaking his head in disbelief. "Fitton, on God's sooth I'm sorry I even asked the question, but back to the business in hand, remind me again, what is the nameth of the renegade priest?" "William Daniels is the name, and he is presently a legendary in Christchurch Cathedral and planning the opening of a university on the site of Saint Trinities' Church with the patronage of her gracious Majesty, and is already appointed as the first scholar on the opening of the college." "A strange fellow indeed Secretary Fitton," the Lord Deputy replied. "And the only one of his kind, a papist clergyman rejecting the religion of the anti-Christ, and giving valorous service to the Crown and our established church. A fine example of the rich rewards to be hadst by such wise and prudent actions. Fitton, send a messenger and fetch him hither, I dost wish to speaketh to the servant of the true God."

The Reverend William Daniels, of previous times Uilliam O Domhaill and a member of the Roman Catholic Church, stood before the Lord Deputy of Ireland, Sir William Fitzwilliam. The reverend was a tall man of strong build, black hair, and dark complexion with the natural features of the Irish race. "Mine own Lord," he began. "I am at thy service, and prithee tell me how I canst be of assistance to thee?" The Lord Deputy stared keenly at the man wondering why he had changed his allegiances with such gusto and fervor to rise to such lofty heights in the state church. "Reverend Daniels, prithee come hither, sit and partake in a little wine and toast and we shalt make discourse, there art several important matters I wisheth to discuss with thee. Now they dost tell me thou art the man who translated *The Book of Common Prayer* into the Irish language and that I dost findeth strange surely the native Irish cannot read?" "Ay, mine own Lord, many art indeed illiterate but most of their schools and colleges hast been destroyed by the soldiers as were their churches and monasteries. It is reported in Munster alone the soldiers burned over fifty schools during the Desmond revolt." "Dost the natives hast schools, Reverend Daniels?" The Lord Deputy queried. "Ay, Lord Deputy Fitzwilliam, and many scholars of high standing. I didst receive excellent assistance from one of the few Irish universities still in existence in remote County Leitrim where the head of the college, Master O Higgins assisted in the accurate translation of Irish words and showing me the proper script for the print type when we printed the bible in Irish. But mine own Lord, one of their greatest skills is in medicine and healing and many trained in Spain and France making fine surgeons and there art many people in the towns willing to payeth for an Irish doctor because of their skill at healing all sorts of maladies." The Lord Deputy sat forward an expression of vexation on his face. "Reverend Daniels, I wouldst warn thee in dealing with papists as I am well informed by her Majesty herself they hast a new religion taught by their priests that they hast no duty nor promise is to be kept to Protestants, queen, prince or other. However, I dost wish to converse with thee on a matter of interest to myself, and indeed to our gracious Majesty. Thou art a renowned scholar, fluent with the Irish tongue and knowledgeable with the customs of the people art thou not?" Reverend Daniels sat back uneasily, curious as to the true nature of the question. "Ay, Lord Deputy, it wast indeed mine misfortune to be born into the irregulous uncivilized Celtic race called the Irish, but by the valorous counsel of Bishop Nicholas Walsh of the true church I discovered mine errors and with the guidance of the Lord above I sitteth before thee a true Protestant man to giveth much valorous service to our Majesty and her church," he replied, a look of self-satisfaction on his face. "But Lord Deputy, liketh thyself I also wouldst seriously question the purpose and validity of translating the bible into the Irish language for I dost truly believe the native Irish wilt never be converted to the true religion of Christ." "Wherefore so Reverend Daniels, wherefore so, for I am curious to understand the reason they clingeth so fervently to their blasphemous Roman Catholic faith even under the pain of torture and at risketh of death." "Lord Deputy," Reverend Daniel replied. "Thou must understand that Catholicism in Ireland differs from elsewhere, for example, the recusants in England art different from the Catholics in this country." "But wherefore reverend, I am much intrigued, prithee, tell me wherefore?" "Well mine own Lord, the Irish were converted to Catholicism by Saint Patrick over a thousand years ago, and he completed this task by incorporating many of the old Celtic pagan beliefs into Christian practices. For example, water was sacred to the Druids as the symbol of fertility and regeneration, so the concept of baptism with water was understood by the Irish as wast Saint Patrick's use of the shamrock which to the Druids represented faith, hope, and love, to illustrate the concept of the father, son and the Holy Ghost as one and the same. Also, Saint Patrick conducted the liturgy of the Catholic Church in the Irish language rather than the proscribed Latin which nearly had him excommunicated from the church, so Irish Catholicism developed as a transitional faith between the old pagan beliefs and the new faith, different from other Catholic countries and thou could sayeth without contradiction, mine own Lord, a hybrid Celtic Christianity both in the literal and figurative sense." "Reverend Daniels, howbeit everything in this backward country is always difficult and nothing ever straightforward or as meesemes, however, I wisheth to discuss another matter with thee. A papist priest wast captured by Captain Lee, and under torture told of a prophecy he discovered in an old manuscript regarding, Red Hugh O Donnell son of the Lord of Tyrconnell, the youth who escaped recently from the castle, couldst thee relate to me all thou knoweth about the prophecy, dost thee hast knowledge of this matter?" Reverend Daniels, eyebrows raised sat back surprised at the question. "Ay, mine own Lord, I dost knoweth of the prophecy for when I wast with Master O Higgins in Leitrim he told me he had a copy of *The Prophecies of Saint Colmcille* which he gave to King Brian O Rourke for safekeeping afraid the soldiers might find it, and apparently it wast smuggled to Spain and is probably the same book." The Lord Deputy raising his hand stopped the conversation in mid-sentence and questioned sternly. "Reverend, didst thee report this prophecy to the Crown authorities at the time?" Reverend Daniels shrugged his shoulders and replied indifferently. "But, wherefore mine own Lord, there wast no need for this is only papist superstition and of no concern and more importantly, O Higgins told me that Brian O Rourke when drunk hadst informed the Lord Deputy, John Perrot of the prophecy, so it wouldst be known to the Crown or at least John Perrot wouldst it not." A surprised expression crossed the Lord Deputies' face. "What Reverend Daniel," he responded sharply. "Art thou telling me that John Perrot kneweth of the prophecy but didst not adviseth the Queen or the Privy Council? I cannot comprehend wherefore he wouldst keepeth the matter secret, but prithee continue with thy discourse I wisheth to learneth more." "Ay, mine own Lord, when I didst visit the college, O Higgins told me there wast several variations of the ancient prophecy which originates in the book of prophecies of Saint Colmcille or known in English as Saint Columba who founded the place called, Doire Colmcille, a monastic and Episcopal seat in Ulaidh, or as we call it now Ulster. The name Doire or Derry in the anglicised form refers to the vast amount of ancient oak trees that abound at the place. *Although,* he thought, laughing silently to himself. *The ancient forests of oak trees of Doire Colmcille won't last any length of time when the English settlers arrive.* The place whither her Majesties' troops landed in 1566, intending to march south against Shane O Neill, but an explosion occurred destroying the entire camp and the army hadst to desert the place. Strangely, the people said it wast the great Saint Colmcille taking revenge on the soldiers for using his church for storing gunpowder and weapons. It was reported a wolf came out of a forest and entered the church sparks emitting from his mouth setting fire to the building resulting in a massive explosion destroying all the munitions and killing seven hundred men. Now, mine own Lord, I cannot sayeth if the story is true but I canst confirm an explosion didst occur killing all those men and Captain Randal one of the survivors stated *The Irish God, Saint Columba killed all my soldiers on that day.* The saint was a man of visions, and the Irish called him the saint of many miracles also he wrote three famous books of prophecies with one concerning the O Donnell Clan of Cen Kinnellin in Donegal, and the prophecy states as I recall as thus:

When two Hugh's lawfully and lineally succeed each other

The Black Hugh and the Red Hugh as the O Donnell

The last Hugh shall be a monarch of Ireland

And banish forever all foreign nations and conquerors

"Prithee, Reverend Daniels, tell me now, what is the meaning of these words?" "Well, mine own Lord, simply when Black Hugh O Donnell hands over power to Red Hugh O Donnell the clans will unite and riseth under the leadership of Red Hugh and drive the English out of Ireland." "Reverend Daniels, Black O Donnell is the Lord of Tyrconnell is he not, and Red Hugh his son." "Ay, mine own Lord, and there art rumours the father hast handed his title to Red Hugh who hast been proclaimed chief of the O Donnell dynasty dropping the title Lord of Tyrconnell in favour of the Irish title in a show of contempt." Seeing the look of trepidation on Sir Fitzwilliam's face he continued reassuringly. "But, Lord Deputy, this is but superstition the Irish chiefs wouldst never join forces and unite. The O Donnell and the O Neill art mortal enemies, is that not true?" "Ay, tis true," the Lord Deputy replied. "The Irish art too disjointed and their only motive is self-interest and greed and many of them despise the O Neills and the O Donnells to which they art forced to payeth tribute and fight for in times of war. I agree the prophecy is the pure superstition of a savage, uncivilised people, and the wishful thinking of a defiant race. The O Neills and O Donnell's art mortal enemies and the Earl of Tyrone supposedly loyal to her Majesty, as indeed were the O Donnells until John Perrot kidnapped the boy. Ay, Reverend Daniels, tis indeed all poppycock, and remember the failure of the Irish chiefs is always jealous envy and that is their downfall, and that is the end of the matter."As Reverend Daniels rose to leave the Lord Deputy gestured for him to sit. "Reverend, thou art indeed a man of much learning and before thee depart I wisheth thee to tell me about this Irish Law called, Brehon Law, which I knoweth is the causeth of much rancor and discord amongst the Irish chiefs, prithee tell me for I dost wisheth to learneth more." "Well, mine own Lord, tis said Brehon Law is the oldest codified legal system in Europe and is a civil, not a criminal code which many scholars sayeth originates from *The Hindu Law of Manu*. I had a conversation with Edmund Spenser in Cork who believes the Irish race originates from India or at least a country connected with Hinduism, but it is the widely held belief the Irish people came from Galicia in northern Spain with the Milesian invasion over 2,500 years ago. Brehon Law is concerned with the payment of compensation for loss, inheritance, property, and contracts, and hast many remarkable features in comparison to English Law." The Lord Deputy leaned forward eyebrows raised. "And what art these remarkable features Reverend Daniels, prithee tell me now?" "Well, Lord Deputy, the greatest difference is regarding what the Irish call, Tanistry, and Gavelkind, whither unlike English Law under the Brehon Law of Tanistry the oldest son is not legally entitled to inherit his father's title or lands as the land is not owned by the chief but shared by the people of the clan, and the leading clansmen decideth who is the best in line to be appointed as their new chief. Under Gavelkind the chief's personal property is divided into equal portions amongst his sons, the only exception being a disobedient son, who is automatically disinherited. But, Lord Deputy," he continued. "What I dost findeth most interesting is the treatment of women, under Irish law whither men and women art equals and under their system women hast property rights and the rights of divorce under certain conditions." The Lord Deputy banging his fist on the desk exclaimed loudly. "Jesu Christi, art thou telling me reverend, the barbaric Irish laws dost giveth rights to women, what utter madness the sooner we civilise these irregulous Irish savages the better but to conclude, Reverend Daniels, prithee tell me, who dost administer this Brehon Law." "Well, Lord Deputy, they hast Brehons or judges who art highly trained lawyers, but it is not a written law but oral, and the concept of state administration and state punishment is alien to the Irish as their system is deeply entwined in their culture and customs, respected and adhered to by all classes of the people from the richest to the poorest, and on the rare occasion a person doth not conform to the Brehon Law they art cast out or exiled from Ireland, a remarkable system." Shaking his head in disbelief the Lord Deputy replied sharply. "A ridiculous system in mine own mind, but Reverend Daniels, prithee tell me who doest train these so-called judges?" "Mine own Lord, they hast schools of law in every province run by families such as the O Daverns in Connaught and the Mc Eagans in Munster." Pushing back his chair the Lord Deputy rose abruptly ending the conversation. "Reverend Daniels, I hast heard enough, thou hast been most informative and I dost thank thee kindly." "It was mine own pleasure Sir William, and if I canst ever be of assistance I am at thy service but before I depart there is one small but important item I didst not mention. The Irish law forbids capital punishment in the first instance and the murderer must instead pay fines to the family of the victim to compensate for any monetary loss, but if he defaults on payment of the agreed compensation the family hast the right to killeth him by hanging with a willow with, and that be Irish Brehon Law, Lord Deputy." "I dost thank thee, Reverend Daniels, thou hast been most helpful and I value thy knowledge, now a good day to thee, sir."

Lord Deputy Fitzwilliam reflected on Reverend Daniels's words' regarding the prophecy. *It was all papist superstition, a farrago of nonsense and absolute balderdash of course. The boisterous exaggerations of a childlike people but if the Irish believed it they would gain hope and courage which could be dangerous and if the clans united. And John Perrot, the cunning and wise old fox, knew of the prophecy and kept the information to himself but took it seriously enough to recklessly kidnap the young O Donnell and threaten the fragile peace. But the kidnapping of O Donnell by Perrot had turned the family against the English, and what if O Donnell allied himself with O Neill. The Privy Council informed him spies had brought news O Neill was secretly importing black powder and firearms from Scotland to arm and train his people who were growing stronger by the day and strength or the appearance of strength ruled in Ireland. And while the O Neills and O Donnells were traditional enemies the scheming devil O Neill would use the prophecy to bring the O Donnells into an alliance to forget the enmity between the two clans and fight for a common cause. He would use the same rationale with the smaller clans and if they defeated the English reignite their feud, as all the other clans would, and the natives would fight amongst themselves and lose everything and O Neills would become the most powerful clan and rule as High Kings of Ireland. Yes, it was Hugh O Neill the Earl of Tyrone who was the greatest threat to the Crown and not the hot-headed, aggrieved young O Donnell. O Neill was reared and educated as a noble in the Pale by the settler Giles Hoveden, and well tutored from an early age in the tactics of English warfare and the art of diplomacy and had served in the army against the Desmonds and always sworn, at least on face value, allegiance to the Crown. A dangerous creature with his Irish blood and English heart, and too wise to believe in such foolish things as prophecies but would use this fallacy for his own ends. Yes, the two-headed Janus had turned Turk. He knew he must act decisively and ensure that he, Sir William Fitzwilliam, the Lord Deputy of Ireland, would not be recorded in history as the Queen's man to lose Ireland for the Crown as the bloody papist Queen Mary Tudor lost Calais the last English town in France. No, he would not bring utter disgrace and shame on his family's honorable name.*

Chapter Nine

Secretary Fitton tapped lightly on the office door and stepping into the room stopped in his tracks on seeing the Lord Deputy slumped over his desk, deathlike pallor on face, and carefully placing the breakfast tray of wine and toast on the floor rushed over. "Lord Deputy, Lord Deputy." What is the matter sir, art thou feeling poorly, thine countenance is whitely, I wilt summon Surgeon Maplesden to attend to thee at once?" The Lord Deputy, without lifting his head, waved his hand dismissively. "Nay, Secretary Fitton, nay, I am upon the pitch of sixty-nine years, I am old, mine own body is weak, mine stomach weaker and the stone oft torment me, and now the gout hast utterly lamed me in the leg." Fitton, concerned for the Lord Deputy pleaded. "Prithee, mine own Lord, I beg thee, alloweth me summoned Surgeon Maplesden this minute to attend to thy needs." "Nay, Fitton nay, be patient sir, I hast not finished relating to thee mine own ailments. Now, firstly I shalt partake in refreshments go fetch me the tray." Pausing briefly he nimbly dipped toast in his wine and taking a dainty bite continued. "Mine own sight and memory doth both faileth me, so I am less than half a man, and not much more than a dead man, mine life candle is nearing its end, and that is all. Now, Secretary Fitton, prithee bid me there is news from the Queen about mine request to be relieved of this burdensome role, for I doth wisheth to returneth to the land of good meat and clean linen, and I crave sorely for the love and attention of mine own dear wife, Agnes." "Nay, Lord Deputy, nay reply as yet but I am certain in recognition of thy valorous service her gracious Majesty shalt grant thee a recall to England and alloweth thee to retire peacefully to Milton Hall." The Lord Deputy slapped the palm of his hand feebly on the desk. "Jesu Christi, Secretary Fitton, wherefore doest the Queen not answer me for I cannot last another winter here and methinks Fitton, the malady of this godforsaken land is the constant rain for I doth believeth England is a much drier country. Doest her Majesty wisheth me to die in this dreadful place, to be buried in Ireland and slandered in England?" Secretary Fitton, placing a weighty bundle of documents on the desk replied. "As advis'd, Lord Deputy, no news regarding thy request but we hast this day received half a dozen dispatches from the Star Chamber, they came in on *The Falcon* from Bristol which wast delayed for two weeks but the ship got wind and it arrived this morning they art from Sir Francis Walsingham, the Queen's secretary." "Ay, I knoweth well enough who he is," the Lord Deputy replied curtly. Breaking the royal seal on the first dispatch he opened the document headed **The Troubles in Ireland** which stated: The Queen and her Privy Council hast held long discourse on the state of affairs in Ireland and we doth instruct the Lord Deputy to execute the following orders:

Soldiers Pay and Supplies

1) Soldiers pay to be reduced to eight pence per day.

2) Soldiers' daily allowance of beef to be reduced to two pounds of fresh beef or one and a half pounds of salted beef.

3) Included with above to be a penny loaf to weigh not more than twenty ounces.

4) Deliver each month to every Captain: half apeck of wheat, a peck of malt money for himself, and fish days.

5) Captains Bills 7s.6.d sterling.

6) Soldiers allowance 3s.4d sterling

7) For 1000 lead fire shot for, officers, and soldiers, in the Queen's pay.

Total £14,484.1s.2 d wages sterling

State of the Army of Ireland

Attendant on Lord Deputy Horsemen Footmen

293 555

Connacht Horsemen Footmen

	41	20
Munster	Horsemen	Footmen
	41	139
Knockfergus	Horsemen	Footmen
	4	204
Inwards of the Pale	Horsemen	Footmen
	28	98
In Dublin Castle	Horsemen	Footmen
	9	29 (artificers)
Pensioners	3	
Injured soldiers	13	

Total   367 Horsemen   942 Foot 200 **Kern**

Cost to the Queen per month   £1,766. 32s.4d sterling

Certificate of Grains transported from Bristol

Lord Deputy to confirm to Auditor Jennings receipt of the following as supplied by victualler Mr. Sackford merchant of Bristol

1) 306 quarters of wheat

2) 78 quarters of malt

3) 240 quarters of masseline

4) 72 quarters of beans and peas

5) 258 barrels of meal

6) 16 butts and 2 dry vats of biscuit

7) 40 Kinder Kerns of butter

8) 40 hundreds of cheese 27 tons of beer

9) 2 tons of Gascoigne wine

10) 5 butts of sack

Further Supply of munitions for Ireland

Lord Deputy to confirm to Auditor Jennings receipt of following munitions for Queens Army of Ireland

100 sheaf's of crossbow arrows at 2s the sheaf

10 gross of crossbow strings at 6s the gross

24 fodders of lead

3 hundredweight of match

40 cavalry pistols

8 targets plated for Kern

80 brigandines

56 shirts of mail

80 pairs o sleeves of mail

40 hargobusses and crocke

1 hog of salt peter

1 hundredweight of sulphur

6 reaping hook and 10 lbs. of marline twine

20 pairs of powldrones

60 pikes

40 battle axes at 18d the piece

A wooden container to pack the axes at 4 s for the team of horses to draw goods from merchants premises to the quayside at Bristol mules at 4 d the mile for each cart and rope for binding and trussing the container at 24 s.

Running his bony fingers deftly through the hefty sheaf of papers the Lord Deputy glanced briefly at the contents before flinging the bundle down scathingly with papers strewing across his desk. "Fitton," he bawled impatiently. "Tidy up this mess and requesteth the quartermaster to check these items hast been delivered and instruct the paymasters' Samuel Wingfield and Nicholas Skiddle to carry out the Queen's orders that I may report back to Auditor Jennings." He opened the second dispatch which contained approval from the Queen to grant Trooper Tom Churchyard an annual pension and honorable discharge from the army taking into account his long and dutiful service with instructions for the Lord Deputy to prepare and sign a discharge warrant for the said trooper. Smiling, he carefully folded the discharge papers placing them in a drawer, and opened the next dispatch which contained two letters, the first from Francis Walsingham which read:

Lord Deputy,

I hast received the attached correspondence from a gentleman in Dublin, and it doth maketh me most curious as to wherefore it wast sent directly to myself when thou art the Queen's principal man in Ireland. Her Majesty hast received pleadings from a former soldier who fought bravely in the Low Countries against the Spanish under Sir John Norris, a settler named,

Christopher Browne, a Devon man who hast lost his lands and property in the Desmond rebellion in Munster. He and his followers seek to remain in Ireland if, at the Queen's pleasure, he is granted lands; he and his family are currently lodged in Dublin. He is a true puritan and most fervent in the Queen's service and wast ruthless in his dealings with the native Irish in Munster, and on the outbreak of the Desmond rebellion wast the first settler sought out for revenge by the natives losing everything and lucky to escape with his life. Her Majesty hast declared that if the serious accusations against the family named in the attached correspondence be proven thou wilt nullify their Surrender and Regrant Agreement madeth with Lord Deputy Sidney, confiscate their lands and property and remove their titles. The land and castle to be granted to Christopher Browne on reasonable terms and he is to be appointed sheriff with a mandate to clear the lands of the native Irish and stock the county with true loyal Protestant, Englishmen.

Francis Walsingham

He opened the second letter from a Dublin solicitor Patrick Fox which read:

Secretary Walsingham,

It is mine own duty as a loyal subject of her gracious Majesty the Queen in the Kingdom of Ireland to report to thee the treacherous actions of a sept of the O Farrells in the shired county of Longford. The said aforementioned articles of treason and disloyalty to the prejudice of the Crown art as follows:

1) Lord O Farrell and his son Fergal art of acquaintance and familiarity with the arch-traitor Red Hugh O Donnell and didst visit him in Dublin Castle bearing him gifts.

2) Lord O'Farrell didst receive a gift of a stallion from the said O Donnell.

3) The O Farrells didst receive a gift of a Spanish cloak and a pair of gilt spurs from King Brian O Rourke the father of O Farrell's wife, currently in rebellion with her Majesty's forces in Breffni.

4) Lord O Farrell's youngest son Cahir is presently in the service of O Byrne in Wicklow and doth him valorous service against the Crown.

5) Lord O Farrell hath in his service for many years a fugitive Jesuit Priest named O Duffy who doth minister to the O Farrell people and they covertly practice the papist faith

All the above acts of treachery art a breach of the O Farrell's terms under the Surrender and Regrant Agreement as signed with Sir Henry Sidney, Anno Domini, 1570.

Patrick Fox

Solicitor

Dublin

A wry smile crossed the Lord Deputies' face as he summoned his secretary. "Fitton, go to the barrack- room and fetcheth me the record book for I dost wisheth to confirm something." Minutes later Fitton returned, and the Lord Deputy running his eye down the list of names muttered *a most fortunate of serendipity methinks* as a sneer crossed his face. "Secretary Fitton," he ordered. "Sendeth a messenger summoning all the councillors to a meeting of the Privy Council in the King's Hall next week, we hast matters of great importance to discuss."

The councillors' sat impassively watching the aged Lord Deputy shuffle into the council chamber, a man they deeply despised who in turn deeply despised them. Lord Fingal glowered scornfully at the Lord Deputy. *Here we go again; they had seen it all before. Lord Deputy after Lord Deputy fresh-faced out of England or in odd case Wales, all equally ignorant of Irish affairs as the last, all as arrogant and knowing nothing about the country or its people. Most of the councillors on the other hand were of Old English families that came to Ireland hundreds of years ago with Strongbow and the Norman invasion, and they knew the country and the ways of the native Irish. Many of them were fostered by an Irish family and could speak the native language. What did these English upstarts know, whipping the people into rebellion and laying waste the country expecting the Lords of the Pale to pay for the Queen's army of raw recruits? If only they let things remain as they were, allow the native Irish to speak their language and fight amongst themselves as long as they left the Pale alone they were satisfied, a few of them even bribing the Irish chiefs' with black rents not to raid their cattle and destroy their property. It was far more effective and cheaper than paying for an ineffective English army led by pompous English fools.* "Gentlemen of the Pale." the Lord Deputy announced in a commanding voice. "I didst holdeth discourse with a Reverend William Daniels, a gentleman I am sure many of thee wilt be familiar, and although born into the savage race with God's grace he cameth to knoweth the errors of his people and religion, converting to the ways of a true Protestant man and he be the one who, and doth not asketh me wherefore, hath translated *The Book of Common Prayer* into the barbaric Irish tongue." Silence descended over the hall as the councillors' waited eagerly to hear what the Lord Deputy was about to say. "I hadst the Reverend Daniels explain to me in great detail the meaning of the reported prophecy regarding the rebel, Red Hugh O Donnell who escaped from the castle last week." Before he could continue pandemonium broke out as Christopher Nugent jumping to his feet shouted angrily. "Lord Fitzwilliam, we cannot believeth that thee, a true Christian man, wouldst give such superstitious nonsense the light of day in this chamber, and this the speculation of a wild ignorant people and utter balderdash." The Lord Deputy stood hand raised for silence and pointed his shaking finger at Christopher Nugent. "Sir," he yelled in a thundering voice. "Sir, I wouldst remindeth thee thou art in the Queen's chamber, and I am the Lord Deputy, and thou wilt not addresseth me in such an outrageous manner. Prithee be seated and heareth me out or I wilt throw thee in the grate and that shalt cool thine impertinence." Christopher Nugent, chastened by the Lord Deputies' outburst, sat meekly with head bowed cursing silently under his breath. "Gentlemen," the Lord Deputy continued. "Of course this prophecy is pure papist superstition and no more but as William Daniels sayeth the Irish hast blind faith in their saints and they dost take false courage and hope from the prophecy of O Donnell. We hast been informed the Lord of Tyrconnell named Black Hugh hast handed over power to his son Red Hugh, and no dowbt thou art aware of the wording of the prophecy regarding this matter." A low murmur of concern passed across the hall as the councillors' muttered to each other in low, hushed voices. "And," he continued. "We must act to quash any rebellious acts by the Irish against her Majesty and her government, but no matter what the prophecy foretells the Irish canst never defeat us for they art disorganized, undisciplined, and forever fighting amongst themselves but gentlemen," he stopped in mid-sentence casting a stern glance over the sea of faces. "I shalt remindeth thee of the damage a rebellion wilt cause and they shalt attack the Pale so thee hast much to lose for they shalt destroy thine own houses and steal thy cattle. The prophecy is nothing but irrational papist nonsense but it gives them hope and false courage, and if O Donnell unites the clans they wouldst roll across the country liketh a wave of thunder leaving death and destruction in their wake. Ay, they wouldst be crushed and couldst never succeed, but at what cost to the country and yourselves?" The Lord Deputy, seeing a dark cloud of concern cross their faces, reassuringly addressed them. "Gentlemen, I hast devised a plan to avert any uprising and saveth the country." The room fell silent all eyes fixed on Sir William. "But first gentlemen, there is another matter I wish to discuss. I hast received a dispatch from Francis Walsingham in London." He gestured to his secretary who, in a slow, stuttering, barely understandable Welsh accent, read the contents of the correspondence, and when finished Christopher Nugent jumped to his feet proclaiming smugly. "Lord Fitzwilliam, I always knew the O Farrells to be traitors for they swear allegiance to her Majesty on face value with a seething resentment thinly veiled. All the Irish chiefs art the same and at the first chance they shalt rebel and Lord Deputy," he continued barely concealing the excitement in his voice. "May I inquire as to thine intentions for the allocation of the confiscated lands and property of the treacherous O Farrells? As mine own estates art close by, and with the amalgamation of mine lands with the O Farrells, I canst secure a large part of the country for the Crown and extend the control of the Pale." The Lord Deputy sat silent tapping his fingers lightly on the table, cold eyes fixed keenly on Christopher Nugent and responded. "I dost welcome thy offer Mister Nugent, which I dost believeth is for the benefit of her Majesty, however, I must tell thee I gracefully decline as I hast a plan for the O Farrell's lands and castle which wilt be of great service to the country." Christopher Nugent stomped out of the King's Hall, his heart filled with hate and disdain for Lord Deputy William Fitzwilliam and the English in general. When the room emptied Lord Fingal approached the Lord Deputy who sat in discussion with his secretary. "Mine own Lord, may I speaketh to thee on a matter of much sensitivity." The Lord Deputy nodded to his secretary. "Thou may take thy leave, Mister Fitton." "Prithee, continue Mister Plunkett, and prithee tell me of this matter of much sensitivity for I am most eager to knoweth." "Lord Fitzwilliam," Lord Fingal spoke in an urgent voice.

"Regarding the dispatch concerning the O Farrells, I wouldst proffer the charges against this family art false." The Lord Deputy, eyes fixed hard on Lord Fingal, leaned forward and inquired. "Sir is that what thou truly believeth, the O Farrell art loyal subjects of her Majesty." "Ay," he replied enthusiastically. "The Nugent family art mortal enemies of the family and hast been since they settled in this country many years ago and dost thou knoweth that Patrick Fox who sent the letter is from the same parish as Christopher Nugent and works for him as a solicitor, and it be well known the Nugents hast coveted the O Farrell's lands for centuries and hast tried on many occasions to discredit the family, and I dost believe Sir Nugent instructed Fox to send the letter forwarding it directly to Francis Walsingham rather than yourself lest thee learn of Nugent's intentions." The Lord Deputy sat forward, eyebrows raised, clenched hands-on desk. "Mister Plunkett," he inquired. "Prithee tell me now, art thou an ally of the O Farrells, and I wouldst mind thee, sir, to consider carefully thine reply." An anxious look crossed Luke Plunkett's face. "Nay, mine own Lord", he replied nervously. "But I am wise to the devious workings of Christopher Nugent." "So, Mister Plunkett, bid me anon, is it thy true belief all written in the letter is false." "Ay, mine own Lord", he replied averting his eyes from Sir William's gaze. "Well sir, if that is so, prithee tell me anon, what is this?" Luke Plunkett turned pale as he peered at the names on the list.

"Mister Plunkett, messemes thou hast chosen the wrong side in this matter, hast thee not?" Lord Fingal stood frozen on the spot blood drained from his face. "Mister Plunkett," the Lord Deputy continued. "I hast instructed the Solicitor General, Ulick Shrovetide, to prepare the legal paperwork for the nullification of the Surrender and Regnant Agreement the O Farrells' signed with Sir Henry Sidney, and when complete they shalt be driven out their lands and castle confiscated, and their titles rescinded. The nullification of their agreement is purely a formality I couldst most easily dismiss, however, I doth not wisheth to cause further dissent amongst the chiefs who hast signed the Surrender and Grant Agreement and lash them into rebellion, and at what cost to her Majesty. I hast a settler who lost his lands in the Desmond rebellion ready to occupy and control Longford and subjugate the native Irish of the county. I didst hold conference with mine own captains and we have decided to use Longford as a staging post to curtail the wild Irish of Ulster. We shalt not be seeking battle with O Neill or O Donnell instead we shalt cut the head from the viper and destroy their crops before they can be harvested and killeth every beast in the field starving the people into submission. We await new levied troops from Yorkshire and Chester and on their arrival, and when the nullification document is complete, our gallant Captain Tom Lee shalt leadeth our army north to drive out the O Farrells and destroy Tyrone with artificial famine. We intend to march before harvest time in a couple of months with a policy of total destruction crushing the prophecy of O Donnell, and the false hopes of the Irish." Moving deftly he gathered up his scattered papers and rising sharply departed leaving the hall to the sole presence of the much admonished Lord Fingal.

Chapter Ten

In the large room adjacent to the scullery, Lord O Farrell crouched over his desk scrutinising the rent ledgers and in the far corner, Fergal and Father O Duffy, assiduously perusing a Latin composition entitled *The Punic Wars*. Slamming shut the ledgers he placed his elbows on the desk, covering his face with his hands. *What was he to do, for the third year in a row he was in arrears with the taxes due to the government as the quit rents he received did not meet his tax levy, and he was in serious debt. The Crown taxed him three shillings per ploughable acre and he taxed his tenants five shillings but many were in arrears and he was burdened with this accursed English tax system. Under the old Irish way of the Brehon Law, all the men of the clan shared ownership of the land and as chief, he was entitled to a generous portion of mensal land for which he received rents in kind, and could even charge his clansmen a petty tax for the proper upkeep of his wife and everyone benefited even the old, poor, and infirm, received a fair share of O Farrell land. Now everything was different and nobody benefited except the Crown or at least the corrupt Crown officials. His people had always been pastoral farmers and now they were forced to become tillage farmers growing crops, and many reluctant to abandon their age-old tradition of herding. The Queen's Commissioners' ordered him to evict tenants in arrears but where would they go, and the forefathers of his people had lived and shared the land for many centuries. Once the O Farrells were a rich and powerful family respected by the people but now!*

O Hanly approached and tapped his master gently on the shoulder. "My Lord, we have a messenger who wishes to speak to you urgently on a matter of great importance." Lord O Farrell pushed back his chair, a surprised look on his face. "Did he say who he was or what was his business O Hanly?" "No, sir, he didn't, he wants to talk to you of a matter of great magnitude." "Thank you, O Hanly, please show the gentleman in." The messenger stepped into the office, mud-splattered clothes, and speaking in Irish began. "My Lord, I have come from," stopping in mid-sentence on noticing the pair in the corner and Lord O Farrell catching the look on the man's face spoke reassuringly. "Sir, it's alright you may speak freely this is my son and his tutor and I can assure you that you may trust them both now come sit and tell me what is the purpose of your visit for I am anxious to learn." The messenger sat cleared his throat and continued. "Lord O Farrell, I am Sean Nagle, and have come directly from my master, Lord Fingal and I regret this day I am the bearer of bad news, very bad news indeed." Lord O Farrell slumped back heavily in his chair a startled expression on his face. "Mister Nagle, please tell me what the bad news is, tell me now." "Lord O Farrell, a letter accusing you and your family of treachery has been sent to the Queen, and you have been summarily found guilty of treason, and as we speak the Lord Deputy is in the process of nullifying your agreement with the Crown." Stopping momentarily to catch his breath he continued. "They are to drive you and your people out and confiscate your lands." The colour drained from Lord O Farrell's face and with trembling voice asked." "Mister Nagle, please tell me who sent the letter and what are the charges against this family?" "My Lord, the letter was sent by a Dublin solicitor, Patrick Fox but Lord Fingal believes it was the cunning work of Christopher Nugent who's greedy for your lands." Lord O Farrell, jumping to his feet banged his shillelagh hard on the desk and yelled. "The Nugent's always the same, always trying to destroy the, O Farrells. Mister Nagle, what are we to do?" "Lord O Farrell," he replied. "There is nothing you can do the soldiers are coming and you will be driven out, so you must leave this place. I am sorry to bring such bad tidings and may God have mercy on you and your people." Lord O Farrell stood face inundated with rage. "Mister Nagle, I thank you for coming and please thank Lord Fingal, but before you leave can you tell me, what are the charges against us?" "I do not know the full details, but I believe it is mainly because of your visit to O Donnell in the castle, he escaped on the feast of the Epiphany, ten days after your visit, and whether you assisted him or not isn't important you are seen by the Lord Deputy as an acquaintance of the arch rebel O Donnell, and that is the crux of the matter." Sean Nagle, placing his hands on Lord O Farrell's shoulders spoke in a low urgent voice. "The Lord Deputy is expecting fresh soldiers from England, and when the Surrender and Regrant Agreement is legally nullified in a month or two they will march here to depose you, but Lord Fingal will let you know when they are coming, in the meantime you must make your preparations to depart." Lord O Farrell and the priest sat in stunned silence as Fergal nervously paced the floor. "Father," he yelled. "We are done for we are destroyed, has the greed of the Nugents no end?" "Yes, son, the Nugent's greed is endless, and make no mistake about that. Father O Duffy, would you do me a small service and fetch my wife we must tell her the dreadful news we have received this day." "In the name of sweet Jesus," Lady O Farrell screamed hysterically. "What will become of us, are we to die of cold and hunger tramping the road like beggars. Will these robbers and destroyers of our people ever stop before we are all dead?" Embracing his wife Lord O Farrell spoke reassuringly. "My dear Megan, do not worry all is not lost I shall seek the assistance of Lord Fingal, he is sure to help us is he not?" Unconvinced by the lameness of his words she drew back and snarled at her husband. "How can he help us, we are finished, we will flee to Breffni where my father will protect us?" "No, no." Lord O Farrell replied angrily. "We shall not seek help from your father, there is only one thing we can do and it is this." They listened intently as he outlined his proposal. "We shall go directly to the Lord Deputy and plead our case, he is greedy and corrupt and will be influenced by a financial inducement, and that is what I truly believe. I will request Lord Fingal to arrange a meeting with Fitzwilliam and offer him a gold purse to nullify the charges against us for it is widely rumoured he took a bribe for assisting in the escape of O Donnell, and our predicament is small beer in comparison to O Donnell, is it not and the Nugents' sending the letter directly to the Queen may help our case." Turning to the priest he said. "Father, can you arrange for O Hanly to prepare the horses for I intend to travel to the city in the morning and Fergal will accompany me to translate the English, and with God's grace in one hand and a hefty bribe in the other we may succeed in our quest and Father O Duffy, say a mass for the success of our undertaking for if we fail we are all doomed."

Leaving at daybreak they reached Dunshaughlin Castle at dusk to be warmly greeted by Luke Plunkett and his wife Aine. "Lord O Farrell and Fergal, you are both welcome and we are deeply distressed at your grievous situation. The Nugents are purveyors of darkness and misery and may God curse their black souls, and I am sorry I cannot help you in your dreadful predicament." Lord O Farrell nodding in agreement replied. "Lord Fingal, I fully understand we would not wish to endanger you or your family but I have a proposal I believe may succeed." "Tell me, Lord O Farrell, I am much interested." "Luke, this is my plan. The Lord Deputy is a greedy cankered man and I propose to bribe him to drop the charges against the O Farrells for it is rumoured he took a substantial sum for assisting in the escape of O Donnell, is that not true?" "Yes, it is," he replied. "In his last role as treasurer charges were brought against him for corruption, and they say he is in substantial debt and has requested to stand down and return to England, and with all this in mind, your plan could succeed, I'm sure of it." "Thank you, Luke," Lord O Farrell replied, relief palpable in his voice. "Your words fill me with great comfort and encouragement and all I ask of you is to arrange a meeting with Fitzwilliam on my behalf." "Yes, of course, that is easily arranged but tell me now have you enough coins to bribe the man for he will demand a hefty sum if he is to drop the charges against you?" When Lord O Farrell told him he shook his head disappointedly. "No, my good friend, it is not nearly enough here let me increase the odds," and opening a large chest containing his rents and Crown taxes he handed Lord O Farrell a purse of gold coins. "Here, take this to weigh the scales in your favour for your paltry sum would never induce the Lord Deputy to change his mind." "Luke, you are too generous this is a small fortune, you are far too kind." "Lord O Farrell, what price can I place on my life you take this, and with your heavy purse I am certain your plan will work, it's only a small token of my gratitude to you and your son. Come, let us eat and drink and tonight we forget about your woes and celebrate the success of your plan."

Lady O Farrell's heart filled with dread as the days passed without word of her husband and son and Father O Duffy tried to reassure her. "My Lady, the undertaking Lord O Farrell is endeavoring will not be done quickly and he may have to wait for an opportune time to meet the Lord Deputy who is a cautious and cunning man and will not be hasty in accepting the bribe. He will no doubt play a waiting game with your husband be assured of that my Lady, please be of good mind and have faith and hope and I will say a special mass for their safe return." The words gave her little comfort and the following morning she instructed O Hanly to travel to the city and visit the home of the Plunketts to seek news of her family and with trepidation stood silent as the manservant departed. At Dunshaughlin Castle, O Hanly found Lady Plunkett in a distraught state and the bearer of bad news. "O Hanly," she cried "What am I to do, I have no news of my husband and I do not know whether he is alive or dead, and I know nothing of Lord O Farrell and his son." "Lady Fingal," he replied. "Please, tell me now what happened?" Her husband accompanied by Lord O Farrell and his son had departed for the city the week before to arrange a meeting with the Lord Deputy but never returned. The following day she travelled to the castle to be told by Constable Merryman the three men were detained and despite her pleadings, Lord Fitzwilliam refused to meet her. "Lady Plunkett," O Hanly said. "I will go to the castle and see what I can learn and will call on my return journey, be calm now my Lady, I am certain all will be well." On reaching the gates of Dublin Castle, O Hanly soon learned the fate of his master and his son as sixty miles away Lady O Farrell was overcome by a terrible fear which hung over her like a black cloud. On O Hanlys' return the following morning she rushed into the courtyard her heart racing, fearful of the news she would receive. "Mister O Hanly," she yelled at his approach. "Have you any news of my husband and son." Sliding off his horse O Hanly stood uneasily eyes fixed to the ground and raising his head replied in a crumbling voice. "Yes, my Lady, I have news about Lord O Farrell and Fergal." Lady O Farrell rushing forward grabbed his shoulders and screamed. "Mother of sweet Jesus, O Hanly, what has happened have you seen them, tell me now for I must know?" "Yes, my Lady, I have seen them alright, their heads are on spikes above the gates of Dublin Castle murdered in cold blood by the heretic Sir William Fitzwilliam."

The Lord Deputy, having taken their money and their heads, after much pleading from Lady Fingal, released her husband on the strict proviso he would tell all persons of the fate awaiting anyone who attempted to offer a bribe to the Lord Deputy in the course of his business. Sir William Fitzwilliam was also responsible for the death of the servant girl, Emir O

Hanly, who on hearing of the murder of her beloved, Fergal, threw herself from the bridge into the dark waters of the Camlin drowning herself and her unborn baby.

Chapter Eleven

A grey mist descended on the people of the O Farrells at the murder of their Lord and his son, and the tragic death of Emir and her unborn child. They knew *The Soldiers of London* were coming like a wave of butchers to drive them off their land and to resist would mean certain death, but what could they do? In the great hall, the priest asked the question. "Lady O Farrell, what can we do we cannot wait here to be slaughtered?" "Father," she replied. "I want you to go to Wicklow and inform Cahir of the death of his father and brother, and tell him I wish him to return immediately we need him here in his rightful place at this time." Father O Duffy shuddered at the thought of leaving the relative safety of the castle remembering his fellow priests and the terrible torture they endured before their awful deaths at the hands of the soldiers. Seeing the look of dread on his face she addressed him in a low engaging voice. "Father, I cannot send O Hanly, I need him here to help me with the tenants and affairs of the castle for I am helpless without my husband." The priest nodded his head in silent obedience uneasy about the long perilous journey ahead. "Father, you leave at dusk only travel at night and you will be safe from the foreigners, and O Hanly wishes you to take *O Donnell,* he is a fine mount and will carry you speedily outrunning any English horse you might encounter, and with God's help you will be at your destination within two days." *O Donnell was indeed a fine horse* the priest acknowledged as he galloped under pale moonlight swiftly across open ground, and when darkness lifted left the dirt track to enter a copse of trees three miles outside Mullingar on the shore of Lough Ennell. He tried sleeping but every time he nodded off imagined hearing voices close by and waited nervously until darkness to resume his journey forever watchful, and making good progress over the flat open grassy plains of Kildare reached Dunlavin, and after two nights ride pushed hard into the wild fastness of Wicklow. He felt safer in the rugged forested landscape and by late afternoon rode into a deep valley with steep sides stretching for miles into the distance. Strewn along the floor of the ravine he began to notice discarded pieces of ragged clothing faded by the weather with the odd pieces of rusting metal, then he came upon a gruesome sight. Scattered human remains, bones and rib cages bleached white by the wind and rain, and the odd skull staring blankly back at him. He was rudely shaken from his macabre thoughts by the presence of a group of wild-looking youths' surrounding his horse armed with a variety of weapons, muskets, swords, and spears. Their leader, an older youth, grabbed the reins firmly stopping the horse dead in his tracks. "Stranger", he barked, pointing his sword threateningly at the rider. "I am Ronan O Byrne, Captain of Kern, and tell me now who are you and what is your business in O Byrne country?" The priest, startled by the sudden appearance of the savage-looking youths, sat upright in his saddle gazing with astonishment at the raggle-taggle motley band, donned in an assorted hodgepodge of military attire, some with morions, all barefoot with brown-tinted, mud-stained legs, except the young captain who wore a pair of oversized cavalry boots, a mishmash uniform of tattered scarlet tunic with rusty, dented morion on head. "I am," he replied. "Father O Duffy of the Society of Jesus, and come from Annaly on important business, I have been sent by Lady O Farrell of Longford Castle to seek her son Cahir and give him a message, do you know him, Ronan?" The Captain of Kern, relaxing his grip on the reins replied. "Yes, Father, Cahir O Farrell is indeed well known to us for he is the captain of our squadron of hobblers in the service of our chief, Fiach Mc Hugh O Byrne, the scourge of the foreigners. Cahir is a fine captain and well respected by the men and indeed O Byrne himself. Running his eyes over the priest he asked himself why a person dressed in the clothes of a common man of low rank would be mounted on such a fine steed. "Father, I do not for a moment doubt who you are, and your intentions are good but," he hesitated. "Our chief has issued strict instruction that no man passes through this valley of Glenmalure unless he is personally known to us. The foreigners are devious and are forever nipping at the heels of our people and Captain Tom Lee is relentless in his pursuit of the O Byrne, it is more than my life is worth to let you pass." The priest leaning down reached out his arm touching the captain on the shoulder. "Ronan my son," he said in a soft reassuring voice. "While I fully understand your caution, for I know too well the devious ways of the heretics, the purpose of my mission here today is a sorrowful one for I bring news of the death of Cahir's father and brother at the hands of the Lord Deputy, and his mother wishes him home at this tragic time." On hearing the priest's words, Ronan O Byrne stood back the young kern chattering excitedly among themselves. "Father, I understand and I am sorry for doubting you, come at once and I will take you to Cahir O Farrell, he is at our fort further along the valley where you can fulfill your sad deed, come with me now." Barking orders to his small band who resumed their watchful eye on the pass they moved along the valley with the Captain of Kern leading *O Donnell* at a steady pace to bring the bad news to the captain of O Byrne's horse.

The fortress sited three miles further along the narrow ravine and only recently established since Captain Tom Lee razed their principal fort at Ballinacor a year before when the Lord Deputy decided O Byrne must be destroyed and Captain Lee ordered to assemble a couple of hundred of his best men in great secrecy as he was aware O Byrne had his spies. In the dead of night, Lee, and his band of seasoned veterans accompanied by half a dozen of the Queen's Kern marched silently under torchlight towards the fortress to exterminate

O Byrne and his people once and for all. On nearing the fort the soldiers' blanketed their feet and the horse's hooves in sackcloth, extinguishing the torches. Under the strictest orders to remain silent, they reached within a hundred yards of the fort unnoticed, O Byrne's guards either asleep, drunk, or missing, when a drummer boy, one of the Queen's Kern, a boy orphaned by Lord Deputy Grey and forced into English service, took his long-awaited revenge by beating his drum with hard strikes of the stick, his Irish heart too strong for the Queen's uniform before a trooper silenced him with a blow of his sword hilt to the head felling him instantly. The thunderous clatter shattered the silence of the night and reverberated deafeningly down the valley awaking the O Byrnes from their slumber, and fighting a rear action led by Cahir O Farrell supported by the Tyrone musketeers, allowed the people to escape with the loss of two riders and ten Tyrone men. On entering the deserted camp, Captain Lee burned the fort and village to the ground ordering Trooper Tom Churchyard to drown the drummer boy in a nearby bog. The heroic and selfless boy soldier of the Queen's Kern who, by his brave and swift action, saved the lives of the people of Fiach Mc Hugh O Byrne, died without uttering a sound his body sinking noiselessly into the miry waters of the bog as bright stars twinkled like diamonds in the night sky above.

The O Byrne fort at Glenmalure was a lively affair with scores of kern practicing the throwing of spears and swordplay, the blacksmiths sharpening knives and forging spearheads, as the women crouched over open fires prepared food for the soldiers. On entering the fort Ronan O Byrne called to a soldier busy grooming a horse in the stable. "Cahir, Cahir, over here you have a visitor from Annaly to speak with you." Cahir glanced at the mounted figure, a few stones heavier than he remembered but it was Father O Duffy, a man forever interfering in his family's affairs and always with an opinion. He walked over defiantly to the priest sarcastically addressing him. "Well, now Father, what a surprise, and what business brings you here did you come to see the wild Irish in action, the ones who will not bow to their foreign master?" Cahir, seeing the troubled look on the priest's face knew he was the harbinger of bad news. "What is it Father?" he asked anxiously. "I want to know what brings you here this day." The priest dismounted and reaching out grasped Cahir by the shoulders. "My son," he said gravely. "I'm afraid I bring terrible news, your father and brother are dead." Cahir staggered back in shock the news piecing his soul like a sharp dagger. "What," he cried out. "What has happened O Duffy, what fate befell them tell me now?" "They were murdered by the heretic, Sir William Fitzwilliam, and their heads fixed on the gates of Dublin Castle." Father O Duffy answered uneasily. "I warned my father." Cahir shouted, eyes blazing with anger. "I told him not to trust the foreigners for they are sly devious murderers and their true intent is to kill us all and he wouldn't listen and my brother, Father O Duffy. In God's name what threat was Fergal to anyone; the murdering dogs. I will avenge the deaths of my family and I will not stop until I slaughter every foreigner in our country." The priest stepping forward placed his arms around Cahir. "My son," he said softly. "I'm afraid there is more."Cahir reeled back in disbelief. "In God's name, Father O Duffy, what more can there be?" "Your father was charged with treason by the Privy Council and they are sending soldiers to confiscate your lands and castle and to drive your people out, you must come home at once and be of assistance to your poor mother, the unfortunate woman needs you at this time." Ronan O Byrne, overhearing the bad tidings, took Cahir by the arm and led him into the great hall followed by the priest. "Here, sit brother and partake of a dram of whiskey for it will comfort you and not to worry Cahir, we will avenge the murder of your kin and to that, I do swear." The doorway darkened filled by a big muscular figure who, stomping across the hall with echoing strides stood staring blankly at the priest. Father O Duffy glancing around was confronted by a giant of a man clad in battle dress of chain mail and breastplate with heavy broadsword hanging from his belt, ruddy complexion, grizzly beard, and long black curly hair. "Who are you?" Fiach Mc Hugh O Byrne bellowed. "And what's all the commotion?" On seeing the distraught Cahir he knelt down and in a low voice asked. "My son, what is the matter, tell me now why you are so distressed?" Ronan O Byrne introduced the priest and related the woeful tale to his father who listened intently and springing to his feet unsheathed his sword waving it angrily. "Fitzwilliam is a devil and no doubt about that," he roared. "An evil monster and they call us savages, but these foreigners are beyond contempt." He stopped in mid-sentence fixing his stare at his young captain who had done him and his people so much good service. "Cahir, my son, on my solemn oath we will avenge the deaths of your father and brother, mark my words the ground will run red with the blood of the foreigners for their murderous deed." The hall filled with soldiers as the news travelled around the fort the men milling around their distraught comrade with heavy hearts. A hush fell over the room as Chief O Byrne proclaimed. "My brave soldiers, the foreigners have done a great injury to our friend and comrade, Cahir O Farrell, and this night we shall avenge the murder of his father and brother. Prepare your arms and horses and we will raid to the very gates of the castle and destroy everything in our path. We will punish the foreigners make no mistake about that, and leave the Pale awash in Saxon gore." The hall erupted as the soldiers raised their swords and fists in unison heaping black curses and damnation on the killers of Lord O Farrell and his son. "Chief O Byrne," Cahir responded in a ragged voice. "I greatly appreciate your support but with Captain Tom Lee and his troop of cavalry camped at the Glen of Imaal it would be dangerous for you to raid the Pale this night. Lee will take advantage of your absence and destroy the fort and kill all your people, he is a mortal danger to the O Byrnes. No, my chief, the time is not right you must stand ready to defend yourselves." O Byrne nodded in agreement placing his arm around his young captain's shoulder. "Cahir," he instructed. "You must leave and may God's grace be with you my son. I understand your place now is at your mothers' side in Annaly, you will be sadly missed but you must return home." O Byrne turned to the priest. "Father O Duffy, before you depart for Longford would you be good enough to do me a small favour." The priest mildly flattered by O Byrnes's request replied. "Of course chief, anything you wish, tell me now what is it you want me to do?" "Father O Duffy, I would like you to say mass for myself and my people, us unfortunate sinners that we are, would you do it for us now." "I will chief," he replied hesitantly. "But you see I do not have my sacred vestments or chalice with me I mistakenly left them behind in Longford." A broad grin crossed over O Byrne's face as he clapped the priest hard on the back. "Ah sure, Father O Duffy, that's not a problem not at all, and I'll tell you why. Wasn't Father O Rogan, the poor soul who was murdered by Captain Lee, an awful death he had the poor man, and may the Lord have mercy on his soul, but you'll never believe this Father, didn't he mistakenly leave his vestments and chalice behind when he left on his travels just like yourself. Sure I'll go and fetch them for you this instance, it's been a long time since we've had any spiritual comfort in this place." After mass Cahir bid farewell to his comrades in the knowledge, he would never see them again. Men he'd fought with day after day, sharing life and death in equal measure. Manus O Sullivan, placing his arms around his captain said. "Captain O Farrell, it has been a privilege and an honour to serve with you in the defense of our country for you are indeed a fearless warrior and because of you, we have the best cavalry squadron in Ireland. God's grace be with you now and the people of the O Farrells." Tears brimmed in Cahir's eyes as he bid farewell to each of his comrades and to the new captain he proclaimed tearfully. "Manus, you have been the companion of my soul and the blanket of my winter, always a good friend and comrade to me, and now you are the Captain of Horse, and a fine captain you will be, of that I am sure. You look after my men they are good lads and brave soldiers and the one bit of advice I will give to you, Captain O Sullivan. Never ride too close to the English horse their petronels are dangerous but only at close range," he tapped his shoulder gently. "Remember my lucky escape with the big ugly trooper at Glenmalure." Laughing heartily they embraced bidding each other their final farewell. Fiach O Byrne saluted his departing captain and gave him a beautiful gold harp as a gift for his mother. "Cahir," he said. "I thank you for your brave service and loyalty to me and my people and I wish you well. I am sorry I cannot help you but you are right about the relentlessly Captain Lee and his band of thieves who are sharp on my heels." "Yes chief," Cahir replied. "You must protect your people and I must protect mine." As they walked towards the stables O Byrne said. "Cahir, it will not be yourself and the priest riding back to Annaly, O Neill's men will ride with you on your journey home. I am honouring my pledge and releasing them from service allowing them to return to Tyrone in time for the harvest although they are much needed here." They were soon joined by the two Tyrone men the presence of the heavily armed veterans giving great comfort to the priest on their hazardous journey home.

Cahir gazed keenly at the mass of smiling faces assembled at the gate to wish him farewell- the people of the O Byrnes. Wild, black-haired, barefoot women, dressed in shabby worn mantles with their scraggy, dirty-faced, naked children by their side. A kind, simple people, reared hard and rough in the forest, never knowing where their next meal would come from, never knowing which day would be their last, these women who cared for him so attentively when he was wounded. Always in fear of *The Soldiers of London* who could come anytime day or night to exterminate them, man, woman, and child, and the only thing standing between them and the murderous foreigners were the raggle-taggle band of the soldiers' of the O Byrne and the handful of outsiders like himself. Running his face over the smiling crowd a cold shiver ran down his spine thinking of the horrific and brutal fate awaiting these poor helpless people at the hands of Captain Tom Lee.

Chapter Twelve

The journey home was uneventful for Father O Duffy and his three companions and entering the courtyard of Longford Castle, O Hanly, who was working in the stables, was startled believing the riders to be English cavalry then noticing the lack of stirrup and mish-mash military attire of the soldiers approached the men recognizing Cahir. "Master O Farrell," he said jokingly. "It is good to see you fit and well, and I see you bring your own private army to protect us from the foreigners. Tether your horses in the stables and come inside your mother has been waiting anxiously on your return." Lady O Farrell, rushing forward threw her arms' around her son hugging him tightly. "Cahir, Cahir, I am so glad to see you," she cried, eyes brimming with tears of joy. "I missed you so very much my son, thank God your home safe and sound." She looked at him keenly shocked at how much he had changed. Gone the youthful countenance replaced by cold lifeless eyes and the callous look of a seasoned soldier. "Cahir my son, you've all grown up you're a big strong man, just look at you." Her smile faded as a cloud of sadness crossed her face. "Cahir, your poor father and Fergal, murdered by the foreigners and us charged with treason and soon to be driven from our home it is only a matter of time before they come, what are we to do?" "Mother," he replied. "It was my fault wasn't it for what happened to father and Fergal, what with me in the service of O Byrne?" "No, my son, it was the Nugents, they are behind all this they were always seeking an excuse to destroy us and it is what they have done, it's not your fault." A red mist of rage came over him and he returned angrily. "I will kill Christopher Nugent, so I will mother, I despise him and his family, greedy heretics is what they are." "Cahir listen to me," she replied. "Lord Fingal, a friend of this family, believes your father visiting Red Hugh O Donnell in Dublin Castle was our downfall." Cahir reeled back a startled look on his face. "What mother, father visited O Donnell in jail but why?" "Cahir, your father learned of the prophecy regarding O Donnell from Father O Rogan who came here and told your father that Hugh O Neill, the Earl of Tyrone was planning an escape and your father knew the Great O Neill had the power and the influence to do so." "Cahir," Father O Duffy interjected. "Your father believed when O Donnell was free he would be allied with O Neill and the prophecy realised and this family would be in mortal danger for submitting to the English, so to protect us he wished to make the acquaintance of O Donnell, and is why at great risk he brought your brother with him to the prison although Fergal knew nothing of the prophecy." "What, I cannot believe this, I cannot believe what I am hearing," he shouted, shaking his head in disbelief. "My father brought Fergal with him to Dublin Castle, but why did he do such a foolish thing?" "Because Cahir, he felt it was important that Fergal met with O Donnell to ensure this family had his protection if the clans rebelled." A look of bewilderment came over Cahir's face. "But Father O Duffy, tell me this why in God's name did he ever pledge his allegiance to the English in the first place?" "Son, listen to me now," Lady O Farrell interrupted. "Your father did what he thought best at the time. Lord Deputy Sidney was here in this very room and threatened your father, and sure look at what happened to your father's relations and friends who didn't take the English title. Foresight, Cahir, is a wonderful thing, and your poor father was trying to protect this family in the only way he could and that is why he took the English title and the reason he visited O Donnell in jail but always remember Cahir, your father had a weak English title but a strong Irish heart!" Ending the conversation she turned to the manservant. "Mister O Hanly, ask Una to prepare a good dinner for our visitors and arrange their sleeping quarters and this night we shall rejoice and celebrate the homecoming of Cahir."

They dined well that night in the great hall, Cahir and his comrades taking great enjoyment relating tales of their grandiose heroic exploits and dangerous missions chasing and been chased by the foreigners up and down the mountains and glens of Wicklow and over many drinks the woes of the O Farrells were put aside at least for one night. The Tyrone men were affable and agreeable companions although their broad

Tyrone accents difficult to understand at times. "Niall," Father O Duffy inquired. "I'm curious to learn how you and Dermot came to be so far from home fighting with O Byrne." "Well Father," he replied. "When O Byrne sent out the call for assistance to defend his people against the army of Lord Arthur Grey, our chief the Great Hugh O Neill secretly sent twelve of us trained men with a cartload of Spanish muskets and ten barrels of black powder to arm and instruct O Byrne's men in the use of firearms and it is what we did but now we're returning home for the harvest and to drive our cattle to high ground, we're part-time soldiers only." "But," the priest continued. "Why then are only two of you returning home?" "Well Father, our comrades were killed in a skirmish when Captain Lee attacked the fort at Ballinacor where they died bravely but not in vain as they stopped Lee's men butchering the people of the O Byrne, and may God have mercy on their souls, brave men they were too." "Niall," the priest asked. "Please tell us about your famous chief the Great Hugh O Neill, Earl of Tyrone I am keen to learn more?" "Well," Niall replied. "The title the Great O Neill was originally granted to his uncle Shane O Neill or more commonly known as Shane the Proud by good Queen Bess when he visited London many years ago, but Father O Duffy he is indeed the Great Hugh O Neill. A man of vision and a true leader of men and I'll tell you his story. As a child, he was taken by the foreigners from his home in Tyrone to be raised and educated in the English manner outside Dublin, and served in the heretic's army as a cavalry officer in the war against the Desmonds in Munster, and trusted by the Queen and her council. But as the settlers and adventurers confiscated more and more land, destroying the smaller chiefs, he could see Bingham encroaching into his territory and soon realised nothing would stop the greedy colonists except force. He knew even his loyalty to the Crown would not protect him so for many years now he has prepared for an all-out war with the English which he knows will eventually come, and unlike his fellow Irish chiefs he is coolheaded patient, and calculating in his approach, managing to keep the Lord Deputy on his side with many friends of influence amongst the foreigners, always generous to the English officials and in particular with the Lord Deputy to whom he lavishes many gifts." Stopping momentarily to take a swig of beer he continued. "Father, for years now he has been covertly smuggling gunpowder and weapons from Scotland, and swords from Toledo, with every man in Tyrone trained in the use of modern weapons, sure he even obtained a license from Walsingham to import vast quantities of lead on the pretense of building a mansion in the English fashion in Dungannon, but secretly making lead balls. He also buys weapons from English soldiers and pays them twenty shillings if they desert and fight for the Irish, and many the foreigner has done that. Now, Father O Duffy, he has even begun making his own gunpowder, isn't that amazing?" The priest raised his eyebrows in surprise. "It is Niall, it certainly is, but tell me now how does he do that?" "Well Father, he imports sulphur from Scotland, and we make charcoal easily enough, but the difficult bit is making the saltpeter now that takes a lot of hard work doesn't it, Dermot," he replied, throwing a smile at his comrade. "Niall, tell me now," the priest asked. "What's so funny about making saltpetre?" "Well Father," he replied. "We do it the French way." The Tyrone men spluttered into hysterical laughter. "Father," Niall continued a wide grin on his face. "O Neill has a Frenchman in his service, an expert in munitions, and he instructed us in the making of saltpeter and what you do is simply piss into straw and manure, but Father O Duffy let me tell you now you need an awful lot of piss, an awful lot of piss now, to make saltpeter and doesn't the chief have us stand over a trench and us standing there all day long pissing like mad and you could say we were pissing for Ireland, and that's how we make saltpeter and our gunpowder. And tell me, Father, what do yeh think about that now?" he asked, a mischievously gleam in his eye. "Father O Duffy," Niall continued. "I have told you of the preparation of O Neill for war and when allied with O Donnell the smaller clans will join them and become an unstoppable force that will roll like thunder from Donegal to Kerry driving the foreigners before them and when our crops are harvested and the cattle secure we will, a united people, drive the foreigners out of our country once and for all." "You seem very certain of victory, Niall," the priest responded. "Yes, Father, you can be sure of it, and there's much more," he hesitated casting a furtive glance at his comrade. "What more is there I am curious?" the priest asked. "Tell him, Niall," his comrade returned. "We can trust the O Farrells with our lives can we not?" "No, Dermot, I'll let you tell him sure with all this talking isn't me mouth as dry as the village gossip." Dermot leaned over to the priest and spoke in a low voice. "Father, what I tell you now is known to few men," he said, a wry smile on his face. "Father O Duffy," he revealed. "The Great O Neill is truly a gifted leader of men, a man of vision, and when we have dispatched the foreigners to Hades, and our country free we do not intend to stop, no, Father, it is only the beginning." "Beginning of what Dermot, what do you speak of?" Fixing his gaze at the priest he replied in a self-assured drawl. "Father, we have plans for the united Irish armies to invade England, kill the bastard heretic Queen, and restore the true Catholic Church to its rightful place," he hesitated for a few seconds and asked in a low mocking voice. "And tell me, Father, what do yeh think about that now?" Father O Duffy shook his head in amazement. "What foolish nonsense is this, you intend to invade the land of the foreigners, are you crazy such an audacious plan would never work." "Oh yes, it will, Father." Dermot replied smugly. "It will if we have Lord Essex on our side with his powerful allies, and the Scots and the Catholic recusants of England. The heretic Queen and her puritan advisors have many enemies such as Lord Essex who is in league with the Great O Neill, and tell me now, Father O Duffy," Dermot asked. "Can you imagine the wondrous sight of our Irish army led by O Neill and O Donnell, marching through the street of London, banners unfurled and our Irish flags' blowing proudly in the wind to the sound of Irish war pipes and the beating of drums? Then we put Essex a Catholic monarch on the throne and our reward will be that England never invades Ireland again and O Neill shall rule our country as High King of Ireland. And tell me, Father, what do yeh think about that now?" he asked, eyes blazing with mischief. "Now," he continued. "Let us all raise our glasses to the new High King of Ireland, the Great Hugh O Neill, Earl of Tyrone." "We live in strange times," the priest replied smiling. "Very strange times indeed, an Irish chief not preoccupied with the past and his illustrious ancestors but looking to the future, a man of vision who is, without doubt, the Great O Neill." Cahir stood and raising his glass proclaimed." Will all present drink a toast now in memory of absent friends, my poor father and brother, and our fallen comrades for they are sorely missed this night?" Lady O Farrell, reaching over grasped Cahir's hand tightly." Cahir," she announced eagerly. "There is something I have to tell you, something important." "And what would that be now mother, I am intrigued?" "Before your father left for Dublin, he instructed me to inform you if he failed to return he wanted you to have something, something of great significance." A look of surprise came over Cahir's face. "And what is it mother?" he asked inquisitively. "Mister O Hanly," she called, summoning the manservant. "Fetch the casket and bring it here." A ripple of excitement passed over the room as returning minutes later the manservant placed a tarnished metal casket on the table at which they all peered with great interest curious as to what it might contain. "Mother," Cahir inquired. "What is it, what's in the casket?" His mother blushing with pride replied. "Open it my son, open it and you shall see." Reaching over tentatively he lifted the lid of the casket gazing in astonishment at what the box contained. In the casket was an object of great beauty. An ornate gold slipper fashioned with the most delicate embroidered pleats and Cahir was speechless, bedazzled at the beautiful shining item before him. "What is it mother?" he asked excitedly. "What is this?" "This Fergal is a sacred object of great antiquity belonging to the O Farrell clan for centuries, it is *The Golden Slipper* used in the inauguration ritual of a new chief." Cahir stood, enthralled at the golden radiance of the slipper as with trembling hands he gently lifted the object which felt heavy and glittered brightly reflecting the flickering waxy yellow light of the rush torches on the walls. "Mother, where did you get this?" Your father," she replied. "He wished you have it, and he wished you be inaugurated as the new chief in the old rituals on the stone chair at Moatfarrell, the inauguration site of the O Farrell chiefs from ancient times." Cahir placed the slipper carefully on the table and stepped back in disbelief. "Mother," he said in a shaky voice. "I never believed this would happen, I never imagined I would be the Chief O Farrell, never in my wildest dreams. I thought father had deprived me of my birthright when he allied our family to the English and abandoned the ancient ways of the O Farrells." "Cahir, Sir Henry Sidney prohibited this custom at the risk of death and your father was the last chief to be inaugurated at Moatfarrell fifty years ago, and he knew this action would be the greatest act of defiance we can show the Lord Deputy and the foreigners. It is the most singular part of our rituals the English despise as it represents everything about us they hate." Turning to the priest she said. "Father, you will preside over the inauguration, and Cahir your two fine comrades Dermot and Niall will be your guard of honour as we enact this noblest and ancient of our Irish ways. O Hanley will instruct Father O Duffy in the inauguration rituals and there is something else, Cahir, a gift from your uncle, King Brian," she said, handing him a pair of gilded spurs.

The previous week, O Hanly journeyed to the abandoned crannog in Derragh Lough, an ancient manmade island built by the O Farrells in the lake to provide protection in times of danger and to conceal valuables. When Lord O Farrell made his allegiance to the English he had the golden slipper taken to the crannog to prevent English soldiers' stealing the valuable object, and placing it in a casket buried it in a place known to O Hanly as he was present when Lord O Farrell concealed the slipper many years before. The recovered item had lost none of its charm or beauty, and on removing the mud and dirt, it was restored to its full shining glory. In darkness, Cahir, his mother, the priest, and the two O Neill soldiers, rode to the ancient site of Moatfarrell, O Hanly having gone ahead to clear the undergrowth and expose the long-abandoned carved stone seat of the O Farrells. As pale moonlight washed over the ancient site of Moatfarrell, seated on the stone chair under the venerable oak, the new Chief O Farrell was inaugurated. Father O Duffy placed in Cahir's right hand a straight white hazel wand called *Slat Na Righe-The Rod of Kingship* and he pledged his life to defend the O Farrell people. Standing, he turned thrice to the left and thrice to the right, and throwing the golden slipper over his shoulder was proclaimed chief, and speaking the ancient words in honour of the Holy Trinity was pronounced the new chief of the O Farrells, a title higher than the foreigners could grant and the ancient title of his forefathers. It was with sadness the next morning they bid farewell to the men of Tyrone who after their service in the army of O Byrne were returning home.

The frantic barking of the two Irish wolfhounds at dawn, one week after the departure of the O Neill men, awoke O Hanly; someone was at the gates. Grabbing his loaded shillelagh he charged across the courtyard calling out. "Who is there, and state your business?" "Sean Nagle," came the reply. "Open the gates, O Hanly, it is me the servant of Lord Fingal, please open the gate." Face red with exertion he slid off his horse shaking the dust from his cloak. "Christ, Sean," said O Hanly. "I thought it was *The Soldiers of London*." "Not this day," Nagle replied brusquely. "But soon enough they will be here banging at your gates and I can tell you now, O Hanly, that shillelagh of yours won't do you much good." Stopping to catch his breath he continued. "I thought you'd never open the gates, they have spies everywhere. Come, raise Lady O Farrell, we must speak." Taking Nagle into the kitchen he addressed his wife who was setting kindling on the fire. "Una, can you prepare refreshments for Mister Nagle, and I will awake the mistress." Lady O Farrell entered the kitchen Cahir close on her heels. "Mister Nagle," she inquired. "What brings you here at this early hour, and by the way, this is my son Cahir, the new Chief O Farrell who was inaugurated in the old ways last week." Sean Nagel shaking his head cast a disdainful look at Cahir and replied. "I am fully aware of this foolhardy act my Lady as is Lord Deputy Fitzwilliam." A surprised look crossed her face. "But Mister Nagle," she responded. "How could you possibly know of the ceremony it was carried out in secrecy under the cover of darkness?" "My good Lady," he replied. "Nothing is a secret in this land the Lord Deputy has ears and eyes in every place, anyway, my master instructed me to relay to you an urgent message." Pointing his finger at Cahir he said. "When the Lord Deputy was told of your foolish deed he proclaimed in the council chamber that the O Farrells were bestial kingmakers, and took your actions as a serious insult to the Queen and a ritual which the English perceive as a most barbaric act in contravention of all civilized and Christian beliefs declaring the O Farrell's outlaws punishable by immediate death. There will be no legalities or further delays and presently the Lord Deputy is awaiting a new army of levied men from Chester, and on their arrival, the soldiers will march here immediately to decimate you and your people, there will be no mercy, so you must flee for your lives you have but two weeks. They intend to occupy your castle and use it as a base to commence a campaign of laying waste the land and destroy all the crops in Ulster to starve the people and stop sustenance for the armies of O Donnell and O Neill if they unite and there is more," he continued. "The Lord Deputy has granted your lands and castle to an English settler called Christopher Browne, a man with a reputation for cruelty against the native Irish and he brings with him his family and many English colonists to settle on O Farrell land." They stood mutely until Nagle broke the silence. "My Lady, may I rest awhile for I am weary from my travels for I intend to leave at the first sign of darkness, and this is the last time I will come. It is too dangerous and Lord Fingal instructed me to tell you he considers his debt of honour paid by his actions, and he asked me to state he owed your son his life and not his own death." "I thank you, Mister Nagle." Lady O Farrell replied. "And please send my thanks to your master for he has done as he promised and repaid his debt honorably to this family."

With heavy-heart, Cahir strolled along the banks of the Camlin, his father's two dogs running alongside startling the odd bird from the rushes, a peaceful place with the low soft murmur of running waters. He came here as a child when he came home from Breffni on occasion to visit his parents. Fergal and himself would spend long days fishing for trout and swimming to cool themselves in the hot summer sun, and he laughed recalling the day their dog disturbed a swan and her cygnets who chased them right to the castle gates only to be saved by O Hanly's walking stick. But that was a long time ago and those days long gone, and everything changed with his father and Fergal dead, and a host of dark thoughts crowded his mind. *We are a doomed race us, Irish. Death walks by our side -our destiny is extermination and that is what the foreigners have planned. This Surrender and Regrant Agreement only a devious way of destroying us and taking our land, in the end, even my father realised he should never have surrendered his Irish title and capituated to*

Sidney, he might have been killed resisting but at least he would have died at a time and place of his choosing and with honour- he died anyway but as a slave, and in the cruelest manner. But what could he do, he had no army as Sidney forbade his father to keep his Gallowglass guard or armed men. They had no choice but to go to Breffni, he knew his uncle Brian O Rourke would welcome them into his household, but what about their tenants and servants what fate would await them, be murdered, or become slaves to this usurper, Christopher Browne. The prospect of this heretic sleeping in his bed and living in his castle was insufferable, so there and then he made the fateful decision, no, he was not running away, he would stand and he would fight, even if it was to be The Last Stand of the Chief O Farrell.

Rushing back to his mother he informed her of his decision. "Mother, I have made my mind up, I am not running away. I will stand and fight for it is only a fool or a coward who lies in bed while his house is robbed." "Son," she replied anxiously. "These are brave words, but fight with what we have no soldiers and we are no match for the foreigners our only chance is to flee to Breffni, and that way we'll survive at least for a while." Staring hard at his mother he nodded in agreement. "Yes, what you say is true, but should I drown myself in the Camlin or hang myself. Mother, listen to me now, I refuse to wait to be butchered by the bombastic foreigners whose sole aim is to demolish our world, have we not blood flowing in our veins the blood of our forefathers, and are we not better men than the callous, pompous, heretics of England. No, mother, I will make a last stand and die if I must." "And die you will my son, no mistake about it," she replied. "That may be true mother, but I intend to seek aid and I intend to fight." "Seek aid from where you know all the chiefs are hard-pressed at this time and can barely keep the foreigners at bay, and with the Bingham brothers on the loose the chiefs won't help us how could they?" "Mother, I will seek men and weapons from Red Hugh O Donnell, he is a man of honour and would never forget my father's kindness which cost him and Fergal their lives did it not, I will ask him to repay us with assistance. I will travel to his castle in Donegal, I am certain he will help us. I will leave at first light and take O Hanly's horse *O Donnell* and reacquaint him with his master, and with this fine steed I can easily outrun anyone I meet on the road."

Finally, after two day's ride, he reached the castle of the O Donnell overlooking the small town of Donegal. In the courtyard, men busied themselves in preparing for war with the polishing and sharpening of blades, the fitting of javelins, and the blacksmiths busy forging weapons. On stepping into the castle square a heavily built man in the full battledress of a Gallowglass, axe in hand, barred his way addressing him in a barely understandable Scottish brogue. "Who are you stranger and what is your business here?" "I am Chief O

Farrell from Annaly, and I wish to speak to the O Donnell on a matter of importance." "He will see no one this day," the Gallowglass replied sharply. "He is at a council of war with his captains." "My friend, inform him, O Farrell, captain of O Byrne's horse wishes to speak with him urgently." The Gallowglass stood aside instantly. "Captain of O Byrne's horse, come with me and I will take you to him, come follow me." In the great hall on the first floor of the castle before him stood the famous, Red Hugh O Donnell, the predestined leader of the Irish people, a youth with a radiant countenance, tall and handsome, and splendidly dressed in the finest of embroidered silk clothes. As he looked at the man he understood why he was the savior of Ireland, the man who would drive the foreigners into the sea. As Red Hugh walked towards him, Cahir was struck by the man's pronounced limp markedly incongruous to his natural bearing and strong upright physique. "Chief O Farrell, you are most welcome to our home, any man of the O Byrnes is welcome here I owe them my life." "Yes," Cahir replied. "I was absent at the time the O Byrnes' rescued you, a fine and noble people they are too." "Come captain, and tell me why you are here and most welcome you are, come be seated and tell me all." "Chief O Donnell, you knew my father and my brother they visited you in Dublin Castle before your escape." O Donnell's eyes brightened and reaching out he embraced Cahir. "Yes, yes," he responded joyfully. "Your father and your brother came to me at Christmas and what joy and happiness they brought when I was in the depths of my misery and despair. Chief O Farrell, I am forever in your family's debt for their act of kindness I am eternally grateful, and tell me how now is your father and brother?" A dark shadow crossed Cahirs face. "My Lord," he replied in a broken voice. "They are both dead murdered by the Lord Deputy and the O Farrells are to be driven out of Longford, and that is why I am here, Chief O Donnell, to seek your assistance." Red Hugh O Donnell sprung back in disbelief. "I am sorry Cahir, I was not informed, the foreigners have blocked all the roads and little news comes through. Cahir, I am sorry for the loss of your family, Fitzwilliam is a murdering devil of a man but it is my hope soon we will have retribution for I am indebted to the O Farrells and will assist you and your family but I cannot at this time for we must harvest the crops and drive our cattle to safer ground. Richard Bingham has taken the Maguire castle at Enniskillen which we are to besiege. I cannot take the risk of weakening my forces now, but when the time is right I will lead my army to Longford and drive out the foreigners. In the meantime, you must take your people to Breffni and you will have your day with my help in the future. Go now, Chief O Farrell, make your preparations and lead your people to safety. I will send a messenger to you when the time right for us to strike."

Chapter Thirteen

The people of Chester looked on in awe as, to the single beat of a drum, column after column of tired, bedraggled men, most without shoes or doublets, trudged towards the quays' of the River Dee, and the waiting ships *The Surefire, The White Falcon,* and *The Merlin,* to transport them to the wars in Ireland. Raw recruits levied from several English counties each town providing a specified number of men for conscription into the Queen's Irish army. At the river's edge, the ships loaded arms, munitions, foodstuffs, and textiles, as hundreds of men filed up the gangplank under the watchful eyes of the sheriff, John Chatterton. A commotion occurred when a levy of thirty-three men from Norfolk refused to board their waiting ship, and despite the best endeavours of the sheriff's men the recruits adamantly refused to embark oblivious to the shouting and pushing until the sheriff stepping forward singled out the man who appeared to be the leader of the mutinous men. "Villain," he screamed, grabbing the man roughly by the back of his collar. "What is the matter, wherefore doth thee men refuseth to board the ship and disobey her Majesties orders. Thou must be of service to thine country, now get thee on board or I shalt hangeth every man who doest refuse." Turning, the man responded in a low resolute voice. "Sheriff, we art Norfolk men from Norwich and

Great Yarmouth of the Roman Catholic faith the true religion of Christ, and we refuseth to go to Ireland to murder our fellow Catholics, our conscience wilt not alloweth us, and we art entirely of one mind. Doeth what thee wish with us but we shalt not be the murderers of the innocent Irish, and wilt not be bullied." The sheriff, drawing his sword struck the man hard on the shoulder with the hilt and replied angrily. "Thou shalt die as all papists deserve, get thee aboard the ship now, and doth thy duty for England and thy Queen." The Lord Mayor, Hubert Hungerford, arriving at the scene pushed his way hurriedly through the scuffling throng of men and approached the sheriff who yelled. "Mister Hungerford, these men art papists and cowards and refuseth to go to Ireland, we hast seen this before they sayeth tis a matter of conscience." The Lord Major, placing his hand lightly on the sheriff's arm tilted the sword downwards. "They art not coward's sheriff if they truly believeth in their faith, and kindly putteth away that sword, methinks what good wouldst they serve in Ireland, for they wouldst give aid to the enemy and be a hindrance, wouldst they not?" Sheriff Chatterton stood silent a blank look on his face. "And," the Lord Mayor continued. "What good wouldst it be to hangeth them because of their beliefs for I dost not believeth her Majesty wouldst be too pleased as it might unsettle the recusants even further and causeth revolt in certain quarters, wouldst it not. Her Majesty hath issued a proclamation stating. *We hast not a got mirror into a man's soul, and art to judge men only by their deeds and not their beliefs,* so if it is for religious reasons we must alloweth them go." The sheriff, returning his sword to its scabbard, nodded in agreement. "Thou speaketh true words, Lord Mayor. We wilt hold them until the rest of the levies depart to avoid discontentment amongst the men, and then we shalt set them free." When fully loaded the ships set sail for Ireland, and the men released without sustenance to walk over two hundred miles to their homes in Norfolk, lucky to have escaped with their religion and their lives.

Below decks, *The Surefire* brimmed to overflowing with men and the materiels of war. In the background, the whinny and squeals of frightened animals emanated from the hold where twelve mighty warhorses kicked nervously at the timber hull of the ship. It was the first time any of the men had been at sea or more than twenty miles from their homes, some convicts, the rest farm labourers or beggars, everyman pressed into service with the Queen's army to fight in the Irish wars. The crowded mass of levied men lay on hammocks slung close together in the cramped, dark, airless hold, stinking of sweat and vomit. Two recruits in their late twenties snatched from the same village of Holmfirth in Yorkshire were billeted together, both farm labourers and childhood friends. "Amos Hooker," a recruit asked his friend. "Wherefore didst the sheriff levy us two when their art many others in the village he couldst hast chosen instead." "Amos, I canst tell thee," Samuel Zouche replied. "We art poor and hast not the coins to bribe the scurvy, Sheriff Davey Duke, a pox be upon him for his cruel deed for he be a cankered man. He didst drageth me from mine own bedchamber in the dead of night whither I didst sleep and now I dost leaveth behind a wife and young child, and how they wilt survive I dost not knoweth and thee Amos, tell me now who wilt careth for thy aged parents in thine absence and we art bound for two years service in the army before we canst returneth home if we ever dost returneth home?" "It is said Samuel, this vile land of Ireland with its mists and bogs swallow's men and armies is what they doth sayeth, and I canst bid thee anon, I swear to God, I shalt maketh mine own escape at the first opportunity and returneth home." "Amos, thou cannot for if thee doth go absent they wilt hunt thee liketh a dog and hangeth thee as a deserter, and even thy family shalt suffer, we art doomed and the devil's curse on that tilly-vally Sheriff Davy Duke, and he be a swing –buckler and a base man, and I bid thee, Amos, if I ever get home I wilt hangeth for him natter-jack that he be, and tis God's sooth." "Samuel, dost thou hast knowledge of this land we art sailing too and wherefore dost the Queen hast an army at war there. "Ay, Amos," his companion replied. "I dost knoweth a little, I didst heareth a veteran soldier in the *Old King John* tavern in Tewksbury talketh about the place many a time, thou wilt recall old fusty, Matthew Smith, he who hast but one leg. He was a soldier in the Low Countries fighting in the war against Spain until he be sent to Ireland where he didst serve for many a year till a savage didst driveth a spear through the poor bugger's leg which the surgeon hadst to cut off. He didst tell us half of the country wast mountains, bogs, and forests, and the land full of barbarous people who spake no English or other recognisable human tongue, a God-forsaken place whither it never stops raining. They surely art a wretched people Amos, and that be God's sooth and papists to boot, also soldier Smith didst tell I the Irish dress strangely and weareth no shoes or boots and dress in a woollen mantle that covers their whole body which they also useth for sleeping and they dost weareth their hair long and cover their face with what they doth calleth a glib but also he didst tell I the only valorous things in this savage land is the whiskey, and well suited for the cold and rain, and best of all art the women who he didst sayeth art, lush bona-robas and saucy callets, easy with the drabbing, their gowns ill-fitting, and dost expose their mammets without shame or blushes, but Amos none of this matters, it is too late now for we art but doomed men fated to suffer and die in a bog somewhere in Ireland, and never put a foot in the civilised land of England again. Ay, methinks what the hell art we the civilized men of the English doing in this God-forsaken land of bogs and mountains, for surely it be better to leaveth the savages to murder each other without us interfering in their accursed affairs."

On the noisy wooden quayside of Dublin Port, Captain Tom lee and Trooper Tom Churchyard sat mounted on their fine English warhorses staring impassively at the motley crew of raw recruits' shuffling down the gangplank of the ships' newly arrived from Chester. The men, dishevelled appearance and dressed in a variety of ragged clothes, gazed at the unfamiliar surroundings with squinted eyes unaccustomed to the bright morning sunshine after their many days' confined in the dark hold of the ships. "Captain," Trooper Churchyard said contemptuously. "Captain Lee, behold yonder what they doth sendeth us from England to fight the wars, behold them now, old, lame, diseased common rowdies, and these vile creatures hast been taken in prisons, markets, and highways, to supply the place of better men at home. Those dregs of humanity art not fit to be common labourers in this land. Captain Lee nodded in tacit agreement. *Always the same, the Queen wishes to conquer this land but will not spend the money required, sending these poor beggars to their deaths. He knew most of them would not survive the war and die forgotten in some ditch or the middle of a bog of marsh fever, and for what? They would seldom if ever receive their pay and never fire a shot or raise their swords in battle against the elusive Irish. How many campaigns had he been on all over the country chasing the savages through every bog, valley, and forest, with clothes seldom dry and bellies seldom full, and often spent weeks if not months on a wild goose chase running after a bunch of rebels without even catching sight of them? These wild Irish were not proper soldiers and never stood and fought, and he had forgotten the number of good men he had seen butchered. Bog fighters, that's all they were and the only success he'd witnessed was when his men discarded their armour and boots and ran barelegged, knee-deep in mud, from bog to bog and forest to forest after the rebels, lucky to finish a hard day' work with half a dozen Irish heads. He knew this country with its misty bogs and mountains had swallowed him up, changed him, making him more like the savages every day, and their ungodly customs and language had corrupted him, hardening his soul and turning him into a butcher. He couldn't recall the countless number of men, women, and even children he had slaughtered, and killing dulled his soul and the thrill of war faded quickly. No, this was no place for an Englishman or any civilised man for that matter, and why the Spanish wanted anything to do with Ireland was incomprehensible, and he had begun to question the cost, purpose, and morality, of the Queen's bloody enterprise. Even his wife Elizabeth, although of old English stock, was more loyal to the Irish than the Queen, and he knew she was passing information to the mountain woodsman, O Byrne who was always one step ahead of him. He couldn't trust her or any of the Irish, and no matter how much they professed their loyalty they resented us for invading their country, outlawing their religion and customs even though the English had brought law, civility, and the true Christian faith to their miserable, Godforsaken country.*

For an hour they sat mutely observing the hustle and bustle of the quayside with lines of men and horse disembarking from the ships and the unloading of weapons and supplies on to the quayside. "Captain Lee, what measures shalt I maketh for the training and drilling of these men?" "Trooper Churchyard," the captain replied. "Billet them in quarters at the castle and tomorrow hast the quartermaster issue them with weapons and uniforms." "But Captain Lee, what about training and drilling for they be but raw recruits without experience or discipline." "Trooper, we hast little time but enough for thee to teachest them the basics. Showeth them the workings of the musket, they wilt soon learneth to killeth on the field of battle or die learning, and I must bid thee Lord Deputy Fitzwilliam hast added to their miseries for this day for he hast commanded no fire be lit in the barrack room and the daily ration of beer be ceased and tis an order." "Captain," Trooper Churchyard replied angrily. "This is madness, these men are already roughly handled and the small relief of half a gallon of beer and a warm fire is their only comfort for the castle is cold and damp and without heat?" Captain Lee, wheeling around in his saddle retorted sharply. "Fitzwilliam is indeed a meazel and facinorous man, and that he is sure enough, but trooper I dost warneth thee to bridle thy tongue and be careful with thine words, and whilst I dost concur with thee, the man is indeed a damn popinjay and tis true, it is the Queen herself who ordered Fitzwilliam to saveth money as the war in Ireland is bankrupting the Crown, and the war council didst concur this morning, and also the Lord Deputy informed me he wished to speaketh to thee on an important matter. I dost prayeth thy petition hast been accepted by the Queen, methinks it wouldst be valorous if thou received a reward for thy long service in the army. Go, Trooper Churchyard, thou art dismissed, depart thee now and go at once to the castle and after thy discourse with the Lord Deputy, as I hast ordered, seeketh sleeping quarters for the men and tomorrow instruct the quartermaster to issue weapons and giveth them two days training."

"Trooper Churchyard, thou art welcome come prithee sit." The Lord Deputy said, placing the discharge document squarely on the desk. "Trooper, I hast this day received news from the Star Chamber, and it is indeed valorous news. I am averaging to thee, on mine own recommendation, the Queen hast graciously agreed to thy request and granted thee a yearly pension and honourable discharge from the army that thou may returneth to England. I hast this day instructed, Mr. John Pipho, Lieutenant of her Majesty's Gentlemen Pensioners, to draweth up a warrant for a pension payable to thee of three shillings a day, now I wouldst inform thee the normal allowance for non- commissioned men is two shillings and for officers three shillings but, because of thy long service and valorous record, I hast decided to reward thee trooper an officer's pension." Trooper Churchyard sprung to his feet, a wide grin across his face and shaking the Lord Deputies' hand vigorously replied in an energetic voice. "I thanketh thee, Lord Deputy. I doth thanketh thee with all mine own heart, I am forever in thy debt and I am most grateful for what thou hast done for me." The Lord Deputy gestured for the trooper to sit. "Trooper, I hast here thy release papers for mine own signature," he said holding the quill temptingly in his hand. "But, Trooper Churchyard, ere I doth sign this paper," stopping in mid-sentence he placed the quill on the desk. "To conclude thy long military service in Ireland, Trooper Churchyard, I wisheth thee to carry out two important tasks which shalt grant me much satisfaction and thee much honour." "I am at thy service," the disappointed trooper replied, a forced smile on face. "And what service dost thou wish me to fulfill, mine own Lord?" "Thou shalt accompany Captain Lee as far as Longford Castle, and thou wilt bringeth me the head of the arch-traitor, Cahir O Farrell, who hast the temerity to now calleth himself the Chief O Farrell, I wisheth him, or to be more correct, his head to take its rightful place next to his father and brother above the castle gates. A fitting place for the arch-traitor dost thou surmise, and when thee complete this task thy service is fulfilled and thou may taketh thy leave of Captain Lee and depart for England, is that clear trooper?" "Ay, Lord Deputy, I shalt be glad to dispose of the O

Farrell with much satisfaction, but what of the second task what dost thou wisheth me to perform, prithee tell me, mine own Lord." "Ay, a simple but important one, Trooper Churchyard. Before reaching Longford Castle there is a place named Moatfarrell, an ancient site used by the O Farrells for their barbaric rituals. Thou shalt halt at this place, smash their totemic stone chair that sits on the hill to pieces leaving nothing but dust, leaveth no trace of the stone visible." Trooper Churchyard sat back a puzzled expression on his face."But, Lord Deputy," he queried. "Prithee tell me, what is the importance of a rude stone chair?" "Great importance trooper, tis the symbolism it represents to the Irish people and by destroying it thou hast the great honour of ending the rule of the O Farrells of Annaly forever, Trooper Churchyard, and thou may taketh great satisfaction in telling thy companions this wonderous tale at which hour thou art making merry in thine local alehouse back in England."

The people of Dublin looked on in awe as the sundry crew of motley raw recruits' trudged along Wood Quay to a single drum beat towards their billet in Dublin Castle. The following day every second man was issued with a matchlock musket, black powder, and ball, and given a day's instruction in its use by Sergeant Tiptoff under the watchful eye of Trooper Churchyard. "Mine own men," Sergeant Tiptoff barked. "This weapon is an updated Arquebus or more commonly called a matchlock musket and thou art blessed, valorous soldiers of

England, as this new-fangled musket is the most modern and latest weapon in the Queens' service, and madeth by the artisans of the Tower of London that be the skillful men of Humphrey Walker the Queen's gunsmith, and those gents be expert at making these marvellous weapons. This new model hast a trigger for better aiming and tis loaded with these paper cartridges which containeth seventy grams of black powder, and now I shalt instruct thee as to the proper use of these fine muskets. Firstly, mine own soldiers, biteth open the paper placing a small amount of black powder on the priming or firing pan and pulleth back the serpentine, liketh this, the rest of the powder goes into the barrel using this ramrod with a cloth plug." He handed the musket to the bemused recruits who passed it around with a mixture of bewilderment and fear. "Men," he shouted. "Alloweth us to continue with thine instruction. The muskets wilt fireth when the trigger is pulled thus and the slow-burning cord soaked in saltpetre ignites the flash pan and discharges the ball which hast a range of a hundred yards and doest much damage if fired in volleys. But, I doth warn thee soldiers; always removeth the burning match cord when loading the weapon." From his office window, a wide smile of satisfaction crossed the Lord Deputies' face as he watched the training and the weaponry of his recruits. *"Oh, how wise are the words of Aristotle when he says Commonwealths are ruined by leniency and cured by severity and how sweet the words of Marcus Cicero- Send force and then justice."*

Three days later, Captain Tom Lee's troop mustered in the great square cobbled courtyard of Dublin Castle. One hundred cavalry and a thousand untried soldiers from England, supplemented by eighty of the Queen's Kerns who would lead the army to the beating of drums and the loud wail of Irish war pipes. The kern, an unholy assemblage of untamed rambunctious youths, ages ranging from twelve to early twenties dressed in the Irish fashion of saffron shirts, tight-fitting trews, most barefooted with only a handful lightly shod in pampooties. All armed with painted wooden targets and light spears with short swords or daggers hung loosely at the waist. Whooping wildly and hopscotching, they danced like fools around the courtyard to the chanting of pipes and banging of bodhran drums as their young English captain struggled vainly to keep his rowdy horde of boisterous, unruly youths in line. The levied men stood mesmerised, astonished at the fantastic spectacle before them, astounded at the abhorrent nightmarish sight of the strange dog-face masks a handful of the kern wore giving them the supernatural appearance of half-human- half animal-like creatures. Recruits, Amos Hooker and Samuel Zouche stood beside Trooper Churchyard and Hooker inquired. "Sir, who art those wild savage devils, and wherefore doth they fight against their own people." "They art orphans, recruit," replied the trooper dispassionately. "Orphans of the Irish wars, their families and homes destroyed, so they hast no lodging and we doth shelter and feed them and they knoweth nothing else. For the Queen's shilling, food and shelter they doth our bidding and wreak much havoc and death on the enemy." He pointed at the unruly mob of youth. "Those thou see yonder soldier art the orphans of Lord Essex, those Lord Pelham, two Lord Grey, five or six Lord Sidney, and the rest I doth not knoweth but I shalt tell thee soldier, they art all orphans because of the ungodly work we dost carry out for the Lord Deputies." To the wailing of uilleann pipes and loud beating of drums under unfurled banners the company of Captain Lee, led by the kern, followed by sutlers' carts and half a dozen barefooted castle women, trundled across the wooden drawbridge on their journey north to execute the orders of the Privy Council and the Lord Deputy, to take Longford Castle and destroy the people of the O Farrells, with only Trooper Tom Churchyard receiving different orders.

Chapter Fourteen

Lady O Farrell shook her head in disappointment on hearing the news from Donegal. "Cahir", she pleaded. "Hugh O Neill, the Earl of Tyrone, should we seek his help?" "There is no point mother, he would not risk helping us against Fitzwilliam remember he still holds a fragile allegiance with the Crown. He is biding his time and will not make his move until he receives the long-awaited military assistance from Spain, or when the opportune time arrives. The English have landed at Derry with an army under Dowcra and could attack Tyrone from the rear. The reality is mother, we have only ourselves to rely on." "Listen Cahir, do not lose heart I will go to my father and seek his aid, he will assist us I know he will." "But mother, surely he will be hard-pressed at this time even more than O Donnell with the relentless Bingham's snapping at his heels." "Are we not all hard-pressed my son," she replied. "But we must not lose hope. I will go immediately to Breffni in the meantime, you make whatever preparation you can if we are to defend ourselves." "O Hanly," the chief ordered. "I wish you to go to each bothy and summoned the men for a gathering, instruct them to come at first light.

Chief O Farrell sat silent as one by one the men tricked into the courtyard, and from his vantage point ran his eyes over the sea of faces standing mutely before him, ninety men and youth, black-haired, strong and hardy, and in a loud commanding voice proclaimed. "Men of the O Farrells, you know the army of the foreigner is coming to drive us from our homes and off our lands and will kill anyone they find. As your chief, I have made the decision that we stand and defend what is rightfully ours, so we must swallow our fear and fight. We can but die once and let here be the place and this be the time. Our ancestors believed that a man's true pride lies in being able to choose his end, and that is what we will do. Your women and children will go to Breffni where they will find food and shelter, and all men who are able-bodied will stay, it is your duty and your chief's command. We are the brave and noble O Farrells- Men of Valour and will not play the coward in the face of the Saxon invaders." A lone dissident voice rose from the crowd. "My chief, every man here will stand with you and fight, but with what, we have no weapons and only a few have any experience of war, so what chance have we against the onslaught of *The Soldiers of London*." "Aidan O Farrell," the chief responded to the lone dissident voice. "I have sought assistance from O Donnell, and Lady O Farrell is presently on her way to seek aid from her father in Breffni. If we run a foreign heretic will be living in your house and sleeping in your bed and you will be destitute. Men of the O Farrells, I spent ten years in the service of the mighty and fearless Fiach Mc Hugh O Byrne and I am experienced in fighting the foreigners, and they hold no fear for me. I have seen O Byrnes men fight with billhooks and pitchforks, and I am wise to the ways of the English soldiers. So, men, I have devised a strategy to delay their passage until we receive aid from O Donnell, which has been promised." Running his eye over the crowd he found the carpenter. "Eamon O Farrell," he ordered. "I wish you to take a dozen men and go to the ancient Annagh woods near Clonguish beside the Shannon, fell the ash trees and you will fashion sturdy pikes with sharpened ends and make many spears. Many of you are skilled hunters and using the spear and pikes we can bring down their warhorses when dismounted the knights burdened with their heavy mail and armour make easy prey for I have seen the deadly tactics of O Byrne. Go now, make your preparations as necessary and bring the womenfolk and children here tomorrow to make ready for departure and gather up any implements we might use as a weapon against the heretics." As they streamed out of the courtyard, each man lost in their thoughts, the chief struggled to accept his own words but he still had hope. He was certain an army would come from Breffni, he was sure King Brian O Rourke would come to their aid. As he dined that night, O Hanly charged into the great hall shouting excitedly. "Chief, your mother has returned and," he stopped in mid-sentence. "She is not alone." Leaping to his feet, heart thumping wildly, he rushed out of the hall. He knew his foster father would not abandon them in their time of need and for a moment imagined the courtyard filled with the fighting men of O Rourke, brave hardened warriors bristling with modern weapons and with them two full scores of the famous Breffni Gallowglass, giant men clad in heavy mail and brandishing glittering battle axes. With these soldiers, he would destroy the foreigners and kill the heretic usurper, Christopher Brown. Shaking with anticipation, his heavy footsteps echoed down the hallway as he raced out to the courtyard stopping dead in his tracks flabbergasted at the sight confronting him. His mother was accompanied not by an army of fighting men but by a solitary figure, a small balding man of dark complexion, dressed in a dirty saffron shirt, torn trews, and worn-out pampooties, who stood pensive holding the reins of a pair of mules heavily laden with boxes rudely secured with rope. "Mother," he snapped, face inundated with anger as a bitter wind of disappointment swept through his body. "Mother, in the name of sweet Jesus where are the soldiers, where is the army?" he yelled angrily pointing his finger squarely at the lone figure who stood staring back at him. "Who is this man?" "It is, Louis Jose Sanchez," his mother replied briskly, mildly embarrassed at her son's outburst. "Cahir, he is a Spanish officer from the Armada, my brother cannot help us now and all we have is this man." "What", the chief returned scathingly. "What we need is an army, not a single Spaniard." He looked disdainfully at the solitary figure who began to gesticulate madly, whimpering and blabbering incoherently the odd word or two of gibberish Irish. On hearing the commotion the priest raced across the courtyard, red-faced and breathless. "Father O Duffy," the chief yelled. "Do you speak Spanish?" "Yes, of course, I do my Lord," the priest affirmed. "Well, ask him what he is doing here?" The priest conversed at length with the man who with little aplomb exhibited a range of emotions ranging from frantic crying to wild outbursts of raucous laughter ending with him dropping in a sobbing heap at the priest's feet and as quick as he fell jumped up regaining his posture, and for a lengthy period volubly related his story to Father O Duffy. "Chief, this is what the Spaniard has told me. His name is, Louis Jose Sanchez from Seville and Captain of Artillery in the regiment of the Duke of Palma and was with the doomed Armada aboard *The Santa Maria De Vision* an eighteen gun Ragusan merchantman part of the Levant squadron which sailed from Corunna in, 1588. Luckily they escaped the fire ships in the English Channel but were blown around the coast of Donegal running aground on Streedagh Strand north of Sligo Town with two other ships losing eighteen hundred soldiers and sailors. He says he swam ashore to the beach which was littered with the naked corpses of his fellow countrymen, the native Irish having stripped the bodies. He moved inland climbing over the Dartry Mountains, however, at a place called Gurteen he was captured by Bingham's soldiers and held for ransom, and a message sent to the Spanish Ambassador in London seeking monies from his family for his release. Anyway chief, he escaped and was found by O Rourke soldiers and taken to their castle at Lough Gill where he trained the men in the use of firearms. Chief, he told me he is forever in the debt of King Brian O Rourke who saved not only his life but the lives of many hundreds of Spanish soldiers giving them shelter and food at his castle." "But Father O Duffy," the chief questioned. "Ask him why O Rourke sent him here for what help can one man give the O Farrells?" "Chief, he says O Rourke didn't send him he came of his own accord and was already released from service to return home on a Spanish ship anchored in Donegal Bay, but changed his mind and came here." "But why Father, why?" "Chief, when he saw the distressed Lady O Farrell pleading with her father he was curious and told of the imminent attack by the English and how her son Cahir O Farrell intended to make a stand, so he decided to return with Lady O Farrell and assist us in whatever way he could." Cahir stood for a moment intrigued by the man's response. "But why Father O Duffy, ask him why did he come here and not take passage back to the safety of his home and family. I cannot understand his motive, brave and noble as it might be?" On hearing the question the Spaniard rolled his eyes to heaven and shaking his clenched fist in the air screamed. "Venganza,

venganza," as tears of bitterness rolled down his face, mouth twisted in anger. "Venganza," he repeated loudly. "For my lost comrades, my poor helpless comrades, six thousand unarmed men, and boys far from their homes and families in Espana butchered like animals in cold blood by the English heretics, and for what. The murderous cutthroat Bingham butchered a thousand in Connaught, and it is said the barbarous Lord Deputy William Fitzwilliam himself was personally responsible for the hanging of two thousand of these defenseless men, have these English dogs have no compassion. God's curse on their black hearts, so tell me how can I return to home with any honour or dignity if I do not seek revenge for these poor souls who cry out for revenge and I will die doing so for there is not a home in Espana that has not lost a son, brother or father." Father O Duffy placed his hands reassuringly on the man's shoulders. "Captain Sanchez," he said in a consoling voice. "What you say does not make sense haven't you had enough revenge with O Rourke in Breffni, revenge is not a good thing it only eats away at a man's soul." "With O Rourke," the Spaniard responded. "There was not much revenge on the heretics as I was confined to the castle at Lough Gill and took no part in the fighting but when I was told that you," stopping in mid-sentence he pointed his finger at Cahir who stood speechless at the man's passionate outburst. "Planned to make a stand against the heretics I, Captain of Artillery, Louis Jose

Sanchez of the Levant Squadron, decided I would join you in your fight and here I stand today beside the brave warrior Chief O Farrell." Dashing over the Spaniard prostrated himself at the feet of the chief and exclaimed loudly. "Un Abrazo, Un Beso." "Father, what in the name of God is he saying?" "Chief, he says he wants to hug you and kiss you for having the gumption and courage to stand against the heretics and presenting him with the opportunity to avenge his comrades." "Father, tell him there is no need," the chief replied smiling. "But we are grateful he came but what help can one man give us no matter how passionate or brave he is?" The Spaniard, slapping his thigh threw his head back defiantly. "Chief, he says he is not one man but a hundred." "What does he mean Father, I am intrigued?" The Spaniard pulled the canvas off one of the pack animals revealing a brass cannon and four small wooden barrels. "Chief, he tells me this is an effective Spanish naval gun called *A Falconet* which was salvaged by O Rourke off one of the shipwrecked vessels *The La Latvia* a Venetian merchantman and barrels of black powder, enough to charge the cannon ten times." The second pack animal carried a wooden case containing six Spanish flintlock muskets and ten pounds of black powder with a plentiful supply of lead ball. On seeing the munitions the chief cursing under his breath turned to walk away the colour rushing to his face." "Chief," the priest protested. "He says it is not the number of guns you have that is important but the way you use them and he is an experienced veteran of the wars in the Low Countries against the heretic, General Norris." "Father, the chief returned despondently. "Tell him we are grateful he is here and for bringing the weapons, and his experience will be of great benefit to us, and Father O Duffy have the men take the munitions into the great hall." "Chief," the priest said. "The Spaniard wishes to learn of your strategy for defending your people against the onslaught of the English heretics." The Spaniard stood, ears perked, eyes fixed attentively on the chief as he outlined his strategy the priest translating his words. "We have only ninety men most with no experience and a few modern weapons which you kindly brought us and thank you again, Captain Sanchez." The Spaniard with a broad grin nodded in acknowledgment as the chief continued. "Our main objective is to delay the onslaught of the English army for as long as possible. O Donnell has promised to assist us presently but in the meantime, we must fend for ourselves and tell him, Father, we intend to send the women and children to O Rourke, and the crux of our strategy is to destroy the wooden bridge over the River Camlin, the only crossing point in the vicinity. From my experiences in Wicklow the haughty English are impetuous and on reaching the destroyed bridge will immediately attempt to wade across the river, and I intend to ambush them in the water where they would be at their most vulnerable." The Spaniard, as if struck by lightning, flung his arms wildly in the air and shaking his head yelled frantically. "*No, no es Bueno, esto es locura.*" Cahir stood chap-fallen, taken aback at the ferocity of the man's outburst. "What does he say, Father O Duffy, in God's name what is he saying?" "Chief, he says your strategy is no good, it is madness, yes you will kill a few soldiers but they have many muskets and their lead shot will drive you back and they will build a pontoon across the river and you will be lucky to hold them for a day. He says you do not have the men or the firepower and their cavalry will cross the river further up and outflank you and what can spears and pikes do against the English musketeers. He is adamant we must use what little resources we have in the most effective way possible and your strategy is not effective." Chief O Farrell, face reddened, stung by the man's critical words which thrust deep into his heart like a sharp knife. "Father O Duffy," he returned in a low crumbling voice. "Tell him he may be correct but what else can we do this is not Breffni where the mountains and forests are good for hit and run tactics, here we are in the open on flat ground with Cairn Hill six miles away and the only high ground in Annaly and the Camlin our only natural defense, what else can we do, please ask him?" "Chief, he wants to reconnoiter the terrain to determine our best means of defense." "What does he mean by reconnoiter Father, I do not understand this word?" "Chief, he wants to see the lay of the land to devise a more effective strategy for our defense." Late afternoon, having completed his reconnoiter, the Spaniard briskly paced the length and breadth of the courtyard taking careful measurements and at nightfall, he approached the priest. "Father, tell the chief the divine Lord above has come and granted me inspiration and I have devised a strategy that will be most effective. The key to our defense is the bridge; the bridge must not be destroyed at any cost." On hearing the Spaniard's proposal the chief stepping forward shouted angrily. "What Father O Duffy, is this man insane and him an officer in the Spanish army, the foreigners will cross the Camlin and overrun us, tell him the bridge is our only defense." "Chief, he says we will use the bridge to trap and destroy them and you must trust him." "Father," Cahir snapped. "Is he a spy for the foreigners, what he proposes will spell disaster for us, and be sure of that the bridge must be destroyed." As he walked rapidly towards the door the priest grabbed his arm. "Chief, be patient and let us understand what his plans are, please let me ask him." "Father O Duffy," the Spaniard responded. "Inform Chief O Farrell we want them to cross the bridge for it will be the instrument of their destruction." "Father," the chief shouted. "I cannot believe what he is saying, it is madness and will destroy us, tell him we cannot meet the foreigners on open ground." "Yes, you are right," the Spaniard replied. "They would smash us to pieces, but I have devised a plan to inflict much damage on the heretics and avenge the souls of my murdered comrades." Eyes blazing with intent he outlined his proposals. "Father O Duffy, tell the chief this is what we must do, we will form *A Campo de Matanza.*" "What in God's name is he talking about Father?" "Chief, he wants us to create *A Campo de Matanza* which means *A Field of Death.*" "And what in God's name Father, is *A Field of Death?*" "He says this way we can inflict maximum damage and delay the onslaught of the foreigners." "Ask him Father, how we create *A Field of Death* and us with no trained soldiers and only a few modern weapons." "Chief, he says we will create *A Campo de Matanza* in the courtyard." "How, Father, how?" The chief returned sharply. "He says we can create *A Campo de Matanza* by constructing *A Couture*." "What in the name of God is *A Coupure* the chief yelled. "He says he has seen *A Coupure* used many times with great effect in the Spanish Netherlands, and it is simply a false wall. We construct two false walls running from the gates to the front of the castle to form a killing field." "Come chief," the priest beckoned. "He wants to show us what he has planned." The Spaniard stomped up and down the courtyard waving and shouting. "We will build two false walls from the gates to the front wall of the castle to form an enclosure and trap the heretic soldiers in *The Coupure*. The men can hurl spears and missiles and we will kill many of their men, then they will withdraw and bring cannon from Dublin which will delay their attack." "Father, ask him how we lure the English into the trap they are not fools are they?" "Chief, the Spaniard says we will offer feint resistance at the bridge, and they will send in the Queen's Kern to lead the assault and their horse behind, and we will make a false retreat back to the castle." "But Father, we have but two weeks to construct the false walls it would be impossible to finish the work in that time?" "Chief, the Spaniard says we will use the women and children to help before they leave and we will work day and night if necessary." "Father, ask him what is the plan for his cannon and muskets for I am curious to know." "Chief, the Spaniard intends to form gun ports in the front wall of the castle for the musketeers and the cannon to fire at close range into the oncoming soldiers trapped in the enclosure, and this is the most effective and deadly use of our limited firepower." In the great hall, the cannon, muskets, and munitions, were laid on the long wooden table alongside a pile of makeshift weapons brought by the tenants consisting mainly of farm implements including a couple of rusty swords with the odd broken musket. Captain Sanchez looked on bewildered by the assorted hodgepodge of crude weapons. "Father, is this all you have to defend yourselves?" he asked, lifting a billhook disdainfully. "O Rourke has many muskets and pistols." "Captain," the priest replied. "When Lord O Farrell, God rest his soul, pledged his allegiance to Sir Henry Sidney the English soldiers' took all the weapons and forbade him to carry arms stating that O Farrells were now under the protection of the Crown and had no need for weapons or soldiers, so this is all we have." Around the chief stood the priest, the Spaniard, and ten men with previous experience of war having served in the Queen's army and to these men, the muskets were distributed, the remaining men appointed as captains. A tall, aged man stepped into the hall followed by two youths of strong disposition. "Chief O Farrell," he announced. "I am Donal Mc Cabe, and these are my sons Tomas and Conor, and when told of your predicament we came to offer our assistance. We owe a debt to your father and sad to learn of his death and your brothers. Many years ago I came from the Hebrides as a Gallowglass in the service of Shane the Proud and were attacked by Richard Bingham who butchered my folk and I barely escaping with my life and fled here where your poor father took pity on my plight and gave me a cottage and a parcel of land so I could make a living and survive, and I am here today to repay my debt for your father's kindness. We have no modern weapons but we will use anything to hand that might inflict injury on the English. I am old but my sons are strong and brave, and eager to fight the Sassenachs." "You are indeed welcome, Donal," the chief replied. "As are you're fine sons and we appreciate your help, we need all the help we can get. Donal, you will be no doubt acquainted with all present except this man," he said, pointing to the Spaniard. "This Donal, is Louis Sanchez, Captain of Artillery in the Spanish army and now in the service of the O Farrells as our Master of Cannon." A surprised look crossed Donal's face. "Chief, do you mean we have cannon?" "Yes, Donal, there," he pointed at the short cannon on the table and they all laughed except the Spaniard who sat dour-faced not understanding what the chief said. At daybreak, work began constructing the false walls the courtyard becoming a sea of activity as men, women, and children, struggled feverously carting and carrying materials as the stonemason and carpenter commenced construction of *The Coupure* under the watchful eye of the Spaniard who, with the priest as interpreter, barked out orders incessantly to the workers. Trees were felled, cut, and sharpened ends driven into the ground with infill panels of stone from demolished outbuildings built between each heavy timber upright forming a rough five-foot-high makeshift palisade with gaps in the wall to allow the men to pierce those trapped in *The Field of Death*. Fearing the imminent arrival of *The Soldiers of London* they worked nonstop with each person delegated a specific task under the supervision and expertise of the Spaniard who, after much measuring and calculating, instructed the stonemason to cut a series of gun ports in the front wall of the castle on both sides of the front door in which he had the men set his cannon on wooden blocks with three musket ports to each side giving a clear field of sight towards the front main gates, the concentrated firepower to have a devastating effect at close quarters in the confined space. "Father," the Spaniard requested. "Take this and give it to the blacksmith, I need him to make these for me." He handed the priest a sheet of parchment on which were illustrated two finely sketched items fully detailed and dimensioned. "Father, you translate and make sure he follows my exact design for our strategy to work, we must have these devices."

Twelve days later, after much sweat and toil, the palisade walls' forming *The Coupure* in the courtyard neared completion with one infill panel to finish when Rory O Farrell, the scout, galloped into the courtyard horse lathered in sweat. "Is it time Rory?" The chief asked. "Yes, chief, the army of the foreigners left Dublin this morning and will be here in two days." "How many men do they have Rory?" "They have one hundred horse and about a thousand men including a squad of Queen's Kerns, a small army chief but heavily armed with new muskets and equipment and led by Captain Tom Lee."

Chapter Fifteen

"O Hanly." The chief announced. "The time has come, the army of the foreigners will be upon us in two days and as my most trusted servant, I am burdening you with a task of great magnitude. I wish you to take charge of the women and children and lead them to the safety of O Rourke country." "But my chief," O Hanly replied, a lump rising in his throat. "I wish to stay and fight, I seek revenge for the death of my poor Emir and her unborn child, and I seek justice for your unfortunate father and Fergal, may God have mercy on their poor souls. If I can kill but one of *The Soldiers of London* I will die satisfied they cannot be allowed to slaughter our people with impunity, so I wish to stay and fight." "O Hanly," the chief replied. "I know how much you miss Emir, and I understand your devotion to my father and brother, but I need you to take our women and children to Breffni, this is the most important thing you can do, go now and make preparations for departure in the morning. The women and children must be long gone before the English arrive, and one last task you can do for me. Lock Erin and Finn in the storeroom with plenty of food and water for they would make easy prey for the soldiers." The following morning, sixty-three souls with heavy hearts bid their farewells and in two's and three's trudged out of the castle led by O Hanly holding the bridle of *O Donnell* on which sat Lady O Farrell and two young children

The men of the O Farrells began their final preparations for the coming battle with broken rocks piled in heaps behind the palisades, the captains' allocating each man a post, as bundles of ash spears were laid in piles at intervals with half a dozen pikes allocated to each side. As the Spaniard and the musketeers prepared their weapons in the entrance hallway the blacksmith arrived with two young apprentices pulling a wooden cart. "Father, inform the Spaniard I have done as he instructed and have toiled solidly for two days and nights to make these unnatural devices." The Spaniard carefully examined the items and turning to the priest affirmed. "Father, tell him these are acceptable, the workmanship a little rough, but fit for our purposes, thank him and tell him he has done his chief a good service." The priest gazed with curiosity at the contents of the cart and lifted a strange vicious-looking metal object with four sharp spikes. "Captain Sanchez," he inquired. "What is this extraordinary device?" "That Father O Duffy, is called a caltrop." The Spaniard took the object from the priest throwing it to the ground where it landed on three spikes with the fourth pointing upwards. "That Father is our weapon against the English horse." The second object comprised two small metal spheres connected with a chain, the balls two feet apart. "And that object Father is chain shot for the cannon which I have used with great effect against men and horse and if discharged at the right angle and the right distance will cut through the English ranks like a scythe wielded by Satan himself." The priest held a metal ball in each hand imagining the devastating injuries to man and beast dropping the device in silent revulsion.

In the great hall, Father O Duffy solemnly blessed each man before handing them a random weapon from the assorted pile on the table. "Here now Paddy O Farrell, a nice shiny billhook for you my son, and may the Lord above grant you the strength to kill as many of the heretics as possible." To the next man in line he declared. "Ah if it isn't old Seamus O Farrell himself, and here for you is a nice Toledo sword a bit rusty mind you having seen better days but you off go now and kill as many enemies of the true faith as you can like a good man." The priest continued until all the weapons were distributed leaving twenty men unarmed. "Sorry men," the priest exclaimed. "The cupboards bare, we've nothing left, so off yeh go now and grab a spear or two from the courtyard, or if you'd prefer yeh can fight the foreigners with your bare hands." In the entrance hall of the castle, the cannon and muskets were primed with smoldering rope soaked in saltpeter ready for coming action. "Father," the Spaniard requested. "Could you bring me the Gallowglass Mc Cabe, I have important orders for him?" The weakest point in the makeshift enclosure was the castle entrance and he required the Mc

Cabe sons, big strong youths, to be allocated the important task of guarding the door, and to Donal Mc Cabe he handed a sack containing the caltrops. "Tell him Father, when the English horse come we must stop them entering the courtyard these armoured knights would cut us down and the rough timber walls may not withstand a charge of their heavily clad warhorses, so we must stop them it would be too much of a risk to let them enter. On the approach of the riders, he is to sprinkle the caltrops across the entrance and sow the seeds of their destruction, their horse will stumble and dismount their riders and on the ground, they can be dealt with easily. No man who enters our trap must be allowed to survive we have but one chance to deal the foreigners a mortal blow." As he spoke, Rory O Farrell brought news the English army was half a day's journey away marching with banners unfurled to the sound of pipes and drums. "Men," the chief ordered. "The time has come, make haste, and take your posts but first." He turned to the priest. "Father O Duffy, will you be good enough to say mass for the men it will no doubt give them much hope and courage on this day." The men gathered in the enclosure soon to be *A Field of Death* and a low murmur of surprise rippled through the ranks as they saw, for the first time, the priest dressed in his black Jesuit habit, a crude wooden crucifix hanging loose around his neck, and a sword dangling from his belt. On bent knees with heads bowed they listened intently as Father O Duffy recited the mass, and standing over the men proclaimed. "Men of the O Farrells, as the great King Solomon once said *To everything there is a season, and a time for every purpose under the heavens* and men now is our season and now is our time, and our purpose to fight bravely and with courage for the O Farrells, for your country and the holy Catholic faith, and may the Lord be at your side this fateful day." The chief scanned the faces around him. *Was he right to bring these men to their deaths, and them farmers or mostly cow herders with no war experience, and he looked at the men, a handful only boys, perhaps he should have let them go with the women. But so what, they would meet their end soon enough and that was their fate at least this way they chose the time, and the place, and with the skill and expertise of the Spaniard perhaps they could gain a small victory over the English, and hold them for a time that they might receive aid from the O Donnell or any of the chiefs but what if the English didn't fall for their trap and chase the retreating men. He knew they had one of the best English captains in Ireland leading their army, the man who harried and chased Fiach O Byrne around every corner of Wicklow and beyond, a cunning and skillful soldier who would not be easily duped.* His thoughts were broken when the priest, with outstretched hands, offered him a communion host. "God bless you, Chief Cahir O Farrell, and may God protect us all this day and let victory be ours." Tears welled in the Spaniard eyes as he prayed for his dead comrades and turning he glanced at the men around him. *What an unfortunate race of people these Irish, persecuted and doomed to destruction by the murdering English heretics, a people who could never win and even if they surrendered would be slaughtered, a race who carried death with them. No wonder they drank so much aqua vitae, if he had two cups he slept for a week but these people drank half a gallon and did a day's work, but who could blame them, too proud and too passionate a people, too easy a prey for the cunning, perfidious heretics, and God only knows what the future holds for them. They called them the savage Irish, and indeed their language and customs unfamiliar to any civilised man, a childlike people with a kind, generous nature and the reason he was still alive unlike his unfortunate comrades murdered far from their family and homes but,* he raised his eyes heavenward as tears trickled down his face, *this day with God's good grace he would avenge their souls, those who cried out for revenge and justice, and he understood the bond between him and the poor unfortunate men beside him was their religion, the Roman Catholic faith, the true faith of Christ and their common enemy the English, Lutheran heretics.* When mass-finished, the priest blessed the men who filed out in silent contemplation taking their allocated positions behind the palisades. Each man full of anticipation, mingled with uncertainty, as they awaited the onslaught of the foreign soldiers, their minds filled with thoughts of their families, and the fate awaiting them that day. The banner of the O Farrells was unfurled. A golden lion rampant on a field of green below an unleashed hound on a ducal cornet with the family motto *Cu- Reubha - I Have Broken My Hold* which the Chief O Farrell held proudly mounted on his favourite warhorse, a small piebald pony called *Croga,* as he was indeed brave and agile. The banner flying bold and defiant as he led his men to take their positions on the bridge where they threw up a makeshift barricade and waited patiently for the arrival of Captain Tom Lee's, *Soldiers of London.*

Six miles away the English army marched at a steady pace, the kern hopping, dancing, and skipping, at the front of the column to the shrieking of pipes and beating of drums like a cavalcade of dancing clowns. On reaching the place the scouts had pointed out Trooper Churchyard turned to his commander. "Captain Lee, before we progress we must stop here awhile for I hast been ordered by the Lord Deputy to carry out a task, it shalt not taketh much time." "Permission granted trooper, but make haste we hast much bloody work to perform this day and now prithee tell me what task hast Sir William instructed thee to complete?" "Thou shalt observe presently, Captain Lee," he replied. Dismounting, he grabbed a sledgehammer from a pack animal and scurried up the slight hill where, partially concealed by undergrowth, an ancient chair of roughly hewn stone stood beneath a sentinel oak tree. On reaching the chair he removed his armour, jerkin, and shirt, exposing a muscular torso covered with a multitude of battle scars and noticeably a pronounced scar on his chest. The soldiers looked on in amusement as his toned muscles flexed and without stopping to catch his breath, Trooper Churchyard commenced to mechanically smash the chair to smithereens until nothing remained. As sweat trickled down his dust-covered face and torso he dressed and mounted his steed, a satisfied grin on his face. Captain Lee, bemused at the strange spectacle inquired. "Trooper Churchyard, wherefore in God's name didst the Lord Deputy order thee to carry out such a childlike act?" "Sir, if thou please, with the greatest of respect, it was no ordinary stone it wast the ancient stone chair of the O Farrells used in the inauguration of their chiefs for many hundreds of years, and now captain, we hast ensured there shalt be no more O Farrell chiefs created in this unholy place and this unnatural manner." The scouts returning approached Captain Lee. "Sir, there is a party of Irish at the bridge near the castle about twenty men all lightly armed with a lone horseman. They hast thrown felled trees across the road to maketh a rough barricade, we rode close to draw fire but nothing sir, it is probable they art without firearms." Captain Lee wheeled around in his saddle. "Trooper Churchyard, this is what Nugent reported; he stated they had no weapons, but why dost they maketh a hopeless stand when we canst easily destroy them." "Captain," the trooper replied sarcastically. "Thou knoweth these Irish as well as I. Chief O Farrell, puffed full of indignity and stung with lost pride wilt maketh a show but methinks they shalt not stand and fight but shalt run at the first sign of our soldiers, cowards that they be." "Ay trooper, I dost believeth thou art indeed correct in thy judgment." The captain, raising his hand signalled the army forward to the noise of war pipes, the kern running wildly in front of the army banging drums, waving spears and knives, a savage unruly mob in contrast to the orderly ranks of the English soldiers. Coming close to the bridge, Captain Lee barked an order. "Trooper Churchyard, send in the kern." "Nay sir," the trooper responded. "I beseech thee, I hast but one more task to complete on the orders of the Lord Deputy." "And trooper, prithee tell me what is this task?" Captain Lee asked impatiently, but without replying the trooper rode forward to within fifty yards of the barricade and reining in his horse called out in Irish. "I seek, Chief Cahir O Farrell, is he present?" "I am here." An immediate response came from the lone horseman behind the barricade. "I am the Chief O Farrell, and what is your business here this day?" Pushing back his morion, Trooper Churchyard sat upright in his saddle and smiling sarcastically replied. "Listen to me, O

Farrell, you will know my business soon enough, but listen to me now are you not a high and mighty Irish chief, a leader of men and me a humble soldier, poor old veteran, Thomas Oliver Churchyard, of her gracious Majesties army and I challenge you to combat. If you have any honour you will come out and face me one to one like a man or are you the coward like your treacherous father?" A red flash of anger crossed the chief's face. "Felim," he shouted to the man beside him. "Here, take this," handing him the banner. "And don't lose it, I want to see the flag of the O Farrells' flying over Longford Castle this day, now lift the barricade and let me through." Felim, grabbing the reins of the horse implored. "No, chief, do not go over it is a trap they will kill you." "Are you a coward O Farrell?" the trooper shouted insultingly. "To hide behind your barricade and call yourself the chief." Ignoring the pleas of his men he gave *Croga* a brisk kick in the ribs forcing the horse over the makeshift barricade and on to open ground as a ball, whizzing past his head like an angry bee, caused *Croga* to raise its head and shied away from the gunfire. "Soldier Zouche," Captain Lee yelled furiously. "Holdeth thy fire, this matter shalt be settled by Trooper Churchyard." At twenty yards from his opponent, the chief drew in his reins and both men sat motionless facing each other. Trooper Churchyard, mounted on his powerful English warhorse, splendid in shining breast armour over leather jerkin, covered in iron scale with vambrace on arm. On his shield, the red cross of Saint George, and held tightly under his right arm a grey metal war lance its sharp head pointing menacingly at the Irishman. In his scabbard, a cavalry broadsword hung loose with petronel cavalry pistol holstered in belt and beneath him, the war horse nervously pawing the ground with hoof and tail swishing, and nostrils flared in nervous expectation. The trooper gazed contemptuously at the diminutive figure of man and horse before him. The savage slouched back perched in a padded cloth saddle, saffron shirt without armour, dull dented morion on head, ash spears in hand, and clutching a red-painted round wooden target, beneath him a piebald pony its head slightly lowered as if bowed in submission. It was the piebald with its distinctive black and white marking he recognized, yes, he was certain. It was the young savage who nearly killed him at Glenmalure; he still carried the scar on his chest where a spear punctured his armour. Sitting upright on his horse his cold eyes flashed and his teeth snarled with anger as he glowered at his enemy. This day he would teach O Farrell a deadly lesson in the art of war and fulfill his last duty for his gracious Queen and country. For what seemed like an eternity the pair faced each other the stillness of the day broken by the war horse's hoof scraping hard ground as the soldiers and men of the O Farrells looked on gripped by the scene unfolding before them, and muttering under his breath. *"Go to the deuce for a fool, wild Irish savage."* Trooper Churchyard was first to move nudging his mount forward and spurring the horse into a gallop with the beating of pounding hoofs reverberating on the earth beneath him, war lance underarm in readiness to pierce his enemy. Giving the reins a sharp tug, Croga snorted, lifted its head, ear's flicking back and forth, and lurched forward unflinchingly towards the English horse. Trooper Churchyard steadied his aim, eyes fixed firmly on the figure charging towards him, ready to drive his lance deep into the man's chest. Chief O Farrell, raising his spear high above his head placed his forefinger in the leather loop at the base of the ash shaft in readiness for casting and as they came within striking distance of each other let fly his spear which, with tremendous velocity, flew through the air barely missing its target and immediately with a sharp tug swung his horse around narrowly dodging the point of the metal cavalry lance. After a short distance, he charged again and at close proximity let fly his second spear which arched graciously through the air with a whizzing sound striking Trooper Churchyard hard in the face, the sharpened metal point piercing his left eye with such force the shaft carried through his skull protruding from the back of the morion killing him instantly, the sudden jolt forcing him back in the saddle, his feet pushing hard in the stirrups causing the horse to rear, dismounting the trooper who landed heavily on rough ground. For a few seconds, the watching men remained unmoving and silent, no shouts of anger or jubilance, then a tumultuous cheer raised as hoards of kern rushed forward like a swarm of locusts followed by the soldiers, the orderly ranks descending into a seething mass of shouting and screaming men with Captain Lee's horse in hot pursuit, and brushing aside the rough barricade they soon gained ground biting sharply at the heels of the retreating Irish. The chief, snatching the banner rode frantically in front of his men shouting curses and urging them towards their goal. Manus O Farrell tripped and instantly hacked to death, the kern rushing forward trampling over his body then finally sweeping in a ferocious storm through gates the air crackling with excitement as they dashed down the timber palisade enclosure toward the castle, the fleet-footed kern at their back frantically piercing and stabbing. At the door, the sons of Donal Mc Cabe, following their appointed task, stood armed with battle-axes determined to guard the entrance with their lives. As *Croga* stumbled beneath him, spear through side, the chief tumbled through the doorway his remaining men behind but before the door could be secured half a dozen kern pushing and shoving entered the hallway to be immediately set upon by the McCabes, who with determined swing and swipe of axe, hacked the intruders to pieces and slamming the door placed heavy timbers across at top and bottom leaving the floor littered with bloody corpses. In a frenzied mass the Queen's Kern, like the hags and furies of hell, rushing forward stampeded into the enclosure followed by the foot soldiers of

Captain Lee's troop who hurtled pell-mell along the palisades like a fast-flowing tide with mayhem breaking out as the men at the front realised they could advance no further, trapped in the hurly-burly of the enclosure, and unable to turn by the weight of the large number of soldiers pouring in through the gate behind them, screaming and cursing, swords and muskets raised. The kern in blind panic shouted *Culu- Culu- Retreat - Retreat* but the English soldiers not understanding kept pushing forward and maddened with fear and adrenalin tried frantically to break down the door which stayed firmly shut against them then flinging themselves wildly over the rough wooden palisade to be cut down by a hodgepodge of crude weapons. As more and more men poured into *The Coupure* the compacted teeming mass squeezed together tightly unable to turn, unable to draw sword or raise muskets. Their diabolic shouts and dire screams muting the cries and moans of the wounded men as through gaps in the palisade the men of the O Farrell's' spearing, thrusting, and stabbing, at the mass of bodies as missiles were hurled from the tower with deadly effect wounding and killing many. Like hobs of hell they came, the charging English horse. The sheen of polished armor, the blowing of trumpets, lances held high, and neighing horses galloping at a furious pace, the reverberation of iron-clad hoofs' shaking the ground. As they approached the gate the chief shouted. "Now, Donal, now," as Mc Cabe flung half a dozen caltrops across the entrance causing the horses to stumble feet pierced by sharp metal, slinging their rider to the ground as a hail of missiles showered on the fallen knights causing Captain Lee to wheel around leading his cavalry away from the castle leaving behind five horses who limped and snorted, neighing in pain as they trod on their fallen riders who lay inanimate, armour bloody, pierced, and dented. *Fuego- Fuego,* the Spaniard bellowed as muskets barked and cannon thundered, filling the air with an explosive burst of red sparks and a cloud of black smoke, sending a withering fusillade of lead ball down the makeshift enclosure into the entrapped soldiers with the dull thud of ball on flesh. The devastating effect of the raging hail storm of lead shot at such close range on the massed ranks was indescribable as the deadly chain shot of crude forged metal arched clumsily through the air like a boomerang of death cutting bloody swathes through flesh and bone, decapitating and severing limbs, showering the soldiers in a fine drizzle of blood. The muskets and cannon fired repeatedly until after seven or eight rounds they exhausted their powder as black plumes of smoke billowed, like the angry ghosts of the dead, over the tangle of mutilated corpses. From behind the palisade, the men continued their deadly work hurling rocks, jabbing spears and pikes at the mass of soldiers who desperately tried pushing forward tramping over heaps of twisted and mangled bodies. Slipping and sliding on the viscous mess with men faltering, stumbling and suffocating where they fell, weltering in their blood, body piling upon body. In mad desperation, the survivors began thrusting and stabbing sword and pike through the gaps in the palisade at their assailants killing and wounding a handful of O Farrell men. At the castle door, Samuel Zouche, above the noisy din of battle, shouted to his childhood friend and comrade, Amos Hooker. "Amos, we art the last men standing, we art done for, mine own friend. Not the bog or forest for us but hereth and now is our fate, but we must not stand idle and be slaughtered liketh dogs. We shalt die liketh the true Yorkshire men that we be, discharge thy musket into the door that we might enter." With difficulty, they raised their muskets discharging a storm of shot into the ironclad doors with little damage. "Come Amos, get thee over the wall, cometh follow me now." Clambering over piled bodies they hurled themselves over the palisade where a shocked Henri O Farrell stood frozen at the sudden appearance of the men who dispatched him with a deadly blow of musket stock smashing his skull. Father O Duffy, on seeing the soldiers, yelled *Sasson Dearg -Sasson Dearg -Red Coats - Red Coats,* and the priest with Leo O Farrell storming forward stabbed one soldier with sword and decapitating the other with a single swing of billhook.

A blurry haze of dense black smoke clung over the killing ground as the shrieks of the wounded mingled with the pitiful groans of the dying. At Camlin Bridge, Captain Lee sat in disbelief at the day's events. He'd been informed the O Farrells were unarmed and would melt like snow in the hot sun before him, but they had stood and inflicted much damage on his men. He never trusted Christopher Nugent, and he never trusted the half Englishmen of the Pale and turning led his horsemen towards Mullingar to fetch reinforcements and artillery from Dublin, and trundling despondently behind Captain Lee's detachment a party of disgruntled settlers led by a disenchanted Christopher Browne accompanied by his wife and daughter. After a few miles, a rider approached, a scout from President Bingham's, Army of Connaught. "Captain Lee, Lord Bingham hath sent me to convey this news to thee, we cameth upon a group of women and children walking towards Breffni, and they art the women and children of the O Farrells. They informed us the Chief O Farrell intended to stand and fight so President Bingham concluded they might be of use to thee as hostages."

Chapter Sixteen

The President of Connaught, Richard Bingham, was a truculent, pugnacious man, brutal and rapacious even by the standards of the day. A true frontiersman and conquistador in pursuit of land and power, and despised by the native Irish as a sanguinary monster who raged savagely unable to quench his thirst for blood. His career began in the navy commanding the warship *Swiftsure* at Smerwick where his sailors' partook in the bloody massacre of six hundred unarmed mercenaries sent by Pope Gregory to assist FitzMaurice in the second Desmond rebellion. For his good service, knighted by John Perrot in Dublin Castle, and with brother's George and John became Governors of Connaught, the three irascible, bullheaded tyrants ruling with an iron fist, their method of empire building by sword, fire, and the hangman, rolling out a bloody tide of aggression across the country with unimaginable brutality and indescribable savagery. These were the worst kind of colonists, their desire for absolute power lashing the whole west of Ireland into open rebellion and taking no pains to conciliate any one with all opposition checked most ruthlessly. Richard Bingham gained his reputation when he slaughtered three thousand Scottish, men, women, and children of the Mc Cabe clan in the service of Shane the Proud of which only a handful survived fleeing to Longford and he was now in the final stage of the destruction of the rebel, King Brian O Rourke who fled to Scotland, and in the process of destroying livestock and crops to cleanse Breffni of the remaining native Irish. Bingham became O Rourke's nemesis when the Irishman had the temerity to refuse handing over many hundreds of Spanish survivors from the doomed Armada sheltering in his castle at Lough Gill incensing Bingham who, deprived of possible Spanish booty and ransom gold, for two years chased O Rourke incessantly through every bog and forest in Breffni. O Rourke divided his small army of well trained and armed men into two groups striking at the English before disappearing into the forests and mountains. But Bingham's blood was up and with his band of hardened veterans relentlessly pursued the Irish, and finally, it was all over for O Rourke. His army annihilated, his people starving and homeless, cursing him for being the author of their misery.

Richard Bingham and his riders' pushed rapidly through the townland of Mohill on the Longford and Leitrim border leaving a scorching mess of black charred, gaunt ruins, not a grain of corn left unburned and hanging everyone they met. Their progress marked by a trail of death and destruction with clouds of smoke clinging ominously in the air. At Garvagh, they came upon a group of women and children led by a solitary man, the sight of the heavily armed horsemen sending a wave of fear through the people of the O Farrells. With weapons and armour glinting in the late evening sun, the squadron of cavalry surrounded the huddled mass who stood frozen in terror, and Bingham drawing his reins beside O Hanly called out. "Who art thou and state thy destination?" No reply from the throng that stood mutely staring at him, and beckoning to an Irish soldier serving in his ranks he ordered. "Soldier, asketh them who art they and whither doth they journey?" A subdued murmur rose from the crowd but no answer. Bingham barked orders and the soldier's dragged Lady O Farrell and the children to the ground, and grabbing O Hanly tied his hands flinging him roughly into the saddle. A rope, which was at hand for such occasions, was thrown over a nearby tree and the noose tightened around the manservant's neck. Bingham, raising his sword above the horse's flank snarled. "Asketh him again soldier, one more time, and if he doth not answer, he shalt hangeth." As Bingham raised his sword to strike, Lady O Farrell yelled. "We are O Farrell people, and travel to seek refuge with O Rourke at his castle at Lough Gill." On hearing the response Bingham stood tall in his stirrups head thrown back and laughingly replied. "Soldier, tell the O Farrell beldam they wasteth their time, the O Rourkes art destroyed and the arch-traitor Brian O Rourke hast fled to Scotland, and soldier asketh her whither the O Farrell men art to be found." Lady O Farrell, heart filled with anger, rushing forward with clenched fists began striking wildly at Bingham who reaching down grabbed her throat. "Soldier, asketh her again whither art the O Farrells?" As she gasped for breath face reddening he released his grip and she blurted in a rasping voice. "They are at Longford Castle, where my son the Chief O Farrell is making a stand with his people." "Soldier, inform her it shalt be his last stand and that I canst assureth thee." *The Last Stand of the Chief O Farrell* he muttered, laughing silently to himself. "My son is prepared to die," she continued. "Defending his home and people, my son Cahir is a brave man." Bingham slapping his thigh with his gloves replied. "Foolish and not brave I wouldst sayeth, and die he shalt, be sure of that," and wheeling his horse around shouted orders to his captain. "Captain Brabazon, send a scout ahead and inform Captain Lee of our hostages. Taketh two companies of men and deliver this rabble back to whither they cameth from that they might be of good useth. Bingham nudged his horse forward slapping his sword hard on the flank of O Hanly's mount causing *O Donnell* to bolt leaving the manservant hanging in mid-air with awkward jerking and twitching movements, veins popping on forehead, blue-faced, and gasping for breath, to the screams and wailing of the women and children who watched in abject horror aghast at the hideous spectacle.

As quick as it began, the awful clamor of war with the shouting and roaring of men accompanied by the deafening noise of thunderous musket and cannon fire was replaced by the low moans of injured soldiers and the odd cry of a dying man. The Spaniard's plan worked well leaving the enclosure littered with piles of bloody mutilated corpses barely identifiable as human. In the hallway of the castle, the Gallowglass Mc Cabe cradled his dying son Conor, and beside him the body of his son Tomas, both hit when soldiers despite the melee managed to discharge their musket shot into the door, the lead balls easily piercing the timber and finding a target. The musketeers' heady with victory, faces blackened by powder, lay slumped on the floor in exhaustion as the Spaniard, slouched over his cannon as if inebriated by the excesses of his bloody work, muttered with ragged voice as he ran his hand down the barrel. "My Irish Amigos and Camaradas, this is the companion of my best actions, the companion of my success, and this day I have wielded the bloody sword of vengeance." On the tower, Chief O Farrell stood with the priest overlooking the appalling scene in *The Coupure* where a quagmire of headless trunks, torn off limbs, and men twitching in death throes confronted him. A scene of unspeakable horror awash in a fine mist of blood and dust, and turning away in disgust as a cloud of darkness filled his soul he spoke in a solemn voice. "Father, is this we have become, the butchers of men?" "No chief", the priest replied sharply. "This is what the English heretics have made us become, but we had to fight and defend ourselves and it is what we did, have we not as much right to live as they and Chief O Farrell, we destroyed the heretic's army delaying their invasion of Tyrone. Now the crops can be harvested and I truly believe O Donnell will come to our aid and be allied with O Neill and the prophecy fulfilled because you had faith and the courage to stand against *The Soldiers of London.*

The gruesome task of removing the bodies began as the men waded knee-deep through the tangled mess of corpses enclosed by the blood-splattered walls of the wooden palisade smeared with handprints, and festooned with a viscous mess of bloody entrails dangling like dripping red garlands from the sides. Unceremoniously the bodies were dragged from the gore dyed soil, thrown on to carts, and both dead and living dumped into the nearby river turning the waters of the Camlin red. Discarded weapons were gathered and soon the great hall stocked high with random pieces of armour, swords, muskets, and pikes. "Father O Duffy," the chief ordered. "We have twenty-four dead and must bury them without delay under cover of darkness. Have the men take the bodies to the old O Farrell graveyard at Clonguish, you go with them and give them your blessing, we will return someday and give them a proper Catholic burial. We must take them away from here lest the foreigners dig up their graves and desecrate their bodies as is their normal barbaric custom to make a cruel spectacle of our dead. At nightfall, two carts stacked with bodies journeyed to their final resting place, a mass grave in the ancient graveyard of Clonguish, near the village of Lisbrack.

The Lord Deputy dined late in his office, and under flickering candlelight sat diligently reading the numerous reports relating to the progress of the Queen's army in his grand stratagem to stamp out any potential uprising and ensure the prophecy regarding, Red Hugh O Donnell, would die on the vine. By destroying their crops and cattle he would quell any potential rebellion by the Ulster chiefs and England's key possession would be secure. Sergeant Tiptoff knocked politely on the door and stepped into the room. "Mine own Lord, forgiveth me for disturbing thee breaking bread but a messenger hast delivered this," he said, carefully placing a willow basket on the desk and turning left the room. Finishing his supper he wiped his hands, lay his cutlery on the desk, and on opening the basket found staring vacantly back at him with grimacing face the bloody head of Trooper Thomas Oliver Churchyard who, on the orders of the Lord Deputy, William Fitzwilliam, finally found peace of mind and a restful night's sleep.

In the great hall, the men of the O Farrells' lay exhausted from the exertions of battle some eating hungrily, others not having the stomach for food after the bloody deeds of the day, and all partaking in large quantities of aqua vitae to wash away their revulsion at the scenes of carnage witnessed and the appalling deeds committed. Men cleaned weapons, wiping blood from swords and spears, and priming muskets in preparation for the next assault. "Father O Duffy," the chief said. "Inform the Spaniard he was right when he said they would go for artillery to batter the walls but what we did today, bloody as it was, has gained us precious time for it will take them a couple of weeks or more for the foreigners to regroup and haul the cannon from Dublin, and with God's grace O Donnell will soon be here or maybe O Byrne or even the Great O Neill himself will come to our aid, they may have heard of our action. But, no matter what happens we must hold out for as long as possible it is our only chance but when the cannon arrives we cannot defend the castle. My father used to say *A Castle of Stones is a Castle of Bones* and he was right, with artillery we would have no chance. Now we will return to my original plan, tomorrow we destroy the bridge and prepare a trench on this side of the river. Let us rest now and in the morning we commence our work." Imbued by their success the men became elated consuming copious amounts of whiskey recalling the brave tasks they had carried out in battle. Donal Mc Cabe, approaching the chief proclaimed in a loud voice. "Chief, I speak for all the men here this night and we want to tell you were right to make a stand. I am heartbroken at the loss of Conor and Tomas, but they did not die in vain they died with honour, and I will avenge them." Walking along the table Mc Cabe looked closely at the exhausted faces of the men and boys. "Everyone here today," he announced proudly "Did a brave thing in the face of *The Soldiers of London,* and we did swallow our fear and were not afraid to fight, and it was because you, Chief O Farrell, dared to stand and by the good Lord above we did stand and we did inflict much damage on the foreigners and the pride of the Lord Deputy." The men jumping to their feet raised their clenched fists and a tumultuous cheer erupted through the hall *O Fearghail Abu – O Farrell Forever* to the banging of swords and musket butts on the table. Leo O Farrell approached the chief. "Chief, Donal Mc Cabe is indeed correct, you saw what we did today and if we have the courage and belief we can defeat them, and you were right they are not invincible they are only men like us. We have captured swords, armour, and a few scores of muskets. We could attack them as they come with their artillery they will be heavily burdened and would not expect an ambush." Rory O Farrell joined the conversation. "Yes, chief, we could do great things if we captured their cannon. We could attack the Nugents and even march on Mullingar, people would join us and we might raise a mighty army under the banner of the O Farrells. By this time their blood fired by strong drink, ebullient at their victory and heads spinning with fighting talk, the army of the O Farrells had taken Mullingar and now marched on Dublin. Even the chief and his captains were buoyed by the overflowing enthusiasm of the men newly bloodied in the art of killing with each man overflowing with a powerful sense of confidence except, Father O Duffy and the Spaniard, who were not carried away on the fast-flowing tide of hot-headed gusto and bravado as, the priest did not partake in alcoholic drinks, and the Spaniard could not understand what the men were saying.

As darkness descended over Longford Castle, the men of the O Farrells lay sleeping on the stone floor of the great hall, dreaming such dreams only rebels' dream, of the great victories before them when drenched in whiskey and small success.

Chapter Seventeen

Rudely awoken by the distant rattle of musket fire the men, stirring bleary-eyed from their twilight sleep, scrambled unsteadily to their feet and dashing forward snatched musket, sword, and pike, the room echoing to the hurried sound of tramping feet. The door thrust open and the priest charged into the great hall. "Chief, come quickly," he shouted, terror palpable in his voice. "What is the matter, Father O Duffy, what is wrong?" "Chief, they are here, the heretics are outside the gate and there is more come and see." Clambering swiftly up the ladder to the tower he peered over the parapet thunderstruck at the sight confronting him. A short distance from the castle gates, beyond musket range, stood naked the women and children of the O Farrells' flung together pell-mell in a huddled mass uttering dull and pitiful groans, heads bowed low in base humiliation. Surrounding them a ring of steel, soldiers mounted and on foot with the odd flash of steel in the early morning sun as riding forward Captain Tom Lee shouted in Irish. "Listen to me now, this rabble will be executed unless you lay down your arms and surrender, but if you obey my orders you have my word as a gentleman and an officer in the army of her gracious Majesty, no one will be harmed we've had enough slaughter at this place. However, the only persons who will not be spared this day are the Chief O Farrell and the anti-Christ papist idolater O Duffy for these men are beyond redemption and are arch traitors to our Queen. I will grant you half of the hour to lay down your arms and leave the castle." On catching a fleeting glimpse of his mother, Chief O Farrell wheeled away in revulsion his body shaking with rage. "Arm yourselves men," he roared, and grabbing their weapons and donning the odd bit of salvaged armour they raced toward the gate where the priest stood hands in the air blocking their path. "No, men, this is what they want you to do they are too many and too well-armed and will cut us down, you put the women and children in mortal danger." "Father O Duffy," the chief responded. "We cannot stand here behind these walls like cowards and watch the foreigners' murder our families there is only one thing we can do to save our people and it is this, you and I will sacrifice ourselves we have no choice." "But chief, how can we trust the word of the heretics especially after the grave injury we inflicted on their soldiers?" "Father, I know this man it is, Captain Tom Lee, he is married to a Catholic, he speaks our language and they say he is of the true religion. We have no choice but to take his word and trust him what else can we do, surely he would not butcher our people in cold blood?" The men stood silent as the chief told them of his decision. "Men, I cannot let all here die, I will gladly sacrifice my life, we will surrender and you can join your families and go to Breffni, you may never see your homes again but you will live." "But chief," Eamon O Farrell pleaded. "How can you trust the foreigners, their word is worthless they will kill us all?" "Eamon, you may be right but we cannot stand here and watch them butcher our women and children. We must surrender it is the only way what else can we do, lay down your weapons and take our banner from the tower." As Eamon O Farrell stepped forward to open the gate the priest grabbed his arm. "No, Eamon, hold on not yet, I have a task to perform first, I'll be back shortly then we open the gate." Minutes later the priest returned leading a horse with the bloody corpse of Tomas Mc Cabe slung over the saddle. "Chief, only one man need die here today and that is me and I will die a martyr for Christ and the true Catholic faith, death holds no fear for me. We will use subterfuge and cunning against the heretics to make them believe you fell in yesterday's affray and this is your body, the ruse might work. Go at once and hide in the postern gate at the back of the orchard and make your way to freedom at nightfall, go now chief and save your life, go with all haste." "Father O Duffy, I will not desert you for it is wrong for me to live and you to die." Without replying the priest shouted to the men. "Lay down your arms and Eamon, open the gate." The priest, white flag in one hand, reins in the other, led the men of the O Farrells as they snaked in single file out of the courtyard, the blank stare of defeat etched on their faces, and on seeing their families rushed forward embracing their loved ones as the soldiers' looked on impassively. Father O Duffy pondered the scene. *Perhaps Captain Lee spoke the truth and was not like the rest of the heretics and a Catholic. After all, he gave his word as an officer surely the man would not be a liar and act honorably.* Above the clamor of crying women and children Captain Lee barked an order and the soldiers' rushing forward, swords drawn and muskets pointed, encircled the crowd. "Priest," he demanded, jabbing the point of his sword into Father O Duffy's chest. "Where is the Chief O Farrell?" "This is him," the priest responded, gesturing to the body slumped over the horse. "He was shot and died bravely defending his home and people." The captain, head tilted to one side, gazed fixedly at the body studying every detail. "Chief O Farrell had a lucky escape indeed, I had a much slower death in mind for the traitor than a leaden ball, but you shaveling papist priest you are not so lucky and will be no doubt familiar, I'm sure, with our proscribed method of execution for the likes of you. And, tell me now, O Duffy, is the Spaniard still alive?" "Captain Sanchez," the priest called as the Spaniard tottered forward body shaking with fear. "You Spaniard," he barked. "Stay by my side, you are to be sent to Dublin Castle and on to London, your family has paid a handsome ransom for your release, we must deliver you home safely so I can claim the head money." When the Spaniard was told he rushed over to the captain falling prostrate whimpering at his feet as tears of joy ran down his face. With malice aforethought, Captain Tom Lee shouted orders to his men. "Men, commence thine work, killeth them all, and spare no one." Blades flashed, hacking and stabbing at the people of the O Farrells who were butchered mercilessly the soldiers' dispatching men, women, and children, with deadly blows of sword and buttstock. A handful, in frantic desperation, tried to break out of the bloody melee to be cut down by a withering hail of gunfire the lead balls tearing brutally into flesh and bone. When the butchery ceased and the gun smoke cleared stillness descended over the scene of carnage only broken by the sporadic groans of the wounded. Soldiers, slipping and sliding, dispatched all alive with a swift blow and exhausted by their bloody work eagerly swilling greedy gulps of strong drink from flasks, their uniforms blood-soaked, hands and faces splattered with blood. All the storms in the world thundered around the priest's soul as he stood horror-struck at what he had witnessed. "You," he screamed, pointing at Captain Lee who sat staring impassively at the heap of bodies. "You, Captain Thomas Lee, you may speak our tongue and maybe of our faith, but you have the black heart of the heretics and a blood-stained soul, you are a cruel monster. You gave your word to these innocent people of the O Farrells. Have you no honour, have you no conscience, you murdering heretic, you are damned to hell for all of eternity." "Priest," the captain returned defiantly. "I would have you know my conscience is clear and I have done a good days work for our gracious Majesty, who will be much pleased with my endeavors in the extermination of your savage race." Leaning forward he continued in a haughty voice. "Papist priest of the anti-Christ, do you not know of *Greys' Faith*. Do you not realise an English promise to your race is worthless, you Irish are beneath the honour of an Englishman and tell me, priest of Rome, would you have us keep our words with those who have no conscience and break their word daily in rebellion against their rightful Queen?"

Flinging bodies into a rude pile the soldiers laughed and joked as Christopher Brown and his followers strutted by the scene without a sideways glance, and passing through the castle gates strolled indifferently over the blood-soaked ground in high spirits at the prospect of enjoying their newfound wealth and titles. Each room in the castle was ransacked, the fire in the great hall stacked high with Latin books, as jewellery, clothes, and a beautiful gold harp pillaged. The vestments, prayer books, and altar cloth belonging to Father O Duffy were thrown on the fire except for the gold chalice. As they rampaged through the castle in the nearby forge the soldiers began their fiendish work on the Jesuit priest, Father Leo Alphonsus Francis O Duffy, first smashing his arms and legs on an anvil, leaving his broken body overnight to suffer in cruel agony as he waited patiently for morning to come and a quick death to end his misery.

At the top table of the great hall, Christopher Browne sat with his wife Lettice, his eldest brother Digby, and surrounded by his many faithful followers. At the blazing fire, the two Irish wolfhounds lazed devouring scraps of meat feed to them by Sabina the Browne's twelve-year-old daughter. Drinking heartily from the gold chalice, Christopher Browne gazed with satisfaction at his wife and his fellow countrymen, all bubbly and boisterous, laughing and joking, drinking wine and aqua vitae from the ample supplies plundered from the cellar. The priest's vestments he'd discarded as worthless rags, but the chalice was his new drinking vessel and a fine drinking vessel it was put to proper use and not for the superstitious rituals of the papist mass. This special night his heart blazed with a sense of wondrous achievement, his mind overflowing with a multitude of thoughts. *He had followed his instincts and while Ireland was no El Dorado for settlers against all the odds he was sitting in his castle as Lord and Sheriff of Longford. All this was his and would remain his, this would be no Munster and he would make sure of it. He would drive out any remaining Irish, bring more settlers over from Devon and Somerset, and soon the whole of Longford would be civilized, and he would have the new settlers bring over the ruby red Devon cow to replace the scraggy native Irish moiled cow, and he would be rich and powerful and the new world would be his oyster. His family and friends considered him mad when he decided to come to Ireland to settle on the confiscated lands of the Desmonds, even his wife disapproved. But while serving in the Low Countries fighting against the Spanish army of Philip 11, his captain, a fine Berkshire gentleman, Sir John Norris or Black Jack, as his men called him told him all about Ireland, and how a man with a brave heart and iron fist could gain land, plenty of it for the taking and all he had to do was hang onto it and the only thing standing in his way was the savage native Irish who spoke no English with barbaric customs, dress, and their papist religion. And so he journeyed to Ireland with his wife and a party of settlers under Black Jack Norris to the green pastures of Munster and at first, all was well. They settled in the beautiful lush vale of Kilmallock where they thrived on the rich and fertile soil of county Cork with many other settlers. Their neighbour was the poet Edmund Spenser and his young family but the rebellious Irish, the dispossessed persons on whose land the new English settlers now farmed, saw things differently and when the Desmonds' rebelled the whole of Munster exploded like a keg of black powder and in one night he lost everything except his life and that of his wife and child, his neighbors' suffering the same awful fate including Edmund Spenser whose son Peregrine was murdered by the rebels. But he had developed a taste for prosperity and status and had no intention of returning to Devon to exist in poverty as a farm labourer. No, he was staying put and so lodged in Dublin to await the next opportunity and the next opportunity came soon enough. His old commander John Norris canvassed the Queen on his behalf and with good fortune and the good Lord's grace here he was and not a rebel in sight well at least not a living one,* he smiled to himself, *Captain Tom Lee had done his work well. This time it would be different, very different indeed, and he would give no quarter to the treacherous Irish, and drive the O Farrells out and hang everyone he could, there would be no outbreaks of rebellion in Longford. He would rule with an iron fist like the Binghams in Connaught, and by the time he was finished there would be not one person in the county of Longford with an O or a Mac in their names and not one person speaking the accursed Irish tongue, he would make sure of it by whatever means necessary, and would forever be Lord Longford in his brave new world.* With a wide grin of self-satisfaction he raised his goblet, nodding in salutation to his hearty and lively fellow Devonians and their wives, and the future success of their enterprise.

Lettice Browne, face beaming with pride was feeling pleased with herself, very pleased indeed. *Her husband was right and had taken a great risk for himself and his family but it paid off and now they were landowners and him Lord and Sheriff. Back in England, he would be lucky to be a farm labourer ploughing a mucky field in the rain, and her a lowly barmaid in the local inn. Now, she was a Lady, the Lady of the manor. Lady Longford, she couldn't stop repeating the name to herself.*

Lady Lettice of Longford, the title had a certain ring to it and here she sat dressed as a lady in a fine silk gown and kercher she plundered from the bedchamber of Lady O Farrell. A rush of excitement ran through her body and reaching out she took her husband's hand squeezing it tightly. She recalled how she had thought him insane when he said they should go to Ireland, her family, and friends aghast at the idea. She was working as a barmaid in the Speckled Hen, a bawdy public house in Paignton when she met Christopher Browne, a sea dog from Devon, who was serving in the Low Counties against the Spanish, a handsome and dashing young soldier. He made her pregnant and they decided to run away together, she wanted to go to London and him to Ireland. She didn't want to go but he'd decided so she agreed to travel but only as his wife becoming Mrs. Lettice Browne and six months later bore him a beautiful little girl. Then they came in the middle of the night like a raging hurricane, the dispossessed carriers of hate, the savage Irish rebels, evil monsters murdering everyone, cutting off people's noses, and worse. Burying people alive and treating the settlers as animals, and the poor Spenser boy burned to death, how could these barbarians do such dreadful things to an innocent child? Savage murderers the lot of them destroying all their good work and their home and their future. She despised everything about these people, their savage tongue, and their papist religion, and if she had her way she would exterminate them all and make Ireland a civilised land with proper law, religion, and language. She looked at her daughter, so innocent of the evil around her but they would shelter her and protect her from the Irish and make sure this was their home forever, and she knew her husband would make sure of it.

A veil of silence came over the room as they gazed in astonishment at the spectacle before them. No one saw the pair enter until they stood directly in front of Christopher Browne and his wife who glared with astonishment at what appeared to be a scraggy old woman dressed in a tattered black shawl with long dishevelled hair clutching the hand of a young girl, both barefoot, both emaciated. The Browne's daughter, curious to see what was happening, crawled under the table coming face to face with the young girl and holding out her hand asked softly. "What is thy name, I am called Sabina, and this is mine own new home, dost thee liketh it." No response and she called out. "Mother, wherefore doth she not answer?" "Sabina, cometh away quickly doth not be close to the savage for they dost carry the pestilence, cometh quickly to me now." A ragged reply came in a low feeble voice. "*Is mise Grainne Ni Faolain* –I am Grainne Whelan." "Mother, what doth she sayeth I dost not understand her?" The crash of a metal drinking vessel, striking, clattering, and rolling across the stone floor shattered the spell causing the dogs to jump, barking excitedly. Christopher Browne stood and drawing his sword bellowed angrily. "Get thee hence savages this is a place for civilised people, get thee back to the forest or bog whither thee rightfully belongeth." To the jeers and curses of the Browne followers who hurled abuse and threw bits of food at the wretched pair as they shuffled silently, heads bowed, towards the door, disappearing into the darkness of the courtyard which reverberated to the shouts and curses of drunken soldier's staggering and reeling about their dark forms illuminated by the lurid glare of the blazing pyre.

The mother and daughter had come from a cottage three miles away and were not O Farrells, and since her husband was killed at Glenmalure serving in the Queen's army they were shunned by the local people and destitute. For four weeks the mother was bedridden with marsh fever and unable to earn a pittance they starved and only one thing they could do to survive. Go to the castle of the O Farrells and seek help as she had done many times before for they were kind generous people and their door always open for the poor and needy. Approaching Longford Castle, an apocalyptic vision confronted them, as a huge bonfire burned brightly with blackish-grey smoke billowing skyward, and dancing flames casting a hellish glow on the walls of the castle silhouetting the drunken soldiers' who, bottles in hand, staggered and stumbled aimlessly as others standing around the fire screamed obscenities at the funeral pyre and knowing nothing of the fate of the O Farrells, and with survival in mind, the mother and daughter entered the castle.

At nightfall, keeping to little-used tracks and cow paths dimly lit by moonlight, Cahir O Farrell moved swiftly and silently through Gaileanga in the direction of Lough Gill. Father O Duffy had saved his life by his ingenuity, a clever and intelligent man, and the terrible torment he would endure but by morning dead his suffering over. At first light, he reached the shore of Lough Rinn without seeing man or beast, everywhere confronted by scenes of total devastation and destruction. Every building a black charred ruin with fields of crop's smoldering, cloaking the morning air in a mist of smoke with the odd raven feasting on carrion flesh. At Killarga near Lough Gill, he came upon the gruesome sight of a staggered line of corpses swinging grotesquely from a rough wooden gallows. A man, women, and six children their ghastly faces peering down at him with mouths agape as if begging for mercy. In the distance, he saw tiny red dots scudding across the landscape, riders, and soldiers everywhere, and keeping off the well-trodden tracks and common highway, moving only at night he walked until his feet bled and could go no further. Lying under a copse off a dirt track he collapsed into a deep slumber only to be brusquely awoken by a sharp stinging blow to his face. A soldier clad in red tunic, sword in hand, and menace in eyes stood over him. "Get thee up, O Farrell," he ordered gruffly. Leaping to his feet he found himself surrounded by a group of six or seven heavily armed mounted troopers all eyes fixed on him with a look of disdain. Captain Lee reined in his horse and shouted. "O Farrell, we find you at last, did you truly believe you could escape her Majesties' justice and fool me with the weasel words of a papist priest. Today, you will hang like a dog and your head sent to the Lord Deputy for he wishes it to take its rightful place over the gates of Dublin Castle beside your treacherous family." Cahir recoiled in horror as he saw, dangling from a trooper's saddle, the contorted faces of O Hanly and Cormac O Rourke staring mutely back at him, and Captain Lee catching the alarmed expression yelled mockingly. "President, Sir Bingham, pays us ten shillings for every Irish head we bring from Breffni, but do not fear, O Farrell, yours is destined for higher places." Fetching a rope from his pannier, the same rope that hung O Hanly and O Rourke, he barked an order. "Trooper Wingfield, hither take this, secure his hands and hangeth him." Trooper Wingfield, a big muscular man, slid easily off his horse and throwing the rope over a nearby tree placed the noose around his neck, and proceeded to pull hard on the rope, huffing and puffing with exertion. As Cahir O Farrell lifted off the ground, legs kicking in mid-air, reddening face struggling for breath, the last thing he saw before passing out was Captain Lee staring at him, a sardonic grin on his face. Trooper Wingfield, breathless with exertion hauled hard on the rope when a volley of musket shot thundered through the air the storm of lead ball killing him instantly causing Cahir O Farrell to fall in a heap gasping for breath. A second volley and four troopers toppled while Captain Lee, kicking his horse sharply wheeled around, and fled. A group of horsemen approached and one cut the noose cradling Chief O Farrell in his arms. "Here," he said, forcing aqua vitae into his mouth bringing him around instantly with a cough and a splutter to the smiling face of Fergus O Donnell. "You are Chief O Farrell, are you not, I noticed you at the castle in Donegal a month ago. We are O Donnell's men returning from Wicklow, and you are lucky we found you alive. Captain Lee has the whole of Bingham's army scouring the country for you since he learned of your escape." Rising unsteadily to his feet Cahir O Farrell stepped back in disbelief. "But, how did he learn of my escape?" he yelled." "Lee tortured a couple of your men and one broke telling him everything." "But, Fergus, what of my people, Captain Lee promised their lives if they surrendered?" Fergus O Donnell stood head bent without replying. "Fergus," the chief screamed. "You must tell me now, what is the fate of my people, tell me for I must know?" "Chief," Fergus returned sharply. "The foreigners butchered them all, men, women and children, every last one of them." Chief O Farrell drew back the new's blowing through him like a sharp wind." "Sweet Jesus, Fergus," he screamed. "What have I done, I have killed them all by my rash selfish actions trying to save my miserable skin." One of the men grabbed him roughly by the shoulders. "No, Chief O Farrell, you are badly mistaken if that is what you believe. Listen to me now one of O Rourke's spies, a horse boy with Bingham, the lad who told us of your escape said Captain Lee tortured your men because he didn't believe the priest's story. You cannot blame yourself chief, the O Farrells were doomed whether you stayed or not. Nothing could have saved your people and you are lucky to be alive. O Rourke is destroyed and Bingham's men are everywhere, you must come with us if you are to survive. Come, and we will see you safely to Donegal."

Chapter Eighteen

Once more he stood in the cavernous great hall of Donegal Castle, captivated by his majestic surroundings. *What they say is true, this must be one of the finest castles in Ireland, the castle of a rich and powerful family, the magnificent castle of the O Donnell, King of the Fish, Lord of Tyrconnell.* At the oriel window, he stared out over beautiful Donegal Bay savouring the saline scent of the gentle sea breeze wafting through the open window, in the background the squawking of seagulls and the thunderous sound of waves crashing on the pebbled shore. Glancing at the intricate timber beams forming the roof structure and over at the large ornate carved stone fireplace, the centerpiece of the room, he was enthralled at the beauty of the place. The whitewashed bare stone walls reflecting vivid daylight and filling the hall with delicate translucent light. Soft footsteps on the wooden planked floor broke the charm and turning he faced the mother of Red Hugh O Donnell. The Dark Daughter- Ineen Dubh, Lady Fiona Mc Donnell who stood as graceful as a queen and with outstretched arms, embraced him warmly. "Cahir, I am glad to see you alive and sorry to learn of the dreadful act of the foreigners against your people. I regret my son could not assist you but he is presently besieging the Maguire castle at Enniskillen which was taken by the

English, we must retake the castle to prevent Bingham entering Donegal." Sitting on a window seat she beckoned him to join her. "Come here my son and we will talk, and please help yourself to a little wine it is called Jumilla, it came in this week from Spain." As he helped himself to wine she reached over clasping his hand firmly. "Cahir, I share your grief, sadness has been my constant companion since my people were butchered by the foreigners on Rathlin Island, slaughtered by Francis Drake and Essex on the orders of Sir Henry Sidney. Yes, the same one who robbed your family of their lands, the creator of all our misfortunes." Glancing across the swollen sea she imagining a band of English soldiers, big brutish men, throwing women and infants off the cliffs to be smashed to smithereens on the rocks below and for a moment she heard their pitiful screams, shuddering at the thought as large tears welled in her eyes. "Cahir, to this day I still think about my unfortunate family and friends." Stopping in midsentence she began to cry. "Then," she continued. "The Lord Deputy, John Perrot takes my firstborn, my special child, a beautiful child touched by God, an innocent boy loved by everyone, his countenance so handsome that all that looked upon him loved him and to take him so cruelly. Kidnapped and thrown in a dungeon, deprived of his youth, and left a cripple and Cahir, it is what Sir John Perrot did to my beloved son and my husband his friend at all times respectful and generous to the man." Cahir looked out at the foaming sea and rolling waves, and over at the distant dark mountains and soft green hills imagining what it would be like to be suddenly snatched from this wondrous place, away from your family and friends to be thrown in a dark dingy cell fettered in chains in the dreadful Dublin Castle, and him innocent and the O Donnells always good subjects to the Crown – the injustice and brutality of it all. "Cahir," she said, touching him affectionately on the arm. "Do you know my son's grandfather also named Hugh, the man who built this castle, undertook a pilgrimage to Rome and on his return was knighted by King Henry V111 at Greenwich Palace in London, eighty years ago at the christening of Henry and Catherine of Aragon's first son Henry, and surrendered his Irish title for the English title Lord of Tyrconnell to become a feudal knight and no longer an Irish chief as your father did many years later? But King Harry never implemented the English language and customs, and as long as you paid your taxes to the Crown they left you in peace but since the bastard, Queen Bess came to power with her puritanical religion of the Lutheran heretics everything has changed and now we suffer from their greedy land grabbing knights. Cahir," she continued. "When the foreigners took our firstborn son his father and I were distraught and we devoted ourselves to getting him released, and when my husband's eldest son Sir Donal, from his first marriage, with the help of the foreigners, tried to take control of the O Donnell chieftaincy, for which Red Hugh was chosen, I had an army of redshanks send over from Scotland and we defeated Donal in battle and I ordered him killed and Cahir, that is what we have done for Red Hugh and even worse." She hesitated as a cloud of darkness crossed her face. "We brought fifty poor Spanish wretches, survivors from the Armada, under safe-conduct to John Perrot in Dublin Castle, who in turn promised the release of our son and the safety of the Spaniards, but he hung the unfortunate men and kept our son in chains. We trusted the English and now we have these poor men's deaths on our conscience, and may the Lord above forgive us for this awful deed. The kidnapping and imprisonment of Red Hugh badly affected his father who has become infirm and bedridden and can no longer make the long journey to the castle. So, here we are helpless as our poor son languished in that dreadful place of cruelty and suffering without hope or comfort when." Stopping momentarily her eyes brightened and a smile crossed her face. "On a Christmas Eve, as my beloved son lays imprisoned in that awful dungeon in a state of utter desperation and misery, your father and your brother," she blessed herself. "And may God have mercy on their poor souls, come from Longford bringing comfort and bearing gifts and the gift of kindness in another's troubles is a wonderful thing, Cahir, so now I wish to repay you for your father's noble deed." "But, Lady O Donnell," he replied. "There is no need, my father was a good man and kind to everyone."

"Yes, my son, that he was to be sure and by his act of kindness he has saved your life for today I repay your family and give you the greatest gift of all." Cahir sat back intrigued by her words. "And what gift is that my Lady?" "It is, Chief O Farrell, the gift of life I grant to you this day." "My life, Lady O Donnell, what do you mean, I do not understand what you are saying?" "This is what I mean, Cahir," she replied, pointing towards the sea where barely visible in the distance he saw a ship anchored far out in the bay, a tiny black dot bobbing on the ocean waves. "That, is a Spanish ship named *The Rada* which is sailing for Corunna on the evening tide, and you will be aboard, all has been arranged." Cahir sprung to his feet. "No, my Lady, I cannot leave, I must stay and avenge my people even if it means losing my life." "And," she replied, nodding her head in agreement. "If you stay you will indeed lose your life for you are a marked man and the relentless Fitzwilliam will track you down and kill you." "But my Lady, what of the prophecy regarding your son which predicts he will free our people and drive the heretics into the sea?" "Cahir," she replied. "I lost my faith many years ago and do not believe in such things, and you will recall the prophecy of Saint Colmcille states that my son will be king for nine years. Do you truly believe the foreigners will be beaten, they have no choice but to defeat us, and every Irish person of rank will be killed or driven out of the country and the lower ranks will remain enslaved to toil as hewers of wood and drawers of water for the English settlers? We are a knife to their back and our curse, Cahir, is England, and we are Catholic and they are heretics and you," she pointed at Cahir. "You are the same as my son, seeking revenge but in the end, it will only destroy you and when I look at you, Cahir, I can see the future burning brightly in your eyes, but not in my sons. Listen to me now, you stood with your people and defended yourself bravely and honorably and made *The Last Stand of the Chief O Farrell* and now it is time to live. It is God's will, it is meant to be, so you must leave this land forever or you will die. We Irish are of the ancient race of *Milesians – Mil Espaine* the soldiers of Spain who came here from the city of Corunna in Galicia over two thousand years ago and now you must return to survive, to carry on your noble and proud name and be safe from the heretics." The door opened and two men stepping inside the room approached Lady O Donnell. "Cahir, this is our family scribe, Friar O Cleary, and this gentleman master of *The Rada,* Captain Alphonso a Venetian mariner who can outrun any English warship and carry you safely to Corunna. Friar O Cleary," she instructed. "I wish you now to draw up letters of introduction from the O Donnells for Chief O Farrell to be presented at the court of the King of Spain stating, Cahir O Farrell is a man of valor and has fought bravely as a commander of Irish forces in the name of the true church of Rome against the army of the heretical, Queen Elizabeth of England. For his safety he wishes to make his home in Spain and seeks a position of officer rank in the King's service." Turning to Cahir she said. "My son, Friar O Cleary will be your companion on the voyage for he carries important messages from the Great Hugh O Neill to the King and will teach you Spanish, enough to be understood. You will leave here in an hour but first, follow me there is something I wish you to have." Leading Cahir up a winding stone staircase they entered the bedchamber of Red Hugh, the stone walls adorned with a variety of swords and shields , but what caught Cahir's eye was a pair of beautiful ornate silver dagges or duelling pistols sitting on a table and lifting them gazed admiringly at the elaborate engravings and fine workmanship. "Those Cahir were a gift from the King of Spain to my son and this," she pointed to a chest sitting on the bed. "Is a gift from the O Donnells to you?" Placing the pistols carefully on the table, Cahir opened the chest to reveal an assortment of clothes of the finest quality, a cloak with ermine trimmings and shirts of the finest linen. "Lady O Donnell, I cannot accept this gift these are the clothes of an Irish prince." "But, Cahir my son," she replied proudly. "You are indeed an Irish prince, are you not?"

Blessed with good fortune one month later, Cahir O Farrell, dressed as an Irish prince was formally introduced to the King of Spain, Phillip 11, at the Royal Palace in Madrid, and with his letters of introduction from the O Donnells giving an account of his exemplary service in Ireland in the war against the heretics was appointed an officer in the Spanish army, but to his initial disappointment not in active service but as a junior officer in the royal household guards under the command of a fellow Irishman, Richard O Neill, son of the famous Shane the Proud who had been exiled to Spain many years before. O Neill served in the wars in the Netherlands against the Protestant Alliance excelling himself as a captain in the Irish Brigade. The Duke of Alba, his military commander, was so impressed with the skill and bravery of the young Irishman he recommended him to the King for the role as head of the royal bodyguard in recognition of his loyalty and devotion, and so he held the highest military rank in the court responsible for the Kings' personal safety. Richard O Neill was pleased with his new officer who became his protégé and ten years later, Cahir O Farrell, on the retirement of his commander, was appointed as head of the King's household guard. He married the Countess of Cartagena and the best man for the occasion his old friend and comrade Captain Louis Jose Sanchez long retired from the Spanish army. Don Cahir O Farrelli, commander of the royal household guard of King Philip, never returned to Ireland, settling in Spain to successfully write the future and to carry on the proud and noble name of O Farrell.

Epilogue

The prophecy of Red Hugh O Donnell was duly fulfilled when in 1594, he joined forces with Hugh O Neill, Earl of Tyrone commencing what became known as *The Nine Years War* representing the greatest threat England encountered by the united forces of the Irish chiefs who almost succeeded in driving the English out of Ireland, and the Irish coming closer to defeating England than any other nation. But, as the prophecy stated, the kingship of O Donnell lasted nine years and when the long-awaited military assistance arrived from Spain it landed in Cork, the opposite end of the country far from the strongholds of O Neill and O Donnell in Ulster. After a gruelling two hundred mile march in winter, the joint forces of the Irish and Spanish were defeated at the seminal battle of Kinsale in, 1601. O Neill and O Donnell, and many important Irish chiefs, fled to the continent where they were warmly received for their efforts against Protestant, England. Red Hugh O Donnell, aged thirty was murdered months later in Spain, and Hugh O Neill died of natural causes in Rome, aged sixty-six thus ending the two great Irish dynasties. Then came the calamitous *Plantation of Ulster* implemented by King James 1 with further plantations under Cromwell and Kings Charles 1 and 11. Before the Cromwellian plantations, Irish Catholics owned over 60% of the land, after the plantation this was reduced to 8% rising again to 20%. Such was the colossal scale of land confiscation in Ireland that Karl Marx wrote a major thesis *Ireland and the Irish Question*. Ironically, King James seriously considered repossessing the six escheated counties because many of the planters' (Grantees) defaulted on payment and did not fulfill the terms of their agreement with the Crown. The wholesale confiscation of land resulted in mass displacement of the native Irish driven out by religious and political persecution. People of rank exiled to mainland Europe, others sold into indentured servitude in Australia and the Caribbean, with many remaining in Ireland as tenants on the land they previously owned paying exorbitant rents to often absentee English landlords with some finding niches in trade. From 1607 until 1829, the Crown introduced the punitive Penal Laws which forbade Catholics, although representing 80% of the population, from all professions, owning firearms, joining the armed forces, from entering Parliament, and more. The Irish, burdened with high rents, heavy taxes, fines, and distresses, were often reduced to the lowest degree of poverty. Edmund Burke the philosopher stated: *The Penal Laws are a machine of wise and elaborate contrivance well fitted for the oppression, impoverishment, and degradation of a people (Irish) and debasement in them of human nature itself as ever proceeded from the ingenuity of man.*

Following years of ferocious opposition, Richard Bingham defeated King Brian O Rourke, who fled to Scotland seeking asylum from King James 1 who, on the request of his half-sister Queen Elizabeth, handed over him to the English (first recorded case of extradition) and was executed at Tyburn by hanging. O Rourke requested he was hung, not with a rope but with a willow withe as was the Irish custom. The lands of Breffni were confiscated and his castle at Lough Gill granted to Captain Robert Parkes, a Bingham henchman, who demolished much of the original castle building a planter's house on the site. Parkes deserted the castle in 1677, which fell into a ruinous state until the Irish government reinstated the building in the 1990s. This was the castle O Rourke sheltered and saved the lives of many hundreds of shipwrecked Spaniards from the Armada and also the Irish survivors, thirty-five out of a thousand, of the unfortunate people of O Sullivan Beare from Kerry, who marched over three hundred miles after the Irish defeat at Kinsale to escape annihilation. Sir Henry Sidney described O Rourke as the proudest man he ever met. King Brian O Rourke is remembered for his courage and daring in the defense of his culture and people, and immortalized in the folk song *Follow Me Up To Carlow* and famously for his witty poem:

When we drink

We get drunk

When we get drunk

We fall asleep

When we fall asleep

We commit no sin

When we commit no sin

We go to heaven

So let's all get drunk

And go to heaven

John Perrot, responsible for the infamous kidnap of Red Hugh O Donnell, found himself in the Tower of London charged with high treason. A Jesuit priest, Father O Rogan, under torture claimed that John Perrot had been involved in the uprising of King Brian O Rourke in Breffni, but the charges dropped however before his release he was poisoned.

It was never proven Sir William Fitzwilliam assisted Red Hugh O Donnell in his escape from Dublin Castle, however, Captain Tom Lee wrote to the Queen stating Fitzwilliam met with O Neill and O Donnell at Dundalk, at which time the Lord Deputy pardoned O Donnell for his escape and a large sum of money handed over to Fitzwilliam who died debt-free and peacefully at his home in Milton Hall his wife Agnes by his side. An incursion by riders of the Great O Neill during

The Nine Years War into north county Dublin, forced Fitzwilliam to send a small body of men to defend the settlers in the Pale who sought shelter at Dunshaughlin Castle. When the castle surrendered O Neill's men slaughtered Lord Fingal and his family, the servant Nagle, the English settlers, and a small party of castle soldiers sent by Fitzwilliam which included Constable Merryman, Sergeant Tiptoff, and a recruit called Throckmorton from Chester. Christopher Nugent surrendered to O Neill's horsemen and on the defeat of the Irish was imprisoned for treason and died in Dublin Castle a year later.

In 1597, Captain Tom Lee finally succeeded in capturing his adversary Fiach Mc Hugh O Byrne in a cave in Wicklow where he beheaded the aged and ailing Fiach and was granted O Byrne's land. The quartered body was hung on the walls of Dublin Castle, and O Byrnes's head sent to Queen Elizabeth who remonstrated that *The head of such a base Robin Hood was brought so solemnly into England.* The worthless trophy was given to a servant and ended up perched in a tree at Enfield Close outside London. Fiach O Byrne is the only Irish chief to be named in a Shakespeare play where he appears as *The Raven*. Earlier in his career in 1594, Captain Tom Lee, to demonstrate his wealth and status, commissioned the Flemish artist Marcus Gheeraert the Younger to paint his portrait which depicts Tom Lee in the attire of a Queen's Irish Kern. The portrait now hangs in the Tate Modern in London. Captain Lee was executed for treason in 1601 at Tyburn, for involvement in a plot with Lord Essex to overthrow Queen Elizabeth.

During the trial of Sir Walter Raleigh in 1618, for treachery against King James 1, one of the charges brought against him was his role in the massacre at Smerwick, thirty-eight years before. His defense was that he was obliged to obey the command of his superior officers but unable to exonerate himself was beheaded. For his services to the Queen, he earlier received forty-two thousand acres of confiscated Desmond land in Munster and the two large towns of Youghal and Kinsale where he famously smoked his Virginian tobacco the first recorded incident of tobacco smoking. These granted lands represented 0.02% of the total land in Ireland making him the principal landowner in Munster. However unable to attract enough settlers from England to tenant the land he encountered serious financial difficulties and forced to sell his plantation for the paltry sum of £1,500. He was also responsible for the introduction of the potato into Ireland and the failure of the potato crop resulting in the great famine in 1845-1849, and the deaths of a million people. In 2002, Sir Walter Raleigh was included in a BBC list of 100 most notable English figures as was, Sir Francis Drake. His protégée, Edmund Spenser, the great apologist for English barbarity in

Ireland, and the denigration of the Irish people served as secretary to Baron Grey de Wilton and granted three thousand acres and the castle of Kilcolman where the poet laureate wrote one of the finest poems (unfinished) in the English language *The Faerie Queene*. However, his newfound wealth was short-lived and during *The Nine Years War* his estate was destroyed by the Mc Sheehys the original owners, and his son murdered. He died in 1599, in abject poverty in London *Of Want of Bread* according to the playwright and poet Ben Jonson, and buried in Poet's Corner in Westminster Abbey where his funeral was attended by all the literary figures of the day including William Shakespeare at which the attendees threw pens and papers into his coffin which was recently excavated but no hidden poems or Shakespeare plays discovered. Ironically his descendants' reoccupied Kilcolman Castle, became Catholics through marriage eventually losing their inheritance because of their new religion. And so Ireland swallowed the Spenser family as it had swallowed English armies and settlers over time. The total area of land confiscated by the Crown from the Desmonds was six hundred thousand acres. A monument to the 600 Italians butchered by Grey at Smerwick was unveiled at *The Field of Heads* in 1980, exactly 400 years after the massacre.

Sir Richard Bingham was recalled by Queen Elizabeth, and jailed for a short time when the famous Irish pirate queen

Grainne O Malley, sailed in her galley to London informing Queen Elizabeth how Bingham murdered her husband and sons in cold blood. Queen Elizabeth conversed in Irish with Grainne O Malley using the Irish primer compiled by, Christopher Nugent. However, as Bingham's' draconian methods worked well for the English, expediency prevailed and he was reinstated returning to Ireland leading an army of three thousand men but died suddenly in Dublin. His cenotaph in Westminster states *To the Glory of the Lord of Hosts* referring to his role in the Smerwick massacre. His brother George, after plundering a religious establishment in Leitrim, refused to share the loot with his Irish mercenaries who hacked him to death. The remaining brother John was granted sixty thousand acres in Mayo where the family settled. It is believed by historians that the greed and brutality of George Bingham was one of the primary causes of *The Nine Years War* which resulted in widespread death and destruction throughout Ireland and impoverished England in the 1590s. It is estimated over thirty thousand English soldiers lost their lives in the war. The Third Earl of Lucan, George Bingham, a direct descendant was the person responsible for ordering the doomed charge of the light brigade at the Battle of Balaclava in 1854 during the Crimea war. He was a notorious landlord known to the Irish as *The Exterminator,* and during the famine demolished three hundred houses, and evicted two thousand people closing the workhouse in Castlebar. Bingham would ride through the town shouting *I would not breed paupers to pay priests*. The infamous George Bingham, the Seventh Earl or Baronet Bingham of Castlebar, Mayo, although he only visited the place once as a child was a free-spending peer and absentee Irish landlord known as Lord Lucan or more appropriately *Lucky Lucan* who disappeared under suspicious circumstances in 1974, after the murder of the family's nanny, and declared dead in 2006, was a direct descendant of the ruthless Bingham family of Elizabethan adventurers in Ireland. In recent time's people purchasing property in Castlebar received bills for freeholds' payable to the Bingham family in London. The former Irish Taoiseach, Enda Kenny received an invoice from the Lucan family when he purchased a property in Castlebar. The son of the disappeared Lord Lucan, also a George, visited the town once collecting ground rents incognito proclaiming. *It was a bit bigger than I imagined, I was a bit nervous and sneaked into town, and nobody knew who I was.* In the typical Irish fashion of forgiveness and generosity, Enda Kenny told reporters: *I wish I had known he was coming –I would have bought him a drink*!

A sept of the O Farrells was sagacious enough to retain ownership of their lands by judicious dealings with the Crown even fighting in Queen Elizabeth's army in *The Nine Years War*. However, their misfortune began on the coronation of

King James 1, the son of Mary Queen of Scots, a man referred to by the Irish as either *The Wisest Fool in the Kingdom* or *The Robber King.* After the initial financial success of his ill-conceived and disastrous *Plantation of Ulster,* James 1 decided to extend the plantations into Leitrim and Longford, and in his munificence granted huge tracts of lands to his friends and favourites at court with scant consideration of the rightful owners many loyal to the Crown. The unfortunate O Farrells became unlucky recipients of the king's generosity when as gentlemen farmers, *Daoine Uaisle,* with no other means of survival were unceremoniously thrown out of their homes and driven off the land they had possessed for over half a millennium beginning the diaspora of many of the O Farrells of rank. The lucky recipients of the king's munificence were many but the leading protagonists in the land grab, Sir Thomas Harman who received 28,779 acres approximately 10.5% of County Longford under the Act of Settlement 1607. His direct descendant the Countess of Rosse, a notorious Catholic hater and English absentee landlord, evicted Catholic tenants in favour of Protestants to ensure a loyalist electorate and Longford suffered the sharpest decline in population in the country with so many people at the mercy of this one sectarian family. One of the king's favourites, Captain Arthur Forbes, graciously received 14,978 acres approximate 5% of County Longford apparently as a reward for his betrayal of his friend the Earl of Argyle who under sentence of death escaped and sought refuge with Arthur Forbes, who had betrayed his friend to the king stated it was for *Reasons of Honour.* The Forbes, with steadfast tenacity, remain one of the few original Longford planter families still in-situ, the incumbent the elusive, Lady Georgina Forbes. In 1626, Lady Jane Forbes, the wife of Arthur Forbes built Castle Forbes when her husband was killed in a duel in Hamburg. When Charles 1 became king in 1625, he rewarded his friends with large tracts of land in Ireland, and Lord Francis Aungier was granted the destroyed Longford Castle, and adjoining O Farrell's land. He rebuilt the castle in 1627, which was recaptured in the 1641 rebellion by the native Irish against the settlers. In 1774, a cavalry barrack was built on the site which was taken over by the new Free State Army in 1922 and renamed Connolly Barracks after James Connolly, a leader of the 1916 rising. The surviving remnants of the castle were demolished in 1971, the barracks closing in 2009. A small section of the original castle wall can still be seen today. After Captains' Edmund and Francis O Farrell captured Longford Castle in 1641, they besieged Castle Forbes which became a refuge for two hundred English settlers for nine months before the English surrendered and Lady Jane Forbes granted safe conduct to Trim by the O Farrells. In her deposition to the Crown, she claimed the sum of £3,744. 7 s. 3 p for loss of materials and cost of feeding winter corn to the settlers with every last penny accounted for in the most astounding and parsimonious manner; she later disappeared to Scotland. With the defeat of the Irish by Cromwell, the O Farrells lost their remaining land and fled to serve in the French army against Spain, and tasked with occupying the important Belgium town of Saint Ghislain. However, at the behest of the exiled, King Charles 11 of England, on the promise of regranting their confiscated lands in Longford, changed sides handing the town over to the Spanish. Two O Farrell's, Captains' Connell and Lisagh (Lewis) were knighted by King Charles, issued with *Decrees of Innocence,* and given rich rewards by King Philip of Spain. On the death of Cromwell, Charles became king and despite his best efforts was unable to fulfill his promise to the O Farrells as the planter families in Longford, disregarding the king's expressed wishes, refused to return the confiscated lands. The Forbes, always dogged in their unflinching loyalty to the Crown and Protestant religion were fervent supporters of William of Orange, and a tenet of the family was *An Irish title with money was little regarded in England.* So, when created Earls of Granard, successive generation of the Forbes served with distinction in the English army or navy, and in Ireland always at hand to ruthlessly crush any attempts at rebellion by the Irish. The Third Earl, an admiral was involved in the capture of Gibraltar and a battery is named after him in the fort. However, the Forbes didn't always treat their subjected tenants well and in 1750, the Fourth Earl refused to allow the

Irish to bury their dead in the ancient burial site of Clonguish situated on the Castle Forbes estate but the local people continued their time-honored practice, and the Earl would dig up the corpses and throw them in the nearby Shannon River. The same gentleman in 1750, changed the ancient name of the village from Lios Breac- Lisbrack to Newtownforbes. In 1824, a convict ship named *The Castle Forbes* carried Irish convicts to New South Wales. In the 1881 Land Wars, Catholic tenants throughout Ireland were subject to cruel taxation with many unable to pay the ever-increasing rents and systematically evicted, someone had to pay for the extravagant lifestyle of the landlords and maintain their homes in England or France. George Forbes, the Seventh Earl evicted 300 persons near Drumlish for non-payment of rents and sent 500 English Lancers to disperse the disaffected tenants. A major bloodbath was averted by Father Tom Conefrey the parish priest who successfully persuaded the Earl not to increase the rents. In 1911, a catastrophic act of environmental vandalism occurred when the incumbent Earl of Granard released into the wild from Castle Forbes estate six pairs of grey squirrels, the invasion of these alien vermin quickly decimating the native red squirrel population throughout Ireland. Castle Forbes estate management company Rawdon (Rawdon from Moira - planters on confiscated O Laverty lands related to the Forbes) was the subject of a magazine article entitled *Castle Foreboding* about the reported wholesale destruction of ancient oak trees and wildlife at Annagh Woodlands, an area protected by European and National Designations, situated in the Castle Forbes estate. This reported environmental destruction was carried out by a forestry firm appointed by Rawdon called Scottish Woodlands. Lady Georgina Forbes refused permission in October 2005, to Longford County Council to survey the ancient and historic graveyard of Clonguish.

Two months after the departure of Cahir O Farrell, Red Hugh O Donnell fulfilled his pledge, and with two thousand riders overran the English settlers of Longford destroying the castle and killing everyone who did not speak Irish. Christopher Browne and his family managed to escape and return to England, where he found work as a farm labourer and his wife a barmaid in the local tavern in Devon. On the defeat of the Irish, the confiscated property of the O Donnells was awarded to a minor English officer, Captain Basil Brooke for his service in crushing the native Irish. The O Donnells largely destroyed their castle to prevent its use and Brooke added a manor wing in the Jacobean style. Never feeling completely secure in remote Donegal, greatly outnumbered by the indigenous Irish, the Brookes' sold the castle to the Gore family and moved to Aghalun in County Fermanagh, to the confiscated lands of the Irish chief Hugh Maguire an ally of Red Hugh O Donnell, where 30,000 acres of land were granted by the Crown to Sir Thomas Brooke for his energetic role in defeating the Catholic uprising of, 1641. The family later built Colebrooke house to the design of the architect William Farrell, and it was here Basil Brooke, the third prime minister of fledgling Northern Ireland lived. He was infamous as Prime Minister for his appeal to Protestants in a 1933 speech not to employ Catholics, and for setting up his private paramilitary group known as the Fermanagh Vigilance, which was later subsumed into the notorious B Specials. In his obituary, the London Times newspaper indirectly blamed him for the continuing troubles in Northern Ireland due to his abysmal political sense, staunch representation of Anglo Irish aristocracy, and Protestant ascendency. Donegal Castle eventually fell into disrepair and was presented to the Irish Office of Public works by the Gore family. In the 1990s, the Irish Government renovated the O Donnell section of the castle in the original style, utilising Irish building techniques of the fifteenth and seventeenth centuries, and is undoubtedly one of the finest castles in Ireland, the restored great hall still retaining its glory and Majesty. The oak timbers used in the restoration of the roof structure were sourced from Colebrooke estate near the village of Brookeborough originally called Aghalun however the ancient name changed by the Brookes.

In May 2020, archeologists discovered what is believed to be the skeleton of Red Hugh O Donnell in the Church of Wonders in Valladolid, Spain, the historic seat of Spanish royalty where the famous Irish leader was buried in 1602, alongside the grave of Christopher Columbus.

Moatfarrell recently opened as a site of historic interest and a small section of the original Pale survives in Syddan, County Meath. The only surviving stone chair, similar to the one used in the O Farrell inauguration ceremony at Moatfarrell, is housed in the Ulster Museum Belfast and belonged to the O Neill's of Clandeboye. Finglas village is a thriving suburb of north Dublin, the Royal Oak Inn closing in recent years, and the maypole long replaced by a commemorative monument to Dick McKee an I.R.A. commander in the War of Independence. The ruins of Finglas Abbey and the ancient Nethercross can still be seen as can Saint Patrick's well now surrounded by the suburbs of the great capital city of Dublin, all as predicted fifteen hundred years ago by, Saint Patrick. Dublin Castle was handed over to the Irish Free State in 1922, and largely restored by the Irish government and the only remaining section from Elizabethan times is the Bermingham Tower. In 2011, Queen Elizabeth 11 made a state visit to Dublin Castle addressing the guests in Irish saying *A Uachtarain agus a Chairde -President and Friends*. President Mary Mc Aleese uttered *Wow, Wow, Wow* on hearing the Queen speak Irish, much to the surprise of nearby journalists. It is speculated Queen Elizabeth 11 acquired her few words from the Irish primer prepared for Queen Elizabeth 1 four hundred years ago by, Christopher Nugent.

In 1921, three hundred years after the Elizabethan conquest, the British government, based on a sectarian headcount, artificially partitioned the island of Ireland, retaining six of the nine counties of the northern province of Ulster under British control, and granting independence to the remaining twenty-six counties. The new Free State, officially known as Eire, became the first Celtic nation to form a democratic government with Irish as the official language, and elements of the Brehon Law incorporated into the modern Irish legal system. Against all the odds the nascent Republic of Ireland survived and prospered, and today is a successful country with progressive laws regarding transgender rights, paternity leave, climate change, etc, and the first country to legalise gay marriage. Since its inception, the British administered Northern Ireland has been subject to civil unrest culminating in what is termed *The Troubles* in which over 3,650 people lost their lives and ended with a settlement known as *The Good Friday Agreement (GFA)* in 1998, with a power-sharing administration. The United Kingdom's chief minister in Northern Ireland known as the Secretary of State (SOS) is appointed by the Queen, as were the Lord Deputies in Elizabethan times, and come to Northern Ireland each with less knowledge and less interest in Ireland or the Irish people than their predecessors.

THE END

AN DEIREADH

Printed in Great Britain
by Amazon